FOUND AT SEA

Found at Sea

A Jewel Cruise Line Adventure

Christine R. Whitlock

DEDICATION

To my beautiful mother, Kathy Robertson.
Thank you for showing me the Light.

"For it is by grace you have been saved, through faith—and this is not from yourselves, it is the gift of God—not by works, so that no one can boast."
Ephesians 2:8-9

PART ONE

Calm Seas

"I have come into the world as a light,
so that no one who believes in me should stay in darkness."
John 12:46

CHAPTER ONE

November 7, Thursday

"Malaysia? Why would you want to go to Malaysia, Steph?"

"We have friends who are missionaries there. Benny thinks you can find us a nice resort with a view at a good price. We aren't too picky but would like something adults-only and all-inclusive. And on a beach, of course. Benny would like to golf but doesn't have to."

"This will be pricey, even with Benny's airline employee discount, but I will make it work. I'm excited to start researching this one. We haven't worked with Malaysia yet. I'm sure I can find something grand."

"Thanks, Morgan. I'm excited too. And tell your mom I said hi. I miss her."

"Will do."

Morgan Stevens ended the call and scanned the photo frames across her desk. She and her husband, Bob, were in each picture, sporting huge smiles with exotic backgrounds. Her brown hair was a different length in each photo, and Bob sported a beard in half of them. His blue eyes were the first thing she noticed about him when he walked into her adult Sunday school class eighteen years ago. On her desk, they sparkled in every picture that didn't involve sunglasses.

As an independent travel agent, Morgan enjoyed regular opportunities to travel around the world—literally. She lived in Jacksonville, Florida, which hosted an international airport and a major highway that led to fabulous cruise ports. Her favorite trips over the past twelve years involved palm trees, but she and Bob had also seen polar bears, the Northern Lights, and Egyptian pyramids. They even watched a bull chasing five years ago.

Morgan had enough clients at Live It! Travel Agency to need two part-time employees to work during the lunch hours each day. Allison was a college student majoring in International Law. She kept her Mondays, Wednesdays, and Fridays free from classes during 10:00 to 2:00 so she could help Morgan with her business. Allison's personality worked well with the older clientele, but she tended to get "creative" when filing paperwork. Morgan made sure to follow up on everything she recorded. Mikey, on the other hand, was a detail beast. A bona fide computer whiz, he streamlined their booking process and kept all their files organized and secure. Mikey worked at home as a programmer, but devoted lunch hours to Morgan on Tuesdays and Thursdays. Both employees took advantage of discount opportunities to take adventurous treks of their own. Mikey was saving up for a trip to New Zealand to see a *Lord of the Rings* movie set.

"How many days?" Mikey walked in, startling Morgan as she was browsing all-inclusive resorts in Malaysia. There were actually a few possibilities.

"Twenty-four! It's getting closer. Not quite time to get the suitcases out, but early enough to start getting excited."

"I read a story yesterday that *Golden Fortune* will add a second-place prize for hunters who get close. That will be cruise credit for a future cruise. What do you think?"

"I'd take it. We'd all take a free cruise." Morgan had scored a balcony cabin on the inaugural sailing of *Golden Fortune*, the first cruise ship of the new Jewel Cruise Line. The "preview" sailing of December first would consist entirely of travel agents and media reporters and their families. Marketed as a modern-day treasure ship,

Golden Fortune was a mid-sized liner with modern amenities. Unlike typical cruises, a Jewel cruise would not promote rest and relaxation. It would not sell fun at sea. Instead, it would promote a real-life treasure hunt complete with a hidden treasure box filled with $50,000 in gold. Passengers would find an initial clue in their cabins at embarkation and must solve further clues to find the one treasure box hidden on each cruise. Most assumed that the box would be buried on the line's private sanctuary, Treasure Island. As the last of three private islands visited during the week, Treasure Island would be the logical place for hidden goods. But the cruise line promised that the location would change weekly, so the gold could be hidden anywhere along the route.

Morgan handed Mikey her well-loved laptop. "It's stalled again. Can you do your magic one more time? It was running earlier but stopped an hour ago."

"Let me see it. You know you need a new laptop? This one really isn't worth your time."

"I know. I'm just used to this one. Thank you for keeping it alive. I'm taking it on *Golden Fortune*. If it gives me trouble, I will take the plunge and get a new one. Maybe you can start looking at some prices for me."

Morgan spent her afternoon booking ten flights for a wedding party and researching resorts in Langkawi, Malaysia. Surprisingly, the area boasted several suitable retreats for Stephanie and Benny to consider. Morgan was leaning to the Selamat Datang, which housed visitors in individual villas with straw roofs. She ran some mock bookings and made a chart of overall costs to share with Stephanie. Next, she looked at airport shuttles in Malaysia and possible flight arrangements with Benny's employee discount. The flights would be lengthy, but the exotic location just might be worth it.

Mikey resurrected the laptop and printed cruise documents for two honeymoons while Morgan continued to look at flight arrangements. She knew that he would file their paperwork correctly and mail the package with all necessary travel information. Honeymoons were fun to plan because Live It! promised to add a romantic surprise to each trip. Last year, they added a swim-with-the-sharks adventure to a Hawaiian honeymoon. The couple sent pictures to Morgan, complete with one open-mouth predator.

Before the day ended, Morgan and Mikey watched a replay of the press conference with *Golden Fortune's* captain. Jewel Cruise Line posted it on their website as soon as it was completed. He answered the questions skillfully and clearly was a master of the seas. But Morgan could tell that he was not enjoying the spotlight. Twice he looked over his shoulder to the company's CEO. The executive did not bite. The captain continued answering questions for another thirty minutes. Mikey thought the captain looked like a famous racecar driver. Morgan thought he could be a chef.

Luciano Barone never liked public speaking. It was the worst part of his job. Today, he was being formally introduced as the inaugural captain of the *Golden Fortune* cruise ship. Coming out of retirement at the age of sixty-two was a difficult decision, but the executives of the Jewel Cruise Line wore him down with appeals for his unmatched expertise. Plus, his home without Dahna in it was just a house. He felt more at home on the sea.

Raised in Naples, Italy, Luciano enlisted in the Italian Navy straight out of college. He traveled the Mediterranean Sea as a *Gardemarine*, or ensign, and rose to the rank of *capitano di corvetta*, or corvette captain, in five years. He planned to give his life to the Navy, just like his grandfather, but a cargo ship company offered to double his salary and pay for the Merchant Navy training program. Dahna prayed for the right answer and pronounced that God wanted Luca to work on the cargo ships. He always suspected that Dahna was the one who wanted him to work on the cargo ships but would do whatever she wanted to keep her happy. With two small children, Dahna dreaded the times that Luca had to leave for months with the Navy. She had little help at home and worried for Luca's safety.

Within two years, Luca moved into the position of "officer of the watch." His responsibility was to ensure that the oversized ship stayed on its designated path and predetermined timeline. He was noticed by the parent company for his amazing focus and solid navigational skills. But the recognition meant that he was given longer routes and more time away from home.

Late one night on a route from Naples to Valencia, Luca was talking with Carlo, a coworker. Carlo was older than Luca and had a wife and children. He shared exciting news with Luca. "I was just accepted as a third mate with Carnival Cruise Line. The pay is slightly lower, but I will be home more and will be able to move up the ranks quicker. Plus, I won't be as isolated on the bridge. A team of officers work together on cruise ships, unlike the solo work here." The idea appealed to Luca, and he discussed it with Dahna the first night he returned home.

Once again, Dahna sought advice from God. And once again, she declared that God supported the change. Luca applied to five different cruise lines and was offered positions with four of them. He decided to work with Royal Caribbean International as a third mate. They had more routes near Italy and would allow his family to travel with him more often than the other lines.

The switch to a cruise line was the best professional decision Luca ever made. He started as a deck hand and earned his captain's license within ten years. The job was stressful yet fulfilling. He was appreciated for his expertise in navigation and maritime safety and enjoyed giving tours to passengers. As a captain, he worked ten weeks on and ten weeks off. This unconventional schedule turned out to be ideal for his family. When he was home, he was able to focus on Dahna and their two teenage sons. Not only did he attend all the boys' soccer matches when he was home, he was able to attend their practices as well. Luca retired after twenty-five years of service, three months after Dahna was diagnosed with ovarian cancer.

Luciano Barone was born to be a cruise ship captain in every way—except public speaking. On each itinerary, he was expected to host a "Meet the Captain" event in the ship's theater. Hundreds of passengers would attend each week to hear stories of the sea and ask questions of the captain. Luca should have been able to handle these events with ease but never did. He became anxious and nervous before each session. His strategy to overcome his unease was to deflect attention to the senior officers also on the stage with him. He later included the heads of the major departments: entertainment, housing, food, and safety. Modern-day cruise ships were temporary cities with thousands of citizens who needed to eat, sleep, and dance. Passengers loved to hear about the endless dishes of ice cream and the logistics of the onboard ice-skating rink. Luca passed these details off to the others.

Dahna and the kids sailed with Luca dozens of times. The ice-skating rinks were her favorite venues. She would watch the athletes practice and would attend any performance she could. Luca could still see the sparkle in her eyes as she watched the skaters glide across the ice. One year, he surprised her with a special anniversary performance by some of the skating team. She was completely captured as the skaters glided in unison to "their" song. Dahna also loved gazing at the vast ocean. From her perspective, it never ended. Of course, from Luca's it was filled with currents, obstacles, and traffic.

"We are delighted to bring you once again . . ." The CEO of Jewel Cruise Line interrupted Luca's memories. ". . . Captain Luciano Barone as the inaugural captain of *Golden Fortune*. Captain Barone's experience in the cruise industry, especially travel in the Bahamas, makes him the perfect choice as our captain. We are thrilled that he agreed to come out of retirement to lead the world's first treasure hunt cruise adventure. Jewel Cruise Line has hired only the best for this journey. Captain Barone will make a few statements and then be available for questions."

Luca stepped up to the podium and was immediately blinded by camera flashes. The flashes did not stop, so he started speaking. "Thank you for attending our inauguration. I am excited to lead such an innovative ship. The advances in comfort and safety will make Jewel Cruise Line second to none." Luca had planned to tell a joke about finding the treasure himself but cut it to minimize his time at the podium. "Jewel has hired the best officers and crew around. It will be a dream to lead them. Passengers can expect an adventure filled with pirate-themed cabins, entertainment, and adventure. We will be traveling to three beautiful and innovative islands. You won't want to miss the fun. Happy hunting!"

When Luca stepped away from the podium, the CEO corralled him and brought him back to the microphone. "Captain Barone would be happy to answer your questions." Luca faced the audience again. Thankfully, the flashes had stopped.

"Where is the treasure?" was the first question yelled by a reporter. The crowd laughed, and Luca smiled.

"Next question."

"Have you ever seen a real pirate?" Luca had heard stories of modern-day pirates but did not share them with the reporters. Instead, he commented on the *Golden Fortune* crew members who would be dressed as pirates throughout the cruises. After ten more questions, the captain turned to the CEO, hoping to be relieved from the podium. Fortunately, the reporters began directing questions to the executives, and Luca was able to move away from the microphone. He stood next to the executives and scanned the crowd. Reporters were holding up recording devices and scribbling in notepads. This type of publicity was not found thirty years ago. Word would spread when the first treasure was found. Luca would ensure that it would be positive advertisement for all involved. Any negative publicity could hurt sales for months.

The questions continued, and Luca wondered if he would have the stamina to sail for ten weeks at a time. He had gotten used to his life of "down time" but decided that he would continue to live, even without his wife. She would be so proud of this new adventure he would be leading. And she would be proud that he didn't stop living.

After dinner with the executives later that evening, Luca went straight to his Miami apartment. Questions about his role continued through dessert and became tiring. He would move into the Captain's Quarters on the ship two days before embarkation. In the meantime, he remained in his apartment near the downtown area. While looking over a list of officers and crew, his phone rang. It was Marco, Luca's older son, calling from the Atlanta area. "Hello."

"Hey, Dad. We just watched your press conference on YouTube. Are you sure you are up for this? It looks like the media will be all over this treasure stuff. They won't let you rest."

"*Ciao*, Marco. It's good to hear from you. And I will be fine. Once the cruises start, I will spend most of my time on the bridge. The media coverage will die down. At least, I hope it does. Are the kids excited to join me for their Easter break? I think you will all enjoy it. This will be different from the other cruises you have taken. They are running the pirate theme with everything. Even the restrooms. And the ship handled brilliantly during the sea trials. The engines, hull, steering, braking system, and noise levels tested perfectly."

"We are all very excited. We want to hear everything you know when you are here for Thanksgiving. I especially want to hear about the food. The kids don't have school that week, so they will be there to pick you up at the airport. And Sonja wants to know your favorite kind of pie."

"My favorite is your mom's ricotta pie, but I would be happy with anything. Tell her not to go out of her way. She is so busy." The conversation turned to sports and then the weather before the two hung up. Luca finished reviewing the crew list and fell asleep thinking of Dahna's ricotta pie.

Morgan stopped at the grocery store on her way home. Thursdays were pizza nights with Bob, and she needed more mozzarella cheese and pineapple chunks. Yes. Morgan fell on the pro-pineapple side of the debate. Her usual pizza toppings were ham, pineapple, and bacon. Bob, on the other hand, mocked her choices and went with the traditional pepperoni pizza most weeks.

"Morgan! Morgan!" A friend from church came rushing toward her.

"Hey, Sadie. How are you?"

"I'm fine. Just a little freaked out. There are live turkeys near the meat department. With little fences around them. I wasn't sure if they were going to kill them, so I got out of there. We will have vegetarian lasagna this week. I'm not going near the ground beef."

Morgan's eyes widened. "Are you serious? Real turkeys? I have to see this."

"Trust me. It's weird. Are people picking them out like lobsters in a tank? I just can't watch that. What are they thinking?"

"I must go see them. Are they cute? Want me to get you some beef? I can grab some quickly."

Sadie crinkled her face. "Nope. Not cute. And no beef, thank you. Be careful over there. See you on Sunday."

"Sure. I'll see you in church. Take care." Morgan made a beeline to the back of the store where the meat was displayed. Sure enough, child gates were set up, and seven live turkeys were walking around inside the pen. They were surprisingly quiet. Morgan assumed the birds were a marketing tactic for Thanksgiving but didn't want to find out. She turned toward the cheese section and moved away from the corral.

Once home, Morgan took the dough out of the refrigerator. She sat it on the counter and went to get changed. As she walked down the hall, her phone rang. Lucy Bond's caramel face appeared on the phone. She was the owner of Global Crusaders, a full-service travel agency in nearby Leesboro, Florida, and Morgan's best friend. Lucy marketed family friendly and often faith-based experiences. Living three years in Las Vegas as a teenager cemented her resolve to provide wholesome experiences for families.

"Hey, Lucy."

"Did you hear? They've added a second-place prize. It's cruise credit, but enough for a family of four to take a week-long cruise on their next ship, *Plunder*. We had two calls today asking about the second prize. Interest is high right now for Jewel Cruise Line."

Morgan removed her shoes and sat on her bed. "We're seeing a lot of interest too. My clients are expecting pictures of everything when I return. Are you still planning to make YouTube videos?"

"Yes. They will be a hit," Lucy added. "Views will skyrocket if I can catch a glimpse of the actual treasure box. What about you?"

"I plan to video a little and really should blog, but I don't want to miss the experience. This will be a one-of-a kind cruise. I'll try to get a lot of pictures and take detailed notes."

"Good plan. Are we still on for lunch Monday?" The women tried to meet for lunch halfway between towns on Mondays. The Green Grill was a favorite place to catch up on life, as well as business.

Morgan mentally reviewed her schedule. "Yes. I may be a few minutes late, but I will be there. See you then."

"See you. Bye."

After a quick change, Morgan rolled out the pizza dough and gathered ingredients. She and Bob would build their pies together and relive their day as the pizzas cooked. Their routines were comfortable and peaceful. At forty-two years old, Morgan had given up on having biological children. Infertility was cruel. But her husband of sixteen years held out hope that God still had an expansion of their family in the plans. Morgan did not have such hopes. In fact, she didn't really trust God the way Bob did. Sure, she attended church with him and helped with the youth group regularly. She believed in God. But she didn't bank her daily happenings on Him. She didn't call on Him with every need the way Bob did. God created the Earth and had little time for Morgan's weeds.

Bob got home on time, and while their pizzas were cooking he shared a funny story. One of his employees found a bird's nest on the ground after trimming some branches. The "tough guy" felt so bad that he built an elaborate platform for the nest in the tree and even lined the nest with one of his handkerchiefs. His fellow workers didn't have the heart to tell him that the nest was probably abandoned. Morgan imagined that some lucky bird family would be living like kings next spring.

After dinner, the couple sat on the back porch looking for the meteors promised by their local weatherman. While looking up at the sky, Bob noted that the cruise was coming at an ideal time. "We never travel on the week *after* Thanksgiving. This will be different. Any family drama will be over, and we can recharge before the Christmas rush. I am really looking forward to getting away. Do we have to do the hunt?"

Bob liked to rest on their vacations. His yard service company employed eight teams with three workers each. He spent his days putting out proverbial fires that continuously reignited. He rarely knew what to expect as he drove out of his driveway each morning.

Someone would run out of weed trimmer string. Another person would be unable to work for one of a thousand reasons. Rattlesnakes made mornings interesting. An unexpected thunderstorm might appear out of nowhere. Bob was good at keeping the teams running. But his days were mentally and physically exhausting.

"Of course. We must do the hunt. I have over a dozen clients eagerly waiting to hear about my experience. And it will be fun. We've never done anything like this. You are good with puzzles. Who knows? We may come back with extra Christmas cash."

"That would be nice. I really think we should nail down a strategy before we arrive though."

"What strategy could we even use?"

"Well, do we want to play offense or defense? I know that we can't bring metal detectors, but can we phone our friends? Should we pack specialized equipment? Sleep during the day, and search at night? Or should we play defense? Keep our neighbors awake so they can't think clearly during the day? Plant fake clues?"

"Oh, my goodness! You have thought of everything. These ships have cameras everywhere, so I don't think we can sabotage others. But the equipment sounds valuable. What do you have?"

"I was thinking that we should bring some sort of shovel. Are those allowed? We could fit a folding shovel in a suitcase. I will get some headlamps in the event we are running around in the dark. And we might need gloves."

Morgan's eyes widened. "I haven't even thought of those things. You're right. We need to be prepared. We have some disposable ponchos somewhere in our travel closet. And bug spray. We will need lots of bug spray. This will be fun. It would be so fun to do this with kids, but let's face it. They would slow us down."

"Ha! They would. Do we still have that butter pecan ice cream from the weekend?"

"Yep. Let's finish it." The couple sat at the kitchen table eating ice cream and planning for their treasure hunt. Bob joked about sabotaging the others, and Morgan rolled her eyes. This trip was going to be different.

CHAPTER TWO

November 10, Sunday

As Bob and Morgan entered Cornerstone Church on Sunday morning, a group of men whisked Bob away to talk football. This was a usual occurrence in the fall. College football was a high priority in the South. Morgan went on to their regular spot in the sanctuary and chatted with her "pew neighbors." Talk centered on Thanksgiving and how unprepared everyone was for the upcoming gatherings. The group laughed when Cindy Foster predicted the age of her mother's most recent boyfriend. "She will find someone—anyone—just so she doesn't have to show up alone. And she will make sure the poor guy is in every picture taken."

Morgan understood. Her own mom didn't like being alone. "Let's hope he is old enough to drive. I'm still not convinced that her boyfriend from two years ago had a license."

"That was bad. My mom hasn't regained her balance since my dad left. Please pray for her. She is hurt way more that she will admit."

"Oh, Cindy. I can't imagine how hard that was for her. To get all her children out of the house and thriving. Ready for the empty nest. And boom! Len walks out with his assistant. She deserves some peace. Maybe someone a little closer to her age though."

"That would be nice."

Bob sat beside Morgan just as the announcements started. Next week was Serving Sunday when the church would leave the building to help the community. Bob always offered his lawn equipment to help maintain the lawns of needy neighbors or remove fallen debris from business landscapes. Morgan's appreciation for the work Bob did was rekindled every November when she worked beside him. Last year, their team planted over one hundred pansy plants and spread enough pine straw to cover a football field.

Brother Greg stepped up to the pulpit and welcomed visitors before the choir led the worship music. The words they sang spoke to Morgan, and she reached for Bob's hand during the last song. Brother Greg started his sermon, preaching about salt and light. He explained that the disciples understood what Jesus meant when He called them the "salt of the earth" in Matthew 5:13. Salt was valuable and used to prevent decay in food, particularly fish. Likewise, believers should stop the moral decay in our world through obedience and forgiveness. But they can lose their saltiness through disobedience and pride. Believers are then "trodden underfoot by men."

Continuing in Matthew 5, Brother Greg shared that Jesus also told the disciples that they were the "light of the world." They should reflect God's love to everyone. Their lights should always be pointed at Jesus. Just as people of that time wouldn't hide their lights under a basket, believers shouldn't hide in isolation. They shouldn't be ashamed of the light. They should lovingly bring their light to the darkness in the world.

There it was. The verse about putting light under a basket. Morgan had issues with this verse. Throughout the New Testament, Jesus testified that the last will be first and the first will be last. He said that we should pray with humility. How, then, should we shine our beacon lights to Jesus for all the world? Isn't that prideful? In past discussions, Bob has countered that the world needs a Messiah. That is why Christians point their beams to Jesus. But Morgan could not get past the seeming arrogance of Jesus to demand the world's attention. Knowing what was on her mind, Bob squeezed Morgan's hand. She smiled, appreciating his faith, but didn't quite agree with it.

During Sunday school hours each week, Morgan and Bob regularly helped with the youth group. They coordinated the student band and participated in the big-group rotation. Today, they had no responsibilities, so they sat in the back row and enjoyed the youth activities. The band consisted of four high school students who took their roles seriously. Morgan felt good about the future of America when she watched these young people praising Jesus through song. The big group activity involved a game called Fusion, in which Luke, the youth pastor, called out numbers. Students had ten seconds to form groups of the called-out number. The noise level was higher than Morgan liked, but she did appreciate that all students were included. Even the quiet introverts were running around, trying to beat the clock. After the game, Luke dismissed the students to the classrooms.

Since Morgan and Bob did not teach a grade-level class, they spent the rest of the hour working with Luke and other adults planning the next few Sunday morning activities. Students were encouraged to work with their parents on Serving Sunday, so the next week was covered. "Who is leading on November 24?" Luke asked. "Attendance may be light for the holiday weekend, so we might want to add a more personal game."

"We are," Morgan said. "I found a cute game called Don't Laugh from a website. I think the kids will like it. We will bring donut holes for snacks and run the game during big group."

"Sounds interesting. Can't wait." After planning, the group dissolved and Bob and Morgan headed to lunch at their favorite after-church spot, Family Fiesta. Several other families went to the "Fiesta" after church, and Morgan waved to them. Seeing the little girls with frilly dresses and matching hairbows made her miss the daughter she would never have. She reminded herself that her life was more comfortable than most of the world. Children just wouldn't be a part of it.

The couple found a booth near a window and waited to give their order. They didn't need menus at the Family Fiesta. Bob always ordered the steak burrito platter, and Morgan got the shredded chicken tacos. After ordering, they went to the tortilla bar up front for chips and salsa.

Back at their seats, Bob could read Morgan's mind, so he steered the conversation to the sermon. "Brother Greg sure did an exhaustive study on your favorite verse today, didn't he?"

"Ha! You know me too well. I don't think I will ever get over the arrogance of the light analogy. It's just a sticking point for me."

"Morg, that is not arrogance. That is mercy. You will see one day. I'm sure of it. This is too important for you to misunderstand. And before I forget, Will invited us to a bonfire cookout on Friday. He and Shae are making chili for about ten people."

"Sounds fun. I'll ask Shae what we can bring. Are we finishing our *Indiana Jones* marathon today?"

"Yep. I think we should. We need all the treasure hunting tips we can get. Can you believe that we sail three weeks from today?"

The Jewel Cruise Line headquarters was in Greater Downtown Miami. Luca took an Uber ride from his apartment to the high-rise building that housed the corporate offices. He made his way to Gayle Parker's office on the tenth floor and waited outside. She was a high-ranking executive with Jewel and was responsible for the final preparations of *Golden Fortune*. He first met her at the ship's christening in France a few months earlier. The cruise industry's week often started on Sunday, so a meeting today was not out of the ordinary.

"Captain Barone! Please, come in. We've been waiting for you." Gayle welcomed Luca and introduced him to the other high-ranking executives in her office. She handed the captain a binder and showed him to his seat in the nearby conference room. Eight others were seated around a large, glass table. A 1/1400 scale model of *Golden Fortune* was placed in the center of the table. Luca naturally focused on the bridge of the innovative pirate ship. It looked like an old-world ship but was a technological marvel.

Gayle directed the group to look at the second page of their binders. "Let's talk about the schedule first. Then I would like to discuss the five departments individually. Please stop me with any questions." Luca noted that Gayle had total command of the room. She would have no trouble speaking to a large crowd. The group opened their binders and reviewed the summary page on the top.

"We have three weeks until our inaugural sailing. Exactly twenty-one days. I have scheduled meetings with Captain Barone and the heads of each division. They will meet here at headquarters."

Luca interrupted, "Please, call me Luca."

"Sure, Captain . . . er, Luca. Let's confirm the dates. You will meet with the officers tomorrow and the hotel staff on Friday. Does that work?"

"Yes. That is fine."

"Then we have the entertainment staff next Sunday and the safety team next Wednesday. I will be at the engine meeting on the twenty-third. We have a lot to share with you covering the welfare of our passengers. You and the senior officers will fly to Nassau the next day for one last tour of the new piers. We will take some promotional photos at Treasure Island. I've scheduled a day at each pier for you to explore and meet with one of the local pilots. You will fly back the evening of the twenty-sixth. This is a packed schedule, but it's necessary before the inaugural sailing."

Luca raised his hand. "Would it be possible for me to fly directly from Nassau to Atlanta? I'm happy to pay for my flight, but I would like to spend the Thanksgiving holidays with my son and his family."

"Of course," Gayle responded. "I will have Martina schedule that. She will contact you tomorrow with details." The group discussed specifics of the schedule and agreed upon the captain's schedule for the next two weeks. He would have an exhaustive itinerary for each meeting and had to be prepared for any unforeseen issues. The final days before a ship launch were never restful.

Gayle followed her notes and discussed each department methodically. The officers were familiar with the challenges of navigating and docking at the busy Miami port. Luca had worked with two of them and felt confident in their abilities. The hotel staff was handling the extreme demand for cabins well. Gayle shared images of the pirate-themed décor of the cabins and the uniforms the room stewards would be wearing. Every detail, from the paint colors to the background music, would be aligned with the theme. The line did their best to make the experience feel like an authentic pirate adventure.

A man sitting on Gayle's left discussed the food and drink department. The diet of real pirates, such as hard biscuits and dried beans and fruit, would not appeal to most passengers, so the menu would include usual cruise food with extra fish options. The drink division developed a special drink of cherry and lime that could only be currently found on *Golden Fortune*. It would be served in a reusable glass etched with a skull and crossbones image. Luca figured that at twenty dollars each, the sales of this drink alone would pay the salaries of half the executives at today's meeting.

Next, a representative from the entertainment staff discussed their plans. The crew would host a "Gold" dance party, complete with guests in shiny outfits, on the third night and a seventies-themed party on night four. Two island-theme productions had been developed. And the ice-skating show would involve comical treasure hunters. Franny Meyers was hired as the cruise director. She had extensive experience with Disney Cruise Line and was a favorite of families.

The last department to be discussed was safety. One of Luca's most important responsibilities would be to ensure the safety of every passenger and crew member on board. From the navigation of the ship to avoid bad weather to the location of life jackets, he had the final say in all safety matters. The department was headed by a retired member of the US Navy. Luca listened to the general plans and started a list of questions to ask at their formal meeting in ten days.

Just as the meeting was ending, a catered dinner was delivered to the conference room. Luca relaxed as he ate. He had a lot of responsibility, but he also had an experienced and competent team. The upcoming meetings to finalize details would be mere formalities. The plans were in place, and the crew would fulfill their roles expertly.

Surprisingly, the dinner was American hamburgers and French fries. They were from a nearby restaurant advertising "gourmet" burgers. Luca had wanted to try them, but just couldn't imagine what a "gourmet" burger would entail. He was pleasantly surprised and made a note to add the hamburger restaurant to his dining rotation.

As she finished a French fry, Franny spoke up. "This pirate theme is really fun. It's been pretty easy to create events to fit. I can't wait for everyone to see the 'real' mermaids swimming at Mermaid Cove. They will be a hit. And the bonfire beach party at Treasure Island will be a favorite memory for all sorts of families. Please thank everyone for their help. We couldn't have pulled this off without our amazing crew."

"All of you have made tremendous efforts to make this a special adventure for our passengers," Gayle replied. "I can't wait to see pictures and hear stories about the pirate fun. I will be bringing my daughters and their families on the ship in February. They can't find the treasure, of course, but plan to solve the clues and see how far they can get. We are all excited to sail on this 'real' pirate ship with Captain Barone."

Luca knew that this was a special assignment. He was doing God's will—for now. The group spoke causally about their plans for the next few weeks. Each person was eager to start the world's first adventure cruise. But they would enjoy their last few days on land. Luca was especially looking forward to a few days with his grandsons before he set sail.

After dinner, the group rode the elevator to the ground floor together. Some of the group decided to walk two blocks to a nearby ice cream shop. Luca declined. He ordered a ride home and rested for the remainder of the evening. Late-night ice cream was a must on the ship. On land, however, it would keep him up all night. His meetings started tomorrow, so he opted for extra sleep. He had learned from the Navy to pick up strength when times were easy. Tonight, he would store up a little strength for the upcoming adventure.

CHAPTER THREE

November 11, Monday

On Monday, Morgan could barely keep up with the phone calls. Clients were thinking about last-minute mountain trips and beginning-of-the-year ski trips. She loved it. Researching and planning trips for singles, couples, and families was more like a hobby to her than a job. She was blessed to be paid for doing something she loved so much. Family reunions were particularly fun, and Morgan had three large ones to plan for the spring.

When Allison arrived shortly before 10:00, Morgan pleaded with her to help with the phone so she could finalize some plans for a multigenerational cruise and honeymoon to Paris. On cue the phone rang, and Allison quickly called from the front desk. "Mrs. Clark is asking about the Malaysia trip."

"Please tell her that I am still working on it. I found something that looks nice."

"Will do." Allison shared the details that she knew with Mrs. Clark and asked about her son Wade. They were in the same economics class and had gone out for coffee twice even though neither actually liked coffee.

After booking two flights to Paris, Morgan grabbed her purse and left for lunch. She would meet Lucy at the Green Grill at 11:45 to beat the noon rush. Known for their abundance of green vegetable sides, the Green Grill was a favorite of diners near and far. Morgan was already thinking about their chicken, bacon, and Brussels sprouts dish.

"I'll be back soon, Allison. Call me if you have any issues."

"Thank you. And I will be fine. Enjoy your lunch." Allison found the stack of documents that needed to be filed and walked to the copier to begin scanning them.

As she pulled into the parking lot of the Green Grill, Morgan spotted Lucy's "mom van." With four kids under ten, the Bond family filled the van quite nicely. Both sets of grandparents lived in Leesboro, so Lucy and her husband, Earl, were able to take two or three getaways each year sans kids. The grandparents took turns caring for the children and did a wonderful job.

Morgan found Lucy seated in a booth and appreciated that she had ordered two large sweet teas. She was wearing a bright green shirt and large hoop earrings.

"Perfect, Lucy. Thank you!"

"Sure thing. Mondays are for sweet tea. Our phones have been ringing off the hook today."

"Same here. People must be home for Veteran's Day." Morgan looked over the menu even though she knew exactly what she would order. "I got to book a honeymoon to Paris this morning. That is so fun. The couple doesn't know, but their room will be covered in rose petals on the evening they arrive."

"Oooh, that is romantic. Earl still doesn't want to go to Paris, but I am wearing him down. We had three requests this morning for plans to see the Ark Encounter. It is strange timing, but easier to plan in bulk."

The waitress took their orders. As expected, Morgan ordered the chicken, bacon, and Brussels sprout dish. Lucy went with the green papaya salad wraps. Talk turned from business to Thanksgiving to the *Golden Fortune* cruise. Morgan shared that she and Bob were bringing a folding shovel. "Do you think we will need more equipment that that?"

"I've been thinking about that. Earl thinks we will need flashlights. And water shoes. They could hide something in water. We are having fun packing for this trip. It will be so different from our other cruises. All the stops are private islands, so we will either be lounging on the beach or chasing down gold. No museums or local restaurants."

Morgan nodded. "We thought about that. Bob even asked if we could skip the hunt. He is really looking forward to the down time. If I know him, though, he will be awake every night deciphering clues. Have you thought about printing maps of the islands? They are new, so we won't know our way around them."

"Great idea! And we should print out the deck plans for each floor on the ship. Even if the treasure isn't hidden on the ship, some of the clues will be."

"I hadn't thought about that. We should be able to pull those maps up on the cruise line app, but printed versions might be handy if we lose service. Or if we are sneaking around in the dark. When are you traveling to Miami?" *Golden Fortune* would be sailing out of a new terminal at the Miami cruise port. The terminal was built with a pirate theme too. Even the parking garage would be fit for a pirate.

The waitress delivered their meals before Lucy could answer. "My parents are staying with the kids this time. They will come over with us on Saturday after Jalen's Pee Wee football game. It's the last of the season, so we don't want to miss it. That will give us a bit of a late start, but we should get to Miami by 6:00 p.m. Just in time for a walk on the beach and a late supper. How about you? Leaving before the sun comes up as usual?"

"Yep. You know Bob. He will be ready to go by 6:00 a.m. We will probably leave around 7:30 on Wednesday and get to my mom's house before noon. I don't expect a lot of traffic heading south that early. We may even stop for a lunch near the Deerfield Beach pier first. It will be fun to have Thanksgiving in South Florida. I'll have two extra days to visit before we leave for the cruise. My mom will love that. Be sure to let me know when you get to Miami. And I will look for you at check in."

"Same to you. I can't wait to see this ship in person. A huge cruise ship designed to look like an old-world pirate ship will be a sight to see. Can you imagine seeing it out in the ocean? It will look like real pirates are attacking."

"Kids will love it. Heck, I will love it. A real adventure."

After lunch, Morgan put together a Malaysian fantasy trip and printed out documents for three upcoming *Golden Fortune* cruises. The announcement of a second-place prize increased interest. The creative marketing was gaining attention from young families, singles, and empty nesters. Morgan was thankful for the sweet tea at lunch. Her afternoon was as busy as her morning. She would go to bed early tonight and get some rest while she could.

Luca returned to the corporate headquarters in downtown Miami on Monday to meet with the deck department. Second in command to the captain, the staff captain could navigate the ship without assistance and could oversee every aspect of the cruise at any time. Jewel Cruise Line hired Jenny Lu as staff captain because of her previous experience as a captain for a river cruise line. Luca hadn't met Jenny previously but was impressed as soon as he saw her. Dressed in a navy suit and four-inch heels, she modeled leadership as well as personality.

"Good morning, Captain," Jenny started. "I've been looking forward to working with you. I am ready to assist you and am prepared for these final meetings."

"It's nice to work with you as well." Luca had a good feeling about the deck department. The line had spared no expense to ensure smooth sailing on their first adventure cruise. Joining Luca and Jenny were the first, second, and third officers, as well as the environmental officer and deck cadet. Each person knew his or her specific role in the overall operation.

After casual chitchat, the team sat down and went over a checklist Luca had prepared. They spent four hours discussing the tricky navigation of Bahamian waters, current safety procedures, and lengthy budget and inventory controls. Luca laid out his expectations for the work environment and shared a few "horror stories" from previous tours.

Once again, the line delivered a catered meal for lunch. Members of the deck department brought up "what-ifs" while eating, and Luca was impressed with Jenny's quick responses. If she performed as well as he expected, she would be promoted to captain soon—probably on a mega-ship. Luca couldn't imagine manning the bridge in high heels but felt confident that Jenny could pull it off.

After lunch, the group pulled up maps of the three private islands. The officers carefully examined tricky features in the navigation to and from each pier. They also discussed how weather might affect docking. High winds were particularly dangerous when turning a supersized vessel. The weather in the Bahamas was generally stable—until a hurricane blew through. In those cases, *Golden Fortune* would have to travel out of the storm's path and possibly forego an island or two. At some point in the year, a storm would be strong enough to divert the ship. Fortunately, these storms provided days of warning.

Luca had experienced a few squalls over the years. They tended to sound more dangerous than they were. Modern sailing vessels were well-equipped to handle rough seas, but many passengers were not. When a ship began to rock too much, crew members had to shut down areas with the potential of flying debris. The medical personnel ran checks on seasick travelers. And the dining crew prepared for more room service than usual. If the crew was prepared ahead of time, stormy seas could be navigated safely.

The meeting ended with more "horror stories." Luca generally did not like to dwell on past surprises and mistakes, but the group was enjoying the discussion. Each had a wonderful story to share about unexpected weather or unruly passengers. Luca was delighted to hear that the crew felt comfortable handling such disruptions.

On the way home, Luca stopped at a nearby market for a few groceries. He found a decent-looking club sandwich for his supper and some ripe fruit for breakfast. After adding some milk, canned soup, and bread to his cart, Luca went toward the greeting card display. He would miss two family birthdays and Christmas during his first leg and wanted to have appropriate cards ready to mail. Guest services collected and distributed the mail on the ship when in port in Miami.

As Luca turned down the card aisle, he saw two boys playing with toy swords. They were clearly pretending to be pirates. Their mother told them to watch out for Luca, and the boys obediently stopped clashing their toys. The younger one looked up at Luca. "We're going on a real pirate ship. After Christmas. And it has real treasure."

Luca grinned. "Oh, really? That sounds like fun."

The mother excused their trio and rushed toward the cash register to check out. Luca found the cards he wanted and checked out too. His smile stayed with him the rest of the evening. God had given him a small glimpse of the joy that *Golden Fortune* was bringing to people around the area, even before stepping onto the ship. He was grateful to be a small part of this excitement and thought about the boys while he ate his sandwich.

CHAPTER FOUR

November 12, Tuesday

Morgan expected today to be slow, and she was right. She thought about calling Mikey and telling him that he didn't need to come in but decided against it. She knew from experience that as soon as she dismissed him, a lunch rush would arrive.

With a few minutes of free time, Morgan found the Jewel Cruise Line website and clicked on the link for *Golden Fortune*. She had looked at the pictures and read the descriptions a dozen times but browsed through them again. The overall décor was amazing. She and Bob would feel like real pirates when they were on the ship. Morgan wondered if there would be pirate music in the background and if there would be any special pirate dishes in the dining room. She had checked the dining section on the cruise line's app but hadn't found any menus posted yet.

As Morgan scanned the deck maps, she heard the bell above the office door ring. The wife of one of her church's deacons walked in. "Good morning, Mrs. Novell."

"Hi, Morgan. Please, call me Dot."

"Well . . . good morning, Dot. How may I help you?"

Dot held her beige purse at chest level with two hands. "I'd like to plan a trip, but I'm not sure how this works."

"You've come to the right place. Please, sit down and give me some details. We can go from there." Morgan flipped her notepad to a clean page and picked up a pen.

Dot sat tentatively in the chair facing Morgan's desk. She kept her purse on her lap. "Sid and I would like to do something special for our fortieth wedding anniversary. We really haven't done anything unique before, and the kids are insisting that we go on a trip. I just don't know where we would go. Sid doesn't like to leave the garden, you know."

Morgan beamed. "Congratulations! You should most certainly celebrate forty years. And I'm sure I can come up with something perfect. What do the two of you like? A beach? The mountains? Museums?"

"Oh, nothing like that," Dot said. "We just like to watch TV. And sometimes play card games. That's about it."

Morgan was surprised at Dot's response. Usually, clients were eager to travel to the ends of the Earth. They wanted adventure and excitement. Rarely did they ask to take a trip to play cards.

"And Sid won't fly or get on a ship," Dot continued. "And he doesn't like to drive very far. His back, you know?"

"Goodness. We'll have to get creative with this one. There is a train that goes to Washington, DC, regularly. Does that sound fun? I could arrange for you to see some of the monuments and museums in the area."

"Oh, that would be too much for Sid. He's never mentioned trains, but I'm pretty sure he wouldn't like that at all."

Morgan smiled and made a few notes on the notepad. "Let me get some contact information from you. I will see what I can come up with and call you back this afternoon. My schedule is fairly free for the rest of the day. Would that work?"

"Why, yes. That would be great. Thank you very much. I really appreciate your help with this."

As Morgan was saying goodbye to Dot, Mikey walked in. He greeted the ladies and went to check on his stack of paperwork. After

Dot left, Morgan asked him to man the phones while she planned a "tricky" vacation.

By the end of the day, Morgan had planned what she hoped would be the perfect anniversary trip for the Novells. She found a cozy home for rent two hours south of Jacksonville. The house was on a river and had an outdoor kitchen area. It was available for the week of the Novell's anniversary. Best of all, the basement had been turned into a large media room complete with two rows of reclining chairs and a state-of-the-art sound system. Morgan figured that the couple would enjoy their normal routine but on a grander scale. They could cook outdoors, play cards by the water, and watch their television programs in style.

Morgan shared the plans with Dot over the phone, and the woman was delighted. Sid agreed to driving two hours to celebrate with his wife. They even asked if the children and grandchildren could visit for an evening. Morgan would surprise them with a basket of popcorn supplies to be delivered on the first day. Days like today were the most fulfilling part of her job.

Luca had nothing planned with Jewel today. The line expected him to rest and begin packing for his first ten-week leg. He had already brought some boxes to his apartment, so today would be a great day to sort through his things. His mind was filled with plans and deadlines. The inaugural sailing of *Golden Fortune* was less than three weeks away. Plans from all departments would have to be finalized soon.

As Luca was sorting through the clothes in his bedroom closet, he saw the box. His box of mementos. He hadn't looked through his memories in over a year. Memories of Dahna were simply too painful. Remembering the better days—no, the *best* days—were difficult. He knew that he had been blessed with two wonderful sons and their equally wonderful families. But the past canceled out today's joy. Losing his wife had been the saddest experience of his life.

Sitting on the wicker chair near his bed, Luca looked at the box and knew exactly what was in there. Three wedding announcements. Baby bonnets. A plastic bottle of dirt from the back yard of their first home in Italy. Dahna's recipe box. His sailing medals. Christmas letters to Santa. Memories. Wonderful memories. And funny memories.

The happy memories included Dahna. And so did the sad ones. The day he first saw her in his college history class was a wonderful memory. She was talking with her friends, and her smile had stayed with Luca until their next class together. He awkwardly asked her to dinner at the fish market and was surprised when she agreed. They talked easily that night and continued for decades afterwards.

Throughout her illness, Dahna was more concerned about others than herself. She made sure that Luca ate and got enough sleep. She called the children and asked about their lives. And she made her way to church until she no longer had the strength.

With so many good times, there was no reason to dwell on the sad times. Luca did his best to only recall the good times. He remembered telling Dahna about the time that he ordered another ship to divert its course twenty degrees to avoid an accident only to discover that the ship was really an immovable oil rig. She laughed and announced that the rig should have moved for him.

Luca laughed about the time that Dahna forgot to add sugar to his birthday cake. It not only looked gray, it also tasted gray. But he didn't want to hurt her feelings, so he ate most of his piece. When Dahna finally ate a bite of the cake, she gasped and asked Luca if he was mad. The two of them laughed until they collapsed onto the floor. They then ate the icing off the "gray cake" with a spoon and declared the birthday a success.

With so many tasks ahead of him, Luca knew that a day of rest would not come around again for a while. He decided to walk down to a nearby duck pond and enjoy the peace and quiet of the area. Today's society was too noisy for the captain. Spending a few hours on a bench near the pond was a perfect afternoon for him. When he returned to his apartment, he would call the boys and remind them how much their mother loved them.

As Luca was watching three birds pecking at the ground, he saw a father and son walking by. The boy had a soccer ball under one of his arms and delighted when the birds took flight in unison as we walked near them. Luca's boys had also been fascinated with birds when they were young. Dahna had bought each of them a field guide for bird identification for Christmas one year. The family had so much fun trying to match local birds with their names. Today, his older grandson used a phone app to name birds. Luca laughed to himself as he hoped that the boys wouldn't be using an app to play soccer some day. Nature was meant to be enjoyed in person—both land and sea.

CHAPTER FIVE

November 15, Friday

Morgan and Bob drove to the home of Will and Shae Denning as soon as Bob got home from work. Their home was down a dirt road and had a large open area in the back, which was perfect for bonfires. Will had built wooden benches in a circle around the fire pit so that guests could sit and chat easily. The area was used as a makeshift chapel one Sunday when a Category 1 hurricane took out power to half of Jacksonville. Tonight, Morgan brought her famous peanut butter chocolate chip cookies and extra marshmallows. She figured that s'mores would be involved in the evening somehow.

As they rang the doorbell, Morgan realized they were the last to arrive. She recognized Will and Shae, of course, as well as Brother Greg and his wife, Marsha—yes, they received plenty of teasing about their *Brady Bunch* sibling names. In a more-awkward-than-necessary movement, Morgan yelled out, "We're here!" and cringed when she saw nine sets of eyes staring back. Attempting to downplay her outburst, she added, "We don't get out much." The eyes laughed.

"I don't know about that," Shae added. "You and Bob travel more than anyone I know. And Brother Greg is on the state mission board."

"True. We do travel a lot. But we don't spend enough time melting marshmallows with friends." The group laughed again, and Morgan learned that the other couples were Lena and Steph Edwards and Risa and Mario Martinez. Both women worked with Shae at a local pediatrician's office. She placed her cookies near the other desserts and turned to Marsha. "We are ready for Serving Sunday. Bob will load up his truck tomorrow. And we have plenty of tools this year."

"That's great," Marsha added. "We appreciate your willingness to get dirty for the Lord."

The couples filled their bowls with chili and topped them with plenty of fixings and ate in the open living room. After twenty minutes, the Dennings' teenage daughter walked into the living room. Morgan knew that Katie was a junior in high school and was surprised at how much older she looked than the last time she had seen her. Time had flown in the past year. Katie walked right by the adults without looking up. She placed some desserts on a plate and walked back to her room. Shae didn't seem surprised by this at all. Morgan was bothered though. Did the girl feel unappreciated? Was she being grounded? Or was she sick? Morgan couldn't imagine the thrill of having a daughter. Surely, she wouldn't waste any time with her like this. Or would she? To be honest, Morgan knew nothing about mothering a teenager. She remembered battles with her own mother but didn't remember sulking. She'll have to ask her mom about that over Thanksgiving.

When dinner was finished, the group headed to the fire pit. Will and Steph had the fire going and were adding more wood. The scene looked like a brochure for a high-end campground, and the smell of burning wood brought Morgan back to her childhood days and camping with her grandparents. Ironically, her family didn't travel much when she was a child. In fact, they didn't travel at all. But Morgan's grandparents had a worn RV that they took to nearby campgrounds several times per year. Morgan looked forward to those trips and still remembered the makeshift campfires her grandfather built.

"I just love autumn. It doesn't get better than this," Shae said. Morgan was a summer person but had to admit that the cool weather and fire were comfortable. The weather was perfect for a cozy sweatshirt, and the bugs were gone for the season. After a few minutes of silence, the men started identifying constellations in the sky. Bob used a star app on his phone to locate the Milky Way.

"Hey, look! There's something out there called Cleopatra's Eye Nebula. I don't think I see it, but the app has something out there labeled as Cleopatra's Eye." Bob held up his phone for the others to see as Morgan covered her face.

Shae put her arm around Morgan. "You are never going to live that down, are you?"

"Nope. Bob is making sure of that." The two women laughed at their inside joke.

"Tell us the story," Risa said. "What's so funny?"

"Oh, it's nothing," Morgan replied. "We don't need to go there."

"Tell the others, Bob. Tell them about your first date." Shae smiled and sat next to Morgan.

Bob began the story, and Morgan continued to cover her face, smiling behind her hands. "Well, Morgan and I met at Jim and Allyssa's Sunday school class. That was eighteen years ago. We started by texting and then talking on the phone at night. Morgan was working at the Henderson's travel agency at the time, and I was working for Clean Cut Landscaping in Lakeside. We had a client who invited the crew to a costume party fundraiser at a big estate house on Trout River. Two of the other guys were going, so I thought it would be perfect for our first date. I wouldn't have to make too much small talk. And the food was free." The guys nodded.

"We decided to dress as Antony and Cleopatra. I don't even remember why."

Morgan dropped her hands and spoke. "I had just booked a river cruise on the Nile for a retirement celebration, and we had been talking about that."

"That's right. We were in our Egyptian phase back then." The group laughed. "Anyways, Morgan was a knockout in her costume. She even decorated her eyes to look like a cat somehow. We made it to the estate, and a valet drove off with my car. But when we walked through the front door, we immediately realized that it wasn't a costume party. It was a "costume fundraiser" party. The client was collecting costumes for needy children at Halloween. Not only were we the only ones dressed up, we also didn't bring a child's costume. I could get away with my pants and loose shirt. But Morgan stood out. I just knew that she would never speak to me again."

"And she shouldn't!" Marsha interrupted. "You men just aren't that interested in the details, are you? Greg used to forget to tell me that he had late staff meetings, and I would be waiting with dinner on the table for hours. Of course, his schedule was stuck on the refrigerator each week, but I'm still going to blame him." That got another laugh from the group.

Morgan finished the story. "It really was an honest mistake. Or at least I think so." She looked over at Bob with a smirk. "But the party got worse. I wanted to leave immediately, but the client's wife wouldn't have it. She had me pose for a dozen pictures to show that they had a queen at her party. Some of the guests were asking me to refill their drinks. It was awful. But it turned out to be one of the best nights of my life.

"When we were finally able to leave, Bob took me out to a lovely pizza restaurant on Jax Beach. Nobody batted an eye at our costumes. We talked until the restaurant closed. That was the night that I knew Bob was a 'keeper.' On our first date."

"That is a great story," Risa said. "Thank you for sharing."

"And guess where they honeymooned?" Shae asked. "Egypt!"

"Really?" Mario was amazed.

"Yep," Morgan said. "The Hendersons paid for half of the trip. We stayed at a resort in Nabq Bay, Egypt, and even saw the pyramids. Now I have a nebula named after myself." Shae laughed and gave her friend a sideways hug.

Talk then turned to Serving Sunday. Shae, Lena, and Risa would be helping with a free mobile clinic hosted by three local pediatricians. Dozens of parents awaited this event each year, and a line always began forming well before the event started. The doctors provided urgent care, well visits, and mental health evaluations. Occasionally, they referred children to specialists. The local community had grown to expect and appreciate the free yearly clinic.

After a discussion about the clinic, Mario brought up tomorrow's college football schedule. The weekend before rivalry weekend did hold many exciting matchups, but that wouldn't stop the men and most of the women from watching their favorite teams. Morgan had already planned to make barbecue chicken nachos tomorrow.

After three days of reviewing the final plans on his own, Luca met with the hotel staff on Friday. The hotel department was known as the "fun department" to many in the cruise industry and housed the entertainment and the food. Led by Barry Manning, the hotel director, and Franny Meyers, the cruise director, the hotel department was the most visible of the major departments to passengers. Luca would meet with the entertainment staff separately next week, so today's meeting would focus on the hospitality details of the cruise. Also attending today's meeting were the chief purser, the casino manager, the housekeeping manager, the concessions manager, and the food and beverage manager. Looking at his checklist, Luca began with the housekeeping manager.

A literal floating city, *Golden Fortune* had 1624 cabins and could hold a maximum of 3422 passengers. The cabins included the interior "Raider" cabins, the windowed "Corsair" cabins, the "Scallywag" cabins with balconies, and the "Buccaneer" suites. Aimed primarily at families, each cabin contained a king-size bed and pull-out couch. The beds could be converted to separate twins, and some of the rooms contained bunk beds or toddler beds. The cabins were decorated with a red, black, and yellow theme. And the cabin numbers in the hallways were shaped like ancient flags. Inside, passengers would find a treasure map painted on one wall and a display of nautical rope knots on another. The first clue and eye patches would be found inside the cabins. Pirate hats and fake gold coins were also placed on the desks for any children. The line tossed around the idea of adding toy swords, but quickly realized they could cause harm to others as well as to the ship.

"Before we get started, does anyone think we are going overboard with the pirate theme? Pun intended." The casino manager looked at Luca. "I know it's too late to make changes, but I think we've gone too far. The slot machines are spitting out golden doubloons, and the servers are dressed like she-pirates. It's just too much. This isn't really a pirate ship, you know?"

"I agree with you that the line has gone a little far." The captain responded. "But only if we are looking at it from our perspective. You see, this will be a once-in-a-lifetime adventure for many of our passengers. They expect the full treatment. Children will remember the pirate adventure for the rest of their lives. They will share pictures with their families and friends. The overboard extras will add to the memories. How are the menus working?"

The grumpy-looking food and beverage manager looked up. He spoke with a heavy, Slavic accent. "Thankfully, corporate hasn't done much with the menus. They are standard. We are adding more fish and pushing the family friendly Cutlass specialty drink with cherry and lime. I've ordered fifteen thousand etched glasses and will adjust our inventory after the second cruise. The head waiter is asking if the bus boys could get away with wearing eye patches only one night out of the week. They are crashing into chairs with them on."

"I think that is a fine idea. Anyone have an objection? If not, we will test the patches on night two and document any issues. If they begin colliding, we will allow them to remove the patches and develop a new plan for next week."

The food and beverage manager continued. "I would like to discuss the desserts. We are trying some new items and have no idea how they will go over with the passengers. I have estimated the consumption on the spreadsheet and will keep it updated daily." Luca thanked the man and asked a few more questions about the new venues.

Pizza was delivered at noon, and the group noted the irony. The department responsible for the fine dining and entertainment onboard *Golden Fortune* was treated to pizza and paper plates for lunch. Of course, the food was delicious, and everyone ate enough to be full. Luca noted that the sweet tea was *deliziosa*.

After lunch, the concessions manager shared a minor concern he had with the main gift shop on board. The shelves near the exit were too close to the doors but could not be moved. Luca made a note to contact a service technician. "I will try to get someone to look at it this weekend. We can't have children in eye patches colliding with the shelves."

Finally, Luca addressed the chief purser. "Thank you for sending me your spreadsheets. I don't know how you do it, but the documents are complete. As you've been told, your team must not share any details about the location of the treasure each week. From what I understand, the clues have been written for the first twenty-five weeks, and staff on the islands will be told two days before they are to hide a chest. Your team will be responsible for keeping this information documented and secure."

"We understand, boss. I trust my team. The hunt will be secure." The chief purser couldn't be older than thirty-five but was very detail-oriented. Luca felt comfortable that he would handle the customary duties of a purser, as well as the much-anticipated treasure hunt.

Luca thanked the purser and the rest of the department heads. He ended with four pages of notes that would keep him busy on Saturday. Media coverage for the initial voyage would come from a firsthand perspective as half of the "preview" cruise passengers would be reporters. The staff must also impress the travel agents on board, so they would encourage their clients to book vacations on *Golden Fortune*. The distinction would be in the details. The "overboard" theming would be the hook to entice visitors from around the world. But the service on board could make or break the interest in the ship.

Luca ordered a ride to take him home after the meeting. When the minivan arrived, he discovered that the driver was a young woman. She greeted him politely. "Good evening, sir."

"*Ciao*." Luca usually didn't speak much to drivers, so he expected his one-word greeting to be enough. Surprisingly, that one word set the woman into a rant.

"Are you Italian? Oh, not Italian. My boyfriend just broke up with me in Hot Tomatoes today. I had just ordered the cheesy bread appetizer when he told me he'd had a dream. I thought it was about parachuting, like I always dream. But it wasn't."

At this point, the girl stopped talking and started to softly cry. Luca was never good with others' tears. He sat quietly, hoping the girl was through with her story. She wasn't.

"I'm Callie, by the way. Are you really Italian?"

"Yes. I was born in Naples."

"Neato. Mosquito!" Callie became excited. "Do you ever go to Hot Tomatoes? They have the very best spaghetti." She suddenly became sad again.

"Oh, man. I didn't even get to my meal. I was waiting for the cheesy bread when Aiden tells me that he dreamt he had a blonde girlfriend. And since my hair is dark brown, we had to break up. Isn't that totally Mickey Mouse? Hello! I can dye my hair blonde. Half of my friends dye their hair blonde.

"Well, he said that the girl in the dream was a natural blonde. Really? How mean. I just don't understand. Then he stood up and high-fived me. What was that about? Well, I didn't text him the whole time I ate the cheesy bread. And I'm not gonna. This is his loss. He's done this before, but I'm not taking him back. He can just keep his naturally blonde bimbo."

Luca didn't know how to respond. He could tell that the girl was clearly upset, but she just continued to ramble on. Something about going back to college. Maybe she just needed someone to listen. He sat there quietly while Callie agonized over her ex-boyfriend's crazy dream and her future without him. When they arrived at Luca's apartment building, she stopped talking.

"I think you should keep your brown hair," Luca said. "It's very Italian." His response must have been perfect, because Callie started laughing and said that he was her new favorite rider. Not bad for an ancient ship's captain who knew nothing about young people these days.

CHAPTER SIX

November 17, Sunday

Serving Sunday had arrived. The weather was perfect, and Morgan was looking forward to spending the morning with Bob. Another couple from church would join them, as well as a handful of high school students whose parents were unable to work that day. She made blueberry muffins earlier and placed two on a plate when Bob walked into the kitchen. "Would you like some coffee?"

"What did I do to deserve this?" He sat in front of the muffins. He was dressed in his work clothes and was ready to serve.

"I know that I usually don't cook on Sunday mornings, but today is different. I feel lighter this morning. It's nice to get out of the building and serve. Together. Marsha said that the Perrys will join us. They can fit the youth students in their SUV and will follow us. Did you pack extra gloves?"

"Yes, we should have plenty of gloves." The couple ate a quick breakfast and Morgan also dressed in work clothes. This was quite a change from her usual Sunday dress. Bob checked the equipment in his truck one last time and drove with Morgan to the church parking lot. They found the Perrys right away and parked next to their van.

The associate pastor was handing out assignments on small cards. Bob's assignment had only two jobs. They were to clean the yard of an elderly church member and clear debris on the property of a nearby start-up church. The tasks should be easy for nine workers.

Once the youth workers arrived, the group drove to Nettie Miller's house. She was homebound and had trouble keeping up with her yard. Neighbors helped when they could, but the leaves had finally taken over. Bob assigned the Perrys to trim the hedges, while the teenagers raked leaves onto tarps and drug them to the curb. At first the young people stared at the rakes, but they eventually got to work. They talked nonstop while working and seemed to be having fun. Bob ran a mower over the grass, and Morgan tackled the weeds with weed killer. The morning was running routinely until Mrs. Miller came out to her porch exclaiming her thanks. The appreciation the woman showed made all the labor worthwhile. She slowly walked to the students and handed each of them a silver dollar. The kids didn't know how to react, but seemed to realize that the woman was giving them as much as she could. The kids tried to refuse the dollars, but Mrs. Miller wouldn't have it. She hugged each one and went back to her porch to watch the work from a rocking chair. Morgan figured that Jesus was smiling down on the busy workers today.

Once finished, the group drove to Grace Community Church. The small congregation had secured a permanent building one year ago, but a strong storm in early September brought down eight pine trees on their property. The kitchen area in the back of the building sustained minor damage, and church members were able to make repairs. But none of the members were able to remove the trees, and the expense to hire a tree-removal service was prohibitive.

The elderly pastor of Grace Community and his wife met the group with a warm welcome. Bob and Mr. Perry worked two chainsaws to cut the trees into small sections. The others loaded the sections onto Bob's trailer. After each tree was loaded, Morgan drove the truck to a nearby waste site where the teenagers helped unload the trailer. The job took nearly three hours to complete, and the entire group was exhausted afterward. Bob and Morgan treated the workers to lunch at Dairy Queen before returning to Cornerstone Church.

There was a buzz of excitement in the parking lot as groups were returning from their jobs. Morgan spotted Shae and Lena and walked over to them. "Hey, ladies. How was your morning?"

Shae spotted tree sap on Morgan's flannel shirt and laughed. "Not as strenuous as yours, I think. There was a line of people when we arrived, and we had to cut off newcomers about thirty minutes ago. It breaks my heart to see some of the kids with problems that could have been solved with simple antibiotics or education. One eight-year-old was addicted to smokeless tobacco. His mom wanted our help getting him to quit."

"Wow, that is sobering. You should have seen Mrs. Miller hugging the kids and thanking them for their help. Her yard looks so much better now. And we hauled away eight pine trees for Grace Community. It feels good to see the fruits of our labor."

Pastor Greg thanked everyone in the parking lot and led a prayer for those receiving help. He reminded everyone that loving their neighbors should happen every day and that they should be looking for "serving opportunities" around them. He added that God just might send a blessing as a job.

Back home, Bob and Morgan fell asleep on the couch while watching football. That evening, they both recognized that their spirits felt lighter. "It feels good to be useful. I'm glad that our church recognizes the importance of serving others," Morgan noted. "There are so many ways to serve, but I truly smile when I see you using your gifts to help others. Mrs. Miller was so thankful."

"She was," Bob chuckled. "Those kids didn't know what to think. I'll keep an eye out for her yard. It didn't take that much work to shape it up. Maybe we can plant a few flowers for her in the spring." Morgan liked the idea and sat out sandwich fixings for supper. The couple ate on the back porch and noted that they would be eating dinner on the *Golden Fortune* two weeks from then.

"Is it too early to start packing?" Morgan asked.

"Ha! Not for you. Let's give it a few more days."

Sunday was "entertainment day." Luca was looking forward to hearing of any changes in the shows and activities. He met with Franny Meyers, the cruise director, and Steven Marino, the music director. The assistant cruise director and director of the kids' club were also present.

"We haven't changed much since we last saw you, Luca." Franny was pulling up videos on her laptop to project on the conference room's pop-up screen. "I'd like to show you clips of our production shows. The performers have perfected their acts in our studio and will fit them onto the ship's venues when it arrives tomorrow. When can we get on board?"

"Let me write Gayle to confirm, but I think crew can board thirty minutes after she docks. Corporate would also like marketing to have opportunities for clean photos before we start boarding."

"Great!" Franny showed the group clips from the main production, *Swiss Family Robinson*. It would be performed in the Swashbuckler Theater. The original songs would appeal to both children and adults, and the acrobatic performers would swoop and sail over the stage.

Franny showed several clips with and without the full costumes. Next, she shared scenes from the ice skating production

Bumbling Treasure Hunters. The talented skaters would perform as clowns in a comical treasure hunting show. The bright colors and cheerful music would thrill adults as much as children. Luca thought about Dahna and how much she would have enjoyed the performance.

The third production show was a mermaid show that involved a state-of-the-art LED screen. The theater would transform into a panoramic space that would simulate the ocean where dancers on wires would portray a school of mermaids. Entertainment technology amazed Luca, but he was responsible for the safety of the performers. He listened to Franny discuss the wire rigging that enabled the dancers "swim" over the stage. After thirty minutes of questions about their safety, attention moved to the kids' club.

Golden Fortune would be popular with all shapes and sizes of families, but those with young children would be especially interested. They would fly down pool slides and gaze on magical shows together. They would eat late-night ice cream and build sand castles as a family. Eventually, though, parents and grandparents would appreciate some "adult time," and kids would appreciate some "play time." Deck Twelve of *Golden Fortune* housed the Ahoy Kids' Club, a full-service facility with age-appropriate activities and programming. Children under the age of eighteen were sorted by age and situated in appropriate environments. While the children were having fun with trained caregivers, parents could enjoy a romantic dinner or dance at a lively night club.

Luca listened to plans for babies in cribs and toddlers with finger paints. He heard the designs for crafts and puppet shows. And he was updated on the placement of six Ping-Pong tables in the teen area. He made notes about all the venues and planned to ask Gayle about extra training for the evacuation of the kids' club in an emergency. The success of the children's program could make or break a family oriented cruise.

After another catered lunch of pizza, Luca addressed the director of music. Dozens of musicians would perform each week in a variety of venues. Solo artists would perform in clubs and the theater. Ensembles would accompany the *Swiss Family Robinson* and *Mermaids Ahoy* shows. Others would provide live music on the pool deck and dining venues. Musicians worked mostly at night and were required to be flexible enough to cover several assignments. Quality performers were in high demand, and cruise lines often had trouble finding enough musicians to fill their needs. Luca was delighted to hear that all the positions had been filled and visas had been secured.

"We are ready, sir. Some of the uniforms are awkward for the performers, but Jewel's tailors are working on alterations as we speak," the director said. "We will be ready for embarkation day. And please don't ask us to wear eye patches."

"Ha! I promise that your musicians will not have to wear eye patches. Thank you for securing the talent on time."

After a few more questions, the meeting ended early.

Luca fell asleep on the couch, watching football. In two weeks, *Golden Fortune* would be sailing. So many preparations were still ahead, but Luca felt comfortable that at this point the crew could handle any emergency. Passengers would be entertained, and they would be safe. He'd bet his life on it.

CHAPTER SEVEN

November 20, Wednesday

The week started out busy but had slowed down by Wednesday. Live It! Travel Agency would only be open for two days next week, so Morgan tried to handle as much paperwork as she could this week. She finalized the ten-day trip to Malaysia for Stephanie and printed travel documents for two more *Golden Fortune* cruises. The new cruise line was instantly popular, and Morgan received inquiries about it on a weekly basis.

Morgan was researching a twentieth anniversary getaway to Jamaica when her phone rang. Lucy's face popped up on the screen. "What's up, Luc?"

"Hey. I had to tell you what just happened. You are the only person I know who would truly appreciate it."

"Do tell!"

"Well, some senior from UNF came in and asked if I could plan a bachelor party in Las Vegas for him. I reminded him that we were a faith-based travel agency, but he clearly didn't understand what that meant. He explained that the trip would be for twelve college buddies, and they wanted to do it up right. They wanted the cheapest rooms I could find. And they wanted me to book strippers for two nights. I was speechless, so he kept talking. They preferred that I find a cocaine supplier for them in Vegas so they wouldn't have to travel with anything illegal from Florida."

"What?!"

"I finally blurted out, 'Stop!' The poor guy looked shocked. I know this is terrible for business, but I explained to him what I meant by *faith-based*. He clearly didn't understand. Apparently, his parents go to church but also introduced him to cocaine. They claim that it helps them on their busy days. So *faith-based* was just a cover to him. I just feel defeated because the guy said a few blue words as he walked out the door."

"You did the right thing, Lucy. I hope I would do the same. I know that a large trip would bring a nice profit, but we can't book strippers. We just can't."

"I know. I probably should have compromised with him and just booked the flights and rooms. We don't know what our clients do on any of these trips. I may have booked someone on a trip to rob a bank or cheat on a spouse. It's possible. Should I give everyone a survey or something? I'm just a little thrown by this."

"Don't beat yourself up. We are traveling through this world the best that we can. I think the Holy Spirit wanted you to know what was going on with this trip. He will reward you for taking a stand. I'm sure of it."

Lucy thanked Morgan. "I needed to hear that. With four kids to feed, it's hard to turn down business. But strippers? Good grief!" The women talked for a few more minutes before getting back to travel planning. Morgan thanked God for her friend. Navigating life is tricky, and Morgan acknowledged that she needed as many like-minded friends as possible.

She ended the day with a few more phone calls, including two about *Golden Fortune*. A high school football coach and his wife wanted to surprise their son with a "real" pirate adventure. They planned to wrap some pirate toys as Christmas gifts and when he opened them add that they would be going on a real ship over spring break. The marketing department at Jewel Cruise Line had created a hit.

Morgan made spaghetti for supper before Bob got home. She still used the recipe her grandmother gave her when she was twelve. It was simple but authentic. She tried to switch to whole grain noodles, but Bob claimed that they tasted like cardboard. Morgan had to agree that they didn't taste like her grandmother's noodles and went back to her traditional pasta. Bob would travel to Egypt for their honeymoon, but he wouldn't fall for cardboard spaghetti.

Perhaps the most important meeting for Luca was with the safety team. Protecting the passengers and crew was his primary responsibility. Today, the team would meet on the bridge of the ship instead of the Jewel Cruise Line headquarter building. Luca shook hands with the chief security officer, the deputy security officer, and the firefighting team leader.

After a general exchange, the ship's head physician walked in. "Captain Stubing! How are you today?" Luca disliked the *Love Boat* reference but went along with the fun. The television show that ran in the 1970s and 80s did more for the cruise industry than he ever did.

"Hi there, Doc. Where are Gopher and Isaac?"

The group laughed before turning to the chief security officer, who was handing out two-hundred-page safety manuals. "Here is our final document. The only changes we made from the last version are in the section on drills. You will notice on page 128 that we have included the medical team in all drills now. Also, we will launch one of the

TorpedoX lifeboats at the regular drills. Since they have new technology for the lifeboats to be dispatched and aimed directly at a person overboard on a Code Oscar, we want to test their speed and distance. I am a little uneasy about shooting an inflatable raft blindly in the ocean, but I do acknowledge that the rapid response is better than the slower approach we have used in the past."

"Let's just keep our passengers on the ship, and we won't have to worry about the TorpedoX," Doc added.

"I agree," the deputy security officer said. "We all agree that 'prevention is better than a cure,' but the treasure-hunting aspect of this ship adds some risk. We have extra cameras in the passageways and on the pool decks. We don't expect a mad frenzy when clues are released, but we need to be prepared for one." The officer also discussed the placement of additional life rings on the top deck and the emergency generator designed to keep lights on in the event of a power loss.

Luca continued down his checklist and quizzed the head firefighter about the alarms, the sprinkler system, and the fireproof doors. Few passengers realized the extensive behind-the-scenes work that was done to keep them safe. The crew had to plan for any possible emergency caused by weather, carelessness, equipment malfunctions, or sabotage. Weekly drills and training kept the staff alert to dangers, as well as proper procedures. With their new ship sailing in eleven days, the Jewel Cruise Line would cut no corners on safety.

The discussion of fire safety continued after lunch. Once all questions were asked and answered, attention turned to Doc and his staff. The medical team was responsible for responding to all ailments affecting passengers and crew. The ship held two examining rooms, an extensive pharmacy, and a modest operating room used for emergencies. It also held a morgue for the possibility of the untimely death of a passenger or crew member while on board. In addition to medical issues, the team was accountable for the general well-being and health of everyone on the ship. They maintained global health standards and sanitation procedures.

Doc ended the meeting by boasting about his team. "Our most common concerns are sunburn and hangovers. But we are fully prepared for any medical emergency—even frostbite. You can trust that the passengers and crew of *Golden Fortune* will be in the best hands possible." Luca was pleased with the safety team and ended the meeting with a group tour of the TorpedoX launch sites.

When he returned to his apartment, Luca decided to find the "gourmet" burger restaurant that served lunch for his first meeting. The Uber driver dropped him off near the shopping center that housed Bessie's, which claimed to have the "universe's greatest hamburgers." Luca hesitated, debating his choice, but eventually walked through the doors.

"Welcome to Bessie's! Have a seat." A grandmotherly woman greeted Luca as soon as he entered. He found a seat near the back and opened the menu. The hamburgers were named with cow references, like the Moo Moo or the Peppered Patty. Luca had to laugh to himself. Here was another business going "overboard" with their theming.

After reviewing the choices, Luca chose the Steer Me Wrong burger. It had three types of cheese and jalapeno peppers. He figured if he were going to eat unhealthily, then do it big, right? Well, sort of. He wouldn't be able to eat the entire sandwich and would only eat a few of the French fries.

A middle-age waitress walked up to Luca's table with a large notepad and pen decorated in black and white to look like a cow's hide. "Howdy! Welcome to Bessie's. We are *udderly* thrilled to have you here. Do you have any questions?"

"No, thank you. I'm ready to order."

"Okay. What'll you have? Our Moo Moo is quite popular. And so is the Bullseye."

"Those sound great, but I will take the Steer Me Wrong. And ice water to drink, please."

The waitress wrote Luca's order on her notepad and looked back at him. "Would you like to have your fries Till the Cows Come Home?"

"Sure. That sounds good."

As soon as Luca agreed, the woman pepped up. She walked to a door near the kitchen and rang a bell. Everyone in the restaurant looked up.

"Holy cow, y'all! We've got a Till the Cows Come Home ordered. Table fourteen!" Everyone in the restaurant began clapping. Luca watched the events unfolding without moving a muscle. What had he ordered? He could only imagine. He sat at his table quietly, waiting for the big reveal.

A couple leaving the restaurant stopped at Luca's table and congratulated him on his fry choice. The man shook Luca's hand as the waitress brought Luca's drink. His water was served in a wide glass with ceramic horns on two sides. Luca remembered the casino manager questioning the over-the-top pirate theming on *Golden Fortune*. He would have to talk with Gayle about his bovine experience. The ship was decorated, and uniforms were ordered. But the names of some activities could be changed. And the eye patches could be eliminated altogether.

After about six or seven minutes, the waitress returned with Luca's oversize hamburger. It looked delicious. Strangely, she did not serve him French fries. He didn't want to take any chances and didn't ask her about them.

As Luca was cutting his cheeseburger in half with a large knife, the lights in the restaurant dimmed, and yellow lights in the ceiling began to flash. A group of ten employees walked out of the kitchen pulling a small cattle trailer filled with French fries. There were enough fries to feed half of Miami. Luca's mouth dropped open.

The group started clapping as they approached Luca's table. Then they began singing.

"*Moooove over for a tasty treat. There's nowhere for you to roam. Sit back and enjoy your meal . . . till the cows come home.*" The entire restaurant began clapping, and Luca knew his face must be crimson.

"Woo-ie! That was fun. Thank you for ordering our specialty. We haven't sold one in three weeks. And remember, we allow tipping in this pasture." Luca later learned that "cow tipping" was an unwanted pastime in farming communities, but at the time he was speechless.

The "fry wagon" came with a small plastic scoop for the fries. Luca scooped a reasonable amount onto his plate and felt ashamed that the rest would be wasted. He looked up to see people at a handful of tables staring at him. Not knowing what to do, he held up the scoop. "Please. Have some fries. I have plenty."

A young couple walked over with a plate and introduced themselves as Mary and Wayne. The girl scooped some fries onto the plate, and the boy thanked Luca. "We *herd* you had some extra taters." Luca could only laugh. Three more people walked over with plates and filled them with hot fries. No one recognized the captain, and he was grateful. The evening turned out to be fun, and Luca decided that he would return. His grandsons would get a kick out of the "fry wagon." And the hamburger didn't "steer" him wrong.

CHAPTER EIGHT

November 23, Saturday

On Saturday, Bob planned to work outside. Since he maintained yards for a living, he didn't enjoy working on his own yard. But he would be away for the cruise the next two weekends, so he needed to get it in order. The leaves seemed to be multiplying, so Bob tackled them first. He raked most of them onto a tarp and drug them to the edge of the yard near the road. He then trimmed the shrubs in front of the house and ran the lawn mower over the yard. Barring a strong storm, the yard would be tidy until he returned.

Morgan started some laundry and sat down with her laptop. The office manager of a dentist's office had called the afternoon before asking for flights and rooms for nine people to attend a conference in Boston in January. She didn't want to put this assignment off, so she made their arrangements while sipping coffee at the kitchen table. She and Bob had a working office in one spare bedroom, but Morgan felt lonely in there, especially when Bob was home. She enjoyed watching him walk by the kitchen windows as he worked outside.

Morgan felt truly blessed by her marriage with Bob. He was her "home" here on Earth. While several things he did annoyed her, she would rather live with these things than without him. They had planned to have two or three children and should be coaching Little League by now, but God had different plans. Her one IVF treatment didn't work, and Bob did not feel comfortable fostering children who had parents out there somewhere. The years just rolled by until it was too late.

Morgan was an only child to older parents. Her father died when she was in college, leaving her mother, Helen, to carry on alone. Eventually, Helen moved in with her sister in West Palm, and the two widows began thriving together. They played pickleball weekly and contributed to their local newspaper's "Senior Moments" section regularly. When Aunt Margaret began getting on her nerves, Helen would drive to Jacksonville and stay with Morgan and Bob for a few days. It didn't take long for her to miss her home and drive back south.

Bob's younger brother had one daughter, Morgan's only niece. Doug and his family lived in northern Alabama, so Morgan and Bob were unable to attend Jessica's dance recitals and soccer games regularly. They made a point to attend her end-of-year recitals in June but spent little time with her the rest of the year. Morgan invited Jessica to stay with them a week or two this past summer, but she declined. Apparently, visiting her aunt and uncle in Florida did not rank above time with her school and church friends. Morgan had been talking with Doug's wife, May, about taking a *Golden Fortune* cruise as a group next summer, but she didn't seem interested in a treasure hunt. Morgan would keep trying. She planned to send May pictures of her upcoming trip. The sunny weather and endless food choices just might coax Doug and May to set sail.

Infertility and a small biological family left Morgan with no children to love at home. Instead, she invested time with the church's youth group and planned fun trips for other families. At times, she became overwhelmed with the thought of a future with neither children nor grandchildren. But those pity parties were opportunities to trust God's plan for her life. He must have a reason, or even something better than grandchildren, if that is possible. She did believe that God knew what He was doing. She just had to accept that He knew better.

After planning for the dental conference, Morgan started making grilled cheese and tomato soup for lunch. Bob had been outside for more than two hours and must be chilled. A cold front had settled over north Florida, making high temperatures huddle near the low fifties for a few days. A week in the Bahamas was sounding better and better.

After lunch, Bob brought the suitcases down from the attic. Bringing them into the kitchen was the ceremonial start to every vacation week. Morgan clapped her hands and picked up the luggage. "It's getting real now. Let's start gathering our hunting supplies."

Bob agreed. "I guess it's time to get serious about this. I made a list on my phone yesterday. Let's find these things and worry about clothes later. Are you sure your mom is okay with us staying for four nights? We usually only stay for two."

"Yes, I think she's looking forward to it. She wants us to meet her pickleball friends. And Aunt Margaret already has our room ready with fresh sheets and chocolates on the pillows. They are so cute together. What do you think about eating lunch at the pier before we go to their house?"

"Great idea!" Bob went to the garage and came back with a folding shovel, headlamps, rope, and garden gloves. "I sure hope we don't get pulled over by the police on the way down. We look like we are planning a serious crime."

"Yikes! We do. What else do we need? I have a magnifying glass. And Shae offered to get a stethoscope if we need to listen through walls."

Bob laughed. "I don't think we will need the stethoscope. But the magnifying glass could be helpful. What about waterproof bags? And a snorkel set? We may have to search under water." The couple nixed the snorkel and mask and managed to fill a large duffel bag with search supplies before heading to the couch to watch college football. Morgan thanked God for her full life, even if it didn't include children.

The final department meeting for Luca was with the engine department. The team walked into the engine room as he introduced himself to the chief engineer, second engineer, chief electrician, and A/C engineer. Gayle Parker was also present but didn't speak much at the meeting. This team was responsible for the maintenance of the ship's mechanical systems, including the air conditioning units, the engines, and the fuel supply. Run completely on LNG, or liquified natural gas, *Golden Fortune* required extra refrigeration and more tank space for its fuel.

Luca began the meeting by addressing the chief electrician. "Has the problem with the elevators been fixed?"

"Yes, sir . . . sort of. Elevator eight is still giving us some trouble. But it does not pose a safety hazard. When a floor button is pressed, the next floor button also lights up. The elevator does not stop at the next floor, but it will be confusing to the passengers. I've been on the phone with the manufacturer, and we have a teleconference with their engineers this afternoon. I think the problem is on our end, but we haven't found it yet. We will check the wiring for a fourth time before the teleconference."

Luca had seen these strange glitches before and wasn't overly concerned. He would have a sign placed near the buttons if the issue wasn't fixed before embarkation day. "Anything else?"

"No, sir. The fire alarms, propulsion systems, and navigation equipment passed their final inspections on Thursday. My team knows their placement during drills and emergencies. And we installed the last of the new motion sensors in the suites. We are good, Captain."

"Thank you. Please keep me updated on the elevator buttons. And I would appreciate a tour of the upper engine room before we embark." Luca next spent an hour questioning the A/C engineer. *Golden Fortune* would be equipped with energy-saving technology, which would conserve electricity in unoccupied rooms. The system would save an estimated fifteen percent in energy expenses by reducing the air conditioning and heat output when not needed. Luca's primary concern was the potential actions to be taken should the systems not resume when passengers and crew returned to their cabins. Passengers expected sufficient air conditioning after their days in the sunshine.

Convinced that the passenger cabins would not become sweltering during a cruise, Luca turned to the chief engineer, who was responsible for the operation and upkeep of all mechanical equipment on the ship and literally kept the ship running. From the engines to the communication procedures to the technology in the lifeboats, engineers ensured that passengers and crew members were transported from port to port safely and comfortably. A ship could not run at all without competent engineers.

The discussion of mechanical issues continued through lunch and into the late afternoon. After the meeting, Luca returned to his apartment. He would leave early the next morning to fly to the Bahamas for a last review of the three ports *Golden Fortune* would visit each week. As he was heating up frozen lasagna, his phone buzzed. It was Marco calling.

"Hello, son."

"Hi, Dad. How has your week been?" Luca shared with his son an overview of the meetings, including the peculiar elevator button issue. As a mechanical engineer, Marco was always interested in the technical issues of a large cruise ship. "Sounds like a simple illumination problem. Are the buttons touchless?"

"No, the engineers decided against touch-free buttons in most of the cars because children often stand too close to the control panels. They end up lighting every button." Luca had received frequent complaints in the past from elevator riders forced to stop at every floor after children knowingly or unknowingly lit up the floor selection panels. Lengthy elevator wait times were a perpetual grievance of cruise ship passengers.

Father and son discussed improvements in propulsion technology and the new TorpedoX lifeboats before talk turned to the Thanksgiving Day plans. Marco confirmed Luca's arrival time and promised to be at the airport when he landed. A cold front would be arriving in Atlanta, so the family might see freezing weather for the holiday. Luca made a quick note to pack some warm-weather clothing for his trip. He didn't see cold weather in the Caribbean very often but was prepared for lower temperatures. His younger son lived in Cincinnati, and he visited his family during his ten-week breaks whenever he could.

"How is soccer going? Anthony must be enjoying it this year."

"He is, Dad. I hope you get to see him play while you are here. We could go to the park one day."

"That would be great, son." Luca could remember Marco and Gio playing soccer. It was only yesterday that he was watching them take one practice kick after another. Dahna would have soup ready when her men returned home. Luca didn't know to appreciate those days as the best of his life. He did now.

After another discussion of the weather, Marco said goodbye and hung up. Luca re-heated the lasagna and ate it in front of the television. He watched an American football game and was impressed with the players who could catch an oval ball flying at a high speed. God dispensed so many different talents. Sailing the ocean was a good one. And kicking a round ball was so much more fun. But catching an oval ball out of the air while running at top speed seemed nearly impossible.

CHAPTER NINE

November 24, Sunday

Church returned to the building on Sunday. Bob and his friends recounted the football rivalry games as Morgan found their seats. Her pew neighbors continued bemoaning that they would not be ready for Thanksgiving. Cindy's mom was being suspiciously quiet about her new boyfriend. And Anna Greer announced that she was expecting baby number three. That last announcement threw Morgan. Why did Anna deserve a third child when Morgan wasn't even blessed with one? Morgan knew that she should not start walking down that road, so she sat up straight and waited for Bob to sit down. She would focus on the sermon, not Anna's precious baby. It still didn't seem fair.

The worship music was exactly what Morgan needed. Singing praises to Jesus out loud made her feel physically rejuvenated. She had so many blessings in her life. Pastor Greg's message was about Rahab's family. The narrative in the book of Joshua tells of Rahab, a prostitute and heroine, saving two spies sent by Joshua. In return, her entire family is spared during the destruction of Jericho. Just like the blood of the lamb spared the Israelites in Egypt, the scarlet cord in Rahab's window spared the inhabitants of her dwelling. They were not saved by their educations, nor their ancestry, nor their wealth. They were saved by their faith. They had to be in the house, just like Noah's family had to be in the ark.

Morgan reflected on the message as she and Bob walked to the youth wing for Sunday school. God did not hold Rahab's public sins against her. He rewarded her faith. How many times had Morgan looked down on others for their public sins? She was quick to judge.

But how did God see it? Our slate is clean if we let down a scarlet cord. If we simply accept Jesus' acts at the cross, God sees us as pure. Morgan said a quick prayer of repentance for seeing people's sins rather than their purity through Jesus. She prayed for Cindy's mom and apologized for poking fun at her young dates. From here on, she would try to focus more on the planks in her own eyes.

Bob and Morgan led big group today, and as Luke expected, attendance was light. They welcomed the students and explained the rules of today's game called Don't Laugh. The oldest student present was selected as the leader. Bob played music, and as soon as he stopped the music the leader would walk around the room trying to make someone laugh. He couldn't talk or touch anyone. The first person to laugh was out and joined the leader. Bob then started up the music for the next round.

The teenagers had fun with the game and asked to play a second one. This time the youngest person started as the leader. After the second game, Bob gathered the group and closed with a prayer. He emphasized how thankful we should be for every blessing we experience, especially the ones that make us laugh. After the prayer, the youth were dismissed to their grade-level classes.

The adults not teaching gathered with Luke to discuss plans. Luke patted Bob on the back. "Our very own Indiana Jones. Don't forget us when you find the treasure."

"Ha! We'll try not to forget you. And we will be out of town the next two Sundays. But we can cover big group when we get back. When will that be, Morgan?"

"Looks like December 15. We'll plan on a Christmas-themed game that day." Luke nodded and continued planning. The students would be visiting two nursing homes on the first Wednesday night in

December. And the group would have a White Elephant Christmas party on the Sunday night before Christmas. The church would provide chicken tenders and fries, while the students brought desserts.

After church, Morgan and Bob ate lunch at Pizza-Rama near the beach. It was too cold to eat outside, but the view was worth the drive. As usual, Bob teased Morgan about the pineapple topping choice. "Just admit that doesn't taste right."

"Do you think I am so stubborn that I would order pineapple even though I don't like it?"

"Yes, I do." He laughed. "I bet you can get really fresh pineapple on your pizza in the Bahamas."

"Ahh, that would be great. I know if you tried it, you would be hooked."

"Nope. I'm sticking with pepperoni."

After lunch, the couple took catnaps on the couch and watched two Bogart movies. Before going to bed, Bob speculated on their upcoming adventure. "One week from now, we could be holding the treasure.

"True. But I seriously doubt it will be found that early in the very first treasure cruise. I'm hoping that we will have figured out the first clue one week from now. Can you imagine if we get stuck on the first clue? That would be so frustrating. But I can see families working together, chatting away at dinner, trying to solve them. That will be fun."

"It will. I really don't know what to expect. Will they have super-obvious clues, like 'look under the Christmas tree'? Or will they involve calculus and complicated codes?"

"Ha! These must be solved by families with children, so they probably don't involve calculus. At least, I don't think they will. I can't wait to read the first clue. It could be anything."

Luca caught an early flight to Nassau on Sunday. Joining him would be Jenny Lu and the first, second, and third officers. This team of five would be most responsible for maneuvering the ship around the islands and docking at the piers. After the one-hour hop, they made their way to a local boat charter company in a nearby marina. Jewel Cruise Line had leased a 140-foot yacht with five staterooms for three days. The craft would carry the captain and the officers to each island visited by *Golden Fortune*. The irony of the crew sleeping on a vessel one seventh the size of *Golden Fortune* was not missed on Luca.

"Welcome aboard, mates! Please stow your gear in a cabin and get comfortable. Our first stop is Cutter Cay. We should be there in about an hour, so make yourself at home." The yacht captain looked quite weathered with tanned skin and wispy blond hair. He seemed at home more on the sea than on land. Luca found a cabin and dropped his carry-on suitcase and backpack on the bed. For the first time, the rapid pace of the preparations was catching up to him. He wouldn't have a real break until his first ten-week stint was over.

Moving his bags to the side, Luca lay back on the narrow bed and closed his eyes. Dahna's face came to his mind. The best part of his busy schedule was that it distracted him from his tremendous loss. It had been seven years since his precious wife was taken from him. God did not save her as he begged. His mooring line had been cut, and he had been drifting ever since. Their sons kept in touch, but he still endured most of his life alone. This endeavor with Jewel Cruise Line would be a welcome distraction to help the days pass. He would give it his all for Dahna.

Luca woke to a knock on his door. "Captain Barone. We're here." The first officer startled Luca, who had fallen into a deep sleep. The thought that he could nap so early in the morning bothered Luca, but he reminded himself that he was keeping a strenuous schedule, even for a person half his age. He quickly readied himself and left his cabin.

On deck, Luca found Jenny and the three officers speaking to the local pilot. Ship's pilots are veteran sailors with expertise on local ports and their surroundings. They precariously board ships from smaller boats by entering via a rope ladder. Once on board, they instruct the ship's officers on current sailing conditions. While each port is different, pilots generally advise on water currents, hazards, and cruise traffic. They speak the local language and are certified to guide the officers in docking. They are also responsible for protecting their country's environment and economy.

"Luciano Barone! My jack. It is God's blessing to see *yinna* again." The pilot rushed to Luca and gave him a bear hug. Luca learned that a "jack" was a friend in the Bahamas. He smiled when he heard Tito say it in his Bahamian accent.

"Tito! It's great to see you. Are you still working?" Luca had known Tito for nearly two decades. They'd developed a professional friendship as Luca docked in Nassau every other week with Royal Caribbean. Tito was a talented port pilot. He prayed for Dahna when she got sick, but the two lost touch when Luca retired.

"Yes. I am based at Cutter Cay now, so I will see you every week. I'm gonna make sure you don't buck that pirate ship. Myrna insists that you come to dinner at our house tonight. A charter will take us to Freeport at 3:30. My nephew can bring us back to your t'ing later. Please say you will come, hey?"

"I would love to see Myrna. Thank you for inviting me." Luca would rather collapse in his tiny cabin, but Tito was a great friend. He would enjoy meeting his family. And he would more than enjoy authentic Bahamian cooking.

"Wonderful! We will eat and go to church services afterward. I've been praying for you, jack."

Church services? Luca hadn't been inside a church since Dahna's funeral. He gave up on publicly worshipping God when Dahna died. Sure. God existed. God created the Earth and the seas. Luca believed that, and he believed in his heart that Jesus paid the price for his sins. But God had not answered his prayers. He did not answer Dahna's prayers. His dear Dahna had more faith than anyone he knew. So why did God take her? And why was Luca left here without her? Luca saw no reason to sit in church and pretend that everything was fine. It wasn't. He would simply ask Tito's nephew to bring him back to the yacht after dinner.

Tito showed the officers a detailed map of the nearby waters. Luca and his crew would have to avoid two sand bars slightly north of their docking location. Since the three islands for *Golden Fortune's* itinerary were leased by the Jewel Cruise Line and *Golden Fortune* was its only ship currently sailing, there would be little traffic to avoid. Occasionally, the line allowed private charters to dock on one of their islands, and Luca knew to pay close attention to these boats. Their captains were untrained in avoiding mega-ships and often traveled too close to them. But the remainder of the time should be smooth sailing.

The four-man crew hopped onto the pier and walked with Tito as he discussed general conditions. Surprisingly, the biggest concern was the ever-present reef sharks. To keep them away from the beach areas, employees ran jet skis throughout the area. They zipped back and forth every few minutes whenever beachgoers might be in the water. The "shark scrubbing" was effective, but a nuisance to docking ships. With *Golden Fortune* being the only ship docking for the first four months, Luca expected the jet skis to be a non-issue. But Tito shared that the young men riding them would start scrubbing one hour before the ship would arrive. The zig-zagging jet skis would now be an issue.

Besides sharks, pop-up storms and evening departures were discussed. Weather was always a concern for docking. The team reviewed a chart listing the wind speeds and wave heights that would prevent mooring. Finally, they discussed at length the strategies for maneuvering in the dark. Not only would the sun set earlier in the winter months, but the line planned for some legs of the treasure hunts to be in the late evening. Luca had vast experience steering at night and felt comfortable as long at the jet skis were not in the water.

Once secure in their plans, the team took a tour of the island. Soon, the area would be teeming with families enjoying a beach day and others eagerly searching for hidden treasure, but today it was quiet. The walking paths around the island were painted in bright colors, and plenty of lounge chairs were found on the island's three beaches. Along each path were signs painted like treasure maps to guide the passengers. At each beach, grab-n-go food stations would serve hamburgers, hot dogs, and tasty sides. The stations were surrounded by colorful picnic tables with oversize umbrellas. Also near each beach were activity centers with playground equipment, volleyball nets, and bean bag toss games. Guests would only need to bring extra sunscreen to enjoy a fun-filled day.

Luca noted numerous places where a treasure chest could be buried. The pursers were responsible for the clues and instructing the island staff on when and where to bury the weekly chests. Luca would be informed of the locations twenty-four hours before a treasure would be found. The photography team would also be informed and would be discretely placed near the hidden treasure to ensure that the excitement was well-documented. Photos and video clips would soon be broadcast all over *Golden Fortune*'s media outlets.

After the tour, Luca freshened up in the charter boat and met Tito on the dock. As they boarded the nephew's boat, Luca stated that he would not be able to make the church service. Tito dismissed his comment. "You een notin tonight. I asked the officers about your schedule. You've plenty of time to worship the Almighty with my family. Now, sit down before we buck-up this boat."

Luca didn't feel like eating, and he didn't feel like sitting in church. That would make him a hypocrite. He didn't even remember that today was Sunday. But Tito was a dear friend, and he could hear Dahna reminding him to be a good guest. Luca would be polite and enjoy the fellowship with his friends. But he did not believe that God had his best interest in mind. God cared about the big things. Not the small details.

Tito's house was a one-story block building with light pouring out of every window. When they walked through the front door, Luca and Tito were surrounded by three yappy dogs. Luca missed having pets, but his schedule did not allow them. He had considered adopting a small dog over the past few years but knew that it wouldn't work. Now that he would be sailing for ten-week blocks, keeping a dog was even more prohibitive.

Myrna appeared from the kitchen wearing a peach-colored apron. She hugged the men and directed them to the small dining room. "Sit down. Have some switcha while I bring the food in." Luca enjoyed the local version of lemonade, which was made with limes instead of lemons. The room was lived-in but homey. How many nights had Tito's family sat around this table sharing good news and bad? Luca knew the importance of eating together as a family.

Myrna brought in a platter of boiled fish and a bowl of conch salad. She added some Johnny bread and pineapple jam. Luca had developed a taste for Caribbean food and thoroughly enjoyed the meal. He noticed that Myrna was walking with a limp but did not mention it to Tito. The woman shared some *sip sip*, or gossip, about Tito's nephew. He had been offered a job as a butler at a large resort on their Grand Bahama Island. Tito thanked God for the provision and high-fived Myrna. During the rest of the meal, questions were asked about the grand pirate ship and its treasure. Luca shared as many details as he could remember about the décor and special activities. Tito added that the ship may alarm some of the locals when it sails by their island.

After dinner, the trio drove to Freeport Worship Center in Tito's small Toyota truck. The congregation met in an open-air courtyard next to a metal gymnasium. Rusty folding chairs were arranged in rows across the brick floor. Luca would later discover that services were held outdoors whenever possible. A petite woman stepped up front and began singing. Luca recognized the tune but did not grasp the foreign words.

Next, a younger couple stood and sang a powerful worship song. Luca had forgotten how much he enjoyed worship music. His heart seemed lighter as he "felt" the song. He looked over at Tito and saw his friend smiling and patting one hand on his thigh. Could God be in the music? Could He be here on this patio? Luca wanted to believe that He was present but had become bitter over the past seven years. The loss of Dahna changed his world, and he would never fully recover.

Next, a tall man with a booming voice stood and welcomed the crowd. He was dressed in a pale blue suit with shiny brown shoes. The man introduced himself as Bishop William and asked his wife, Bernie, to stand for the fellow worshipers. The order of worship was different from the churches Luca had attended, but also familiar.

William began his message and members of the congregation encouraged him with short outbursts. "God has put in my heart the message of light to share with you today. Our world is becoming spiritually dark, and we have the answer. We are to share the light of Jesus to our neighbors near and far. Read with me Matthew 5, verses 14 through 16."

The pastor continued, "'You are the light of the world. A town built on a hill cannot be hidden. Neither do people light a lamp and put it under a bowl. Instead, they put it on its stand, and it gives light to everyone in the house. In the same way, let your light shine before others, that they may see your good deeds and glorify your Father in heaven.'" He paused for the message to sink into the hearts of the crowd.

"You are the lamp, my friends. Jesus had not returned yet, so we must shine our lights. How do we do that? We do it with unapologetic faith. We do that with our actions. It's not enough to be a good person. It's not enough to give to the poor. We must do everything to give glory to the one true God.

"Do we give God credit for our blessings? Do we share our faith with friends who are hurting? Do we invite our lost family members to services? That is what our brother Matthew was telling us. We must stand out. We must be different. If we try to fit into the culture, we are hiding our lamp under a bowl."

William continued, but Luca stopped listening. The message hit home. He hadn't directed anyone to Jesus since Dahna got sick. In fact, he blew out his light and put it away in a drawer. But that was wrong. Luca had been treating God as a genie who granted wishes. Like a small child, he stomped his feet and walked away—because he hadn't gotten his way. He was being selfish by not sharing the answer to sin. The answer to anxiety. The answer to pain. And loneliness. And fear.

But changing his bitter ways would take more than his own understanding. God was speaking to Luca through the pastor in the shiny shoes. He had a choice to make. Before he could rationalize his bitterness any longer, Luca prayed. For the first time since Dahna passed, Luca met with his God. "I'm sorry. I need you more than I realized. And I want to light my lamp again. Please, help me find a spark." The message had ended, and the congregation was singing a lively tune. Most of the people were standing, and all were clapping. A few children moved to the front to dance together. Luca wiped a tear from his eye. He missed Dahna so much, but he needed to remove the bitter roots that had grown around his heart. He decided that moving forward he would "live it!" as Dahna used to tell the children.

After the service, Tito's nephew brought Luca back to the chartered yacht. The captain congratulated the boy on his job offer and asked him about the role of a butler at an all-inclusive resort. For the first time in years, Luca thanked God for a blessing—the blessing of a job for this young man. Back on the boat, Luca dressed for bed and had an unusual feeling. It was peace. He was not ready to attribute the peace to the church service, but he was also not ready to rule it out. He asked Jesus to fill the hole that Dahna left and fell asleep easily.

CHAPTER TEN

November 25, Monday

Monday turned out to be quite slow. Allison went home for Thanksgiving week, so Morgan was on her own. The phones were quiet, so she got caught up on some paperwork and called a hotel representative from a major hotel chain. Morgan liked to stay up to date on the latest deals and promotions. Later, she researched two new resorts in Cancun. She and Bob planned to visit the area in late spring, and they would like to see at least one new location.

"The Flamingo Resort. That sounds intriguing," Morgan said out loud to no one. The vision of beautiful, pink flamingoes created an image of tranquility and tropical relaxation. Morgan discovered that the main building at the resort was painted in flamingo pink, and live flamingoes roamed the property. With three salt-water pools and an expansive beachfront, the resort sounded heavenly. Morgan priced some rooms with her corporate discount and planned to discuss them with Bob at lunch. He also had a light day, so the two planned to meet at the Surfside Café shortly after noon.

In the meantime, Morgan called Lucy to check in on her friend. "Hey, Lucy. Are you as slow as I am?"

"Yep. We may see a rush this afternoon, but it's slow. I'm trying to catch up on my printing."

"Same. I was just looking at that new Flamingo Resort in Cancun. I think I'll try to talk Bob into it at lunch."

"Is that the one with a pink lobby area?"

"Yes, but only the outside. I think the lobby is open-air with lots of palm leaves. Have you started packing yet?"

Lucy sighed. "We got our suitcases down. That's about it. The kids are out of school this week, so I'm not sure we'll get much packing done before Friday. How about you?"

"We got our suitcases down too. And we packed a bag of search supplies yesterday. Bob kept adding things, but I figure one bag full of gadgets won't be too much. I'm going to have Mikey update my laptop tomorrow so I can handle any client emergencies while we are gone."

"A bag of gadgets? Ha! We won't be that prepared. I hope you find it. That would be something to tell your clients."

"Oh, I would have to change the name of the agency if I found a real treasure chest. Maybe Swashbuckler Expeditions." The ladies talked for a few minutes and made plans to find each other at the cruise terminal check in. Morgan read more about the Flamingo Resort and left to meet Bob for lunch.

Morgan spotted Bob's truck as she pulled into the parking lot of Surfside Café. He was waiting for her at the building's door. "Hey, gorgeous. Need company for lunch?"

"Why yes, I do. Have anyone in mind?"

Bob laughed and held the door for Morgan. "How has your morning been? I had three employees call in sick, so I've been helping at three different sites."

"My morning was much quieter," Morgan answered. A waitress seated the couple in the back near windows with a sliver of an ocean view. The weather was unseasonably cold, but Morgan spotted a handful of people walking on the beach with sweatshirts or jackets. After ordering two sweet teas—Mondays are for sweet teas—the two started talking at once.

"You go first," Bob insisted.

"I was just going to talk about our trip to Cancun in May. It's not important."

"No, that is important. Thinking about lounging on the beach will make my chilly afternoon a little better. What are you thinking?"

Morgan told Bob about the roaming flamingoes and pink main building. They discussed the timing and costs of flights and rooms. With Morgan's discounts, the trip was semi-reasonable. "Book it!" Bob declared. "I like the early flights. Oceanfront would be nice, but I'm okay with a resort view if it saves enough money. Or would that be 'flamingo view'?"

"Yeah! This will be fun. I'm going to need a bright pink dress to fit in with the theme. Maybe we can find a Hawaiian shirt with flamingoes on it for you."

"Don't try too hard," Bob snickered. "I'm fine with my usual shirts."

The two ate matching BLT sandwiches with fries and headed back to work. "I'll see you tonight," Morgan said as she hugged Bob. "And I'm proud of how hard you work for us."

"Same to you, Morg. Book that flamingo trip. It sounds fun. Maybe you can show me some pictures of the pink building tonight."

Monday's visit was to Treasure Island, the flagship of *Golden Fortune's* itinerary. It would be the third and final stop for the actual cruises but would be second this week to give the officers enough time to inspect it completely. As with the other islands, Treasure Island was leased from the Bahamian government for ninety-nine years. It held 130 acres of outdoor pirate fun.

The perimeter of Treasure Island was one continuous beachfront. Visitors would find an abundance of lounge chairs and hammocks in the white sand. Treasure chests of complimentary sand toys were found throughout the island, as well as high-top tables and chairs with built-in charging stations. While Cutter Cay was tranquil and quiet, Treasure Island was filled with piped-in pirate music heard over the entire island. Luca found the jaunty tunes annoying but acknowledged that cruise passengers would probably love them.

In the center of the island was a 20,000 square-foot salt-water pool. It featured a twenty-two-foot waterfall and 1,500 lounge chairs. The pool also held twelve stationary boards placed over the surface for children to "walk the plank" into the water. Lifeguards were dressed as pirate crew members, and shuttle drivers sported fake parrots on their shoulders. Luca made a note to ask if the parrots were a distraction to them.

Outside of the pool was a lazy river attraction that threaded around the entire island. Inner tube rafts that looked like nautical lifesavers were provided at intermittent stations, and tropical greenery provided shade for most of the route. The lazy river provided a restful and efficient way to travel from one side of the island to another.

Unlike Cutter Cay, which had three quick-serve food stations, Treasure Island boasted one large dining facility, named The Crow's Nest, in the center of the island. Here, visitors would find a variety of tasty options with covered seating. By including bibs and highchairs, Jewel Cruise Line attempted to cater to all sizes of families.

Luca and the officers were met by the local port pilot at 9:00 a.m. He was a man of few words but managed to demonstrate his proficiency in the condition of the port. He immediately began speaking about the tides and the shipping channel nearby. Luca asked a few questions about sharks and moved on to emergency evacuation procedures. He was informed of the helicopter landing sites and safety measures.

After receiving an hour of detailed information, the first officer asked about the nighttime maneuvering of the ship. *Golden Fortune* would depart Treasure Island at 11:00 p.m. most evenings. The late departure would allow for extra search time for the treasure, as well as a Bonfire Beach Party for the passengers. Franny had organized a ship-wide party that would center around a permanent bonfire structure. Visitors would dance in the sand to the music of a steel drum band. They would roast marshmallows and make s'mores with provided materials. And then they would watch a fireworks display before returning to the ship. The cruise line hoped that media coverage of the nighttime beach party would add to the excitement of the treasure cruise. Luca paid close attention to the details of the local navigation issues.

The individuals ate a box lunch of sandwiches before embarking on a complete tour of the island. Luca knew that his grandchildren would spend hours in the lazy river floating under waterfalls and around foliage when they participated in the cruise in April. He was looking forward to showing them the endless beach and pirate-themed pool on Treasure Island. The children loved watching their Papa "drive" the ship, but the lazy river just might top that.

Once again, Luca noted several obvious locations for a hidden treasure chest. He assumed that those responsible for hiding it would make the spots less obvious but expected a few to be in plain sight. The pilot noted that some palm trees were strategically planted to protect expensive technology from high winds. A hurricane passed over this island in 1966, but none have come close since.

To the officers' surprise, the staff of Treasure Island lit the bonfire and held a scaled-down beach party. They handed out sandwich meals—this time in bags—and joined the crew on nearby chairs. In all his years as a mariner, Luca had never participated in an evening beach party. Franny and her staff hit a homerun with this space. Families would be talking about their Treasure Island experiences for generations.

Back on the yacht, Luca updated his notes on Treasure Island and its navigation. He noted potential hazards, including the permanent bonfire. The rapid pace of the tour was once again catching up to Luca. He would turn in early tonight and be fresh and ready to go tomorrow.

When Dahna died, Luca put his life on pause. He didn't want to live without her but knew that God had plans for him. He still had his beloved sons and their families. But Dahna was the joy of his life. Luca found himself having fun on the tours. And he had something else to hold his focus. A lot of things to hold his focus, in fact. God sent him back to the sea and back to happiness. Jesus should be the Joy of his life. Luca realized that now. He clung to that. Life had always been good to him.

November 26, Tuesday

"Ahoy, Matey!" Mikey entered the office with a spring in his step. "I declare that today will be pirate day. We will talk like pirates and steal each other's pens."

"Shiver me timbers, Mikey. What's gotten into you?"

"Well, my boss is going on the world's first-ever treasure cruise in five days. Five days! I am so excited! Are you? Did you pack a shovel? And a magnifying glass? Please take lots of pictures."

"Yes. Yes. Yes. And will do. Bob and I packed an entire duffel bag with treasure hunting supplies. We probably won't need any of it, but at least we will have it. I need to finish packing clothes and toiletries tonight, but I'm almost ready. We'll leave early tomorrow to drive to my mom's. Are you still spending Thanksgiving with your girlfriend's family in Brunswick?"

"Yes, and my mom is acting like a baby about it. My sisters will be home, but she can hardly stand that I won't be there. I had to promise that I would be there for Christmas . . . and for more than ten minutes. Nora won't be happy, but I can't take both holidays from my mom."

"These things are tricky, but mom's need their babies in the nest. Especially during the holidays. Be sure to call you mom first thing on Thanksgiving. She will be thrilled to know that you are thinking of her."

"I will do that. How's your laptop? Acting okay?" Mikey walked over to Morgan's desk and eyed her outdated machine.

"It's acting fine, but I would appreciate you looking it over. I'm expecting a few inquiries on Black Friday and would like to be prepared to answer questions if needed."

"Sure thing." Mikey powered up the machine and checked the email program. Everything seemed to be in order. He closed the lid and packed everything into a carry case.

The rest of the day was productive for Morgan. She ate lunch at her desk and tried to clear everything on her to-do list before her long break. Between Thanksgiving and the *Golden Fortune* cruise, she would be gone for nearly two weeks. Allison and Mikey would come in next week to return calls and print travel documents. And Morgan would have her laptop for time-sensitive matters. But she couldn't leave any pressing matters hanging for too long.

Before Morgan left for the day, an elderly man entered the office. He walked slowly and carefully to her desk. "Do you plan trips for seniors?" he asked.

"Of course we do. I would love to help you."

The man went on to explain that his late wife's birthday was in January. She would have turned eighty if a careless driver hadn't hit her head-on twelve years ago. The man wanted to celebrate her birthday at her favorite place in the world: Sedona, Arizona. Morgan got some information from the man and sketched out a trip. He was concerned about flying alone and asked about the train from Orlando to Tucson. Morgan explained that the train would take more than four days to get to Arizona but would work. He decided that he would ask his grandchildren if one would accompany him and get back to Morgan after Thanksgiving.

Morgan assured the man that traveling alone was not impossible. "You will be well cared for by the airlines, Mr. Campbell. We can arrange everything."

"I'm sure of that. But I got on the wrong plane coming back from a leave when I was in the service. I ended up three states away and had to hitch a ride to the base. Dell always took care of me after that, and I'm not sure I trust myself anymore."

Morgan smiled. "We will arrange it however you would like. Let me know what your grandchildren say."

"I will. And thank you. My heart is lighter today." The man shuffled out of the office and into a sedan that was longer than Morgan and Bob's first apartment.

After work, Morgan stopped by a local grocery store to pick up last-minute items for Thanksgiving. She agreed to bring the rolls for Thursday and chocolate chip peanut butter cookies for the weekend. Bob had ordered a turkey to be delivered on Thursday morning, so they didn't have to carry anything perishable. She grabbed two premade flower bouquets for her mom and Aunt Margaret. On impulse, she also grabbed a rotisserie chicken for tonight's dinner. With some sides at home, she would prepare a healthy and quick dinner.

One hour later, the couple was finishing the last of the supper dishes. Morgan was wiping down the counter when she declared, "This is it! We are officially on vacation."

"Let's finish packing and put our feet up," Bob agreed. The two filled their suitcases; as usual, Morgan overpacked. Bob rolled his eyes. "I acknowledge that we will be gone for twelve days, but you may have overdone it with the clothes. I'm not sure you can close your suitcase properly."

"Don't worry. I will get it closed. And I may need all of this. December weather can be tricky. And we have no idea if this brand-new ship will be chilly or hot inside."

"It's fine. Pack what you want. We'll just bring it all home after you don't wear it." Morgan threw a folded pair of socks at him. "Hey! You know I'm right."

"Fair enough. Are you sure you packed everything? I don't think you have enough shirts to make it to Sunday."

"I'm good. And you aren't getting your socks back. I'm keeping these." After a final check, the couple collapsed in the living room in front of the TV. Morgan texted her mom to see if she needed anything last minute. All was good. Let the adventure begin.

The third and final island was visited by the officers on Tuesday. Mermaid Cove was aimed directly at the children on board. It would be the second island of the weekly itinerary. Jewel Cruise Line expected adults traveling without children to either remain on the ship when *Golden Fortune* was docked there or to briefly walk around the island and quickly return to the ship.

Mermaid Cove had one large beachfront on the west side of the island and multiple kiddie pool areas. In addition to the pools, the area had five splash parks and an area with twelve water slides. The slides, located in the Whale's Tails section, ranged from a four-foot toddler slide to a fifty-foot "thrill" slide. Kids of all ages would be able to sail down the slides over and over for free.

Much like Treasure Island, Mermaid Cove featured one large dining facility. Landlubber Café served child favorites, such as chicken nuggets, peanut butter and jelly sandwiches, and cheese quesadillas. Parents could enjoy grilled hamburgers and hot dogs plus all the soft-serve ice cream they could stand.

The island was built with larger bathroom stalls and advanced beach showers complete with bodywash and shampoo dispensers. Sandy toddlers could be rinsed before returning to the ship, if necessary. Parents would find beach wagons available to escort children from the ship to the beach. And bubble machines released bubbles all day, adding to the underwater theme.

The same pilot from the previous day met the group at 9:00 a.m. again. He would work all the islands over time and was eager to share the nuances of Mermaid Cove. The island would be frequently chartered by children's organizations, so the primary concern was small-craft traffic. Detailed schedules would be provided ahead of time, so the officers would have advanced knowledge of the vessels' presences.

Like Cutter Cay, the island would be scrubbed of sharks with zig-zagging jet skis. The stay on this island would be the shortest of the three, with *Golden Fortune* usually departing at 4:00 p.m. The line employed extra lifeguards on the large beach and added two first aid stations near the entrance. Children would be overjoyed when they discovered "real" mermaids swimming in the shore.

Luca and the officers enjoyed a brief tour of the island and its facilities before they returned to the yacht. Once on board, the long-haired captain returned the group to Nassau. The five officers took a taxi to the airport and checked in with no trouble. Luca would be flying to Atlanta, while the others would be returning to Miami.

"We really need to watch out for those shark scrubbers," Jenny commented as the group waited in the security line. "I have seen them acting recklessly before. They are usually teenagers hired to drive the jet skis all day. When the ships show up, they occasionally try to show off for their friends."

Luca nodded. "I have seen that too. They have no fear of such a massive vessel. I will mention it to HR and ask that they review the local hires."

"Well, Captain, we will part ways with you now. See you on Saturday. And Happy Thanksgiving!"

"Happy Thanksgiving to you too. See you soon." Luca walked to his gate and sat in an end seat at the terminal. He reviewed the port manuals as he waited to board the plane. Children of tired parents were squirming in their uncomfortable chairs. The woman sitting directly across from Luca was speaking loudly on her phone. Apparently, her boyfriend wasn't giving her enough space. All the people in the area looked up when she called him a "big wobbly dummy."

During the flight, Luca saw a commercial for *Golden Fortune* on the seat screen in front of him. The cruise line had a partnership with the airline to promote one another. Luca saw a brief glimpse of himself at the press conference. He looked older in the clip than he did in the mirror. And he chuckled to himself when he was labeled as a "world-renowned sailor" on the screen.

Luca dozed during the two-hour flight and arrived in Atlanta shortly before 8:00 p.m. He gathered his things and patiently waited to exit the plane. As he got closer to the gate, he heard the chant of "Papa! Papa!" His heart swelled at the sound of his grandchildren. Anthony was ten years old, and Paulo was eight. They looked very much like their father but had Dahna's fiery spirit. When Luca reached the boys, they rushed toward him and caused him to fall on the ground.

Sonja was horrified. "Boys! Be careful with Papa."

But Luca was thrilled. Dahna should be here to love them in her special way, but Luca would try his best to make up for her loss. He wrestled with the boys as they struggled to stand back up. Sonja rolled her eyes and muttered something about the Barone boys. He knew they came from a long line of adventurers and would be wrestling in airports for generations to come.

As the family entered Marco's home, the boys pulled Luca into the guest bedroom. "Look, Papa. We made your room into a pirate's room. Luca could only laugh at the pirate décor. Hand-drawn treasure maps and plastic coins were placed throughout the room. He had already tired of the theme before the first cruise had taken place. A sports theme or outdoor décor would have been a welcome break. But the pirate theme was appropriate, and the boys were proud of their work. Once again, Luca smiled. He could feel peace slowly being sprinkled on his soul, and he silently thanked God for the blessing of family.

As Luca was listening to Anthony discuss his soccer team's upcoming tournament, Sonja entered his room. "Are you hungry, Papa? I made your favorite ricotta pie. It won't be as good as Nonna's, but we want you to have something special before the big adventure cruises." Luca looked at her through blurry eyes. "Oh, Papa. Don't cry. It's just a pie."

"It's not just a pie, dear Sonja. It's a family that God has given to me. I have been so mad at Him for taking Dahna that I have forgotten those who remain. Thank you for making the pie. It will be heavenly." The family ate a late dessert at the kitchen table and marveled as Luca shared details about the *Golden Fortune* cruise. Sonja brought out playing cards and the group played until midnight. Special times called for the breaking of bedtime rules. Luca grinned the entire time.

The boys let him win several of the games before Sonja finally called the night to an end. The boys scurried to their rooms obediently and promised to be up early. Luca helped Marco and Sonja clean up the kitchen and thanked them for a wonderful evening.

"We miss you, Pop. Thank you for taking time from your busy schedule to visit," Marco said as he placed two drinking glasses into the dishwasher.

"Oh, I thank you two for including me. And for those wonderful boys. You are marvelous parents. Mama would be so proud. No. Mama *is* so proud." Sonja gave Luca a hug and ordered him to get some sleep because the boys planned to keep him busy the next day.

<h1 style="text-align:center">CHAPTER TWELVE</h1>

November 27, Wednesday

Bob was awake before the alarm clock rang and had coffee and bagels ready as Morgan walked into the kitchen. He was used to starting his day early to beat the Florida heat on his job, and vacations days were not an exception. He was dressed, and his suitcase was zipped and sitting by the door next to the overloaded duffel bag.

Morgan was also an early riser, but she preferred to get ready at a slower pace. She prayed in silence each morning and read a devotional with her first cup of coffee. Mornings were a time to plan her day and bathe in quiet before the busyness started. Today, Bob was like a puppy ready to go for a walk. Morgan could only smile at his exuberance. Yes, he was exuberant. It didn't matter that he was spending four nights at his mother-in-law's house. Any trip was an adventure to him.

Bob stared at Morgan as she poured a second cup of coffee. "If we leave within twenty minutes, we can completely beat the bypass rush. We might even avoid the Disney World traffic on I-95. Once we pass the Disney exit, it should be smooth sailing. Well, smooth driving."

"Okay. Okay. I'm almost ready." Morgan dressed and closed her suitcase quickly. Bob loaded the car while she walked through the house, ensuring that no faucets were left open and no appliances were running unnecessarily. Convinced that the house would be safe for twelve days, she met Bob in the car. His smile was almost childlike. There must be some primitive yearning in men to load their belongings into a vehicle and drive to distant territories.

Unfortunately for Bob, half of Jacksonville had the same plan to leave before the rush. The 295 bypass was unusually crowded. And I-95 was funneled to one lane near St. Augustine. Thankfully, the slowdown was caused by highway construction and not a holiday accident.

Morgan talked Bob into stopping at Buc-ee's near Daytona. He put up a modest fight but didn't mind stopping. Buc-ee's biscuits were worth the madness, even though he had eaten a bagel not long ago. "We've been driving less than two hours. Are you sure about stopping?"

"Yes. I'm sure. I will always be sure for a Buc-ee's biscuit."

As soon as they exited, Bob regretted the decision. The line of cars ran nearly to the highway. After twenty minutes of inching along, he began the search for a parking spot. Of course, the only spot available was miles away from the store. Well, maybe half a mile. "What were we thinking? Stopping on Thanksgiving weekend? We will lose any advantage we had by leaving at 7:00. I'm getting two biscuits."

"Ha! We're on vacation . . . with ten thousand of our closest friends. Might was well enjoy it. We aren't getting out of here any time soon." The couple joined the crowd in purchasing more food than necessary and found themselves in another line of cars reentering I-95.

Bob became reflective after the second biscuit. "We lost over an hour for this stop. It probably wasn't worth it. But I have you with me, Morg. And I'm not edging the third driveway of the day." As soon as he commented about work, his phone rang. Speaking hands-free, he answered with an extra eye roll.

"Hey, Tony. How's it going?"

"Hey, Bob. We're good. I didn't want to call you, but we have a situation with the East Acres crew. After we did his yard, Mr. Bean told us that he wasn't going to pay and didn't want our services. We did pine straw and everything. I told him that he had to pay today and had to give us a week's notice before canceling, but he just walked back into the house."

"Don't worry about it, Tom. This is the third time he's done that. I will send him a stern letter in the mail. That usually gets him to pay. Did the Allen brothers show up today?"

"Yep. They are working hard. I think they were a good hire. Go have fun. I've got it covered till you get back."

Bob wondered if Tom really could handle the daily crises but had no other option. "Thanks, man. I'll try to bring back some treasure." Before the Palm Beach exit, Tom called two more times. Bob helped him solve the issues and reassured him that he would return in less than two weeks.

Bob and Morgan decided to skip the late lunch at Deerfield Beach because both were still full after the biscuit detour. They arrived at Helen's house shortly before 3:00 and were greeted by two older ladies and two yappy dogs. Family. This was Morgan's family. She teared up as her mom hugged her longer than necessary and admired her flower bouquet. Her mom spoke first. "I'm so happy you're here. It feels like a holiday now."

"I agree. I've missed you and Aunt Margaret. It's so good to be here."

Bob brought the suitcases into the house and set them in the guest bedroom. Helen directed everyone to the screened-in porch at the back of the house. As they were sitting, Aunt Margaret brought out a pitcher of lemonade and glasses of ice. The temperature was in the

70s, and Morgan could smell the grapefruit trees. Florida holidays did not involve snow and fireplaces. But they were quite special in their own way.

Helen sat on the edge of her seat and smiled at Morgan. "Tell me everything that has happened since I last saw you. September was such a long time ago."

"Wow, Mom. That could take a while. We text nearly every day, so you should be up to date. Work is fine. Church is fine. Home is fine. I want to know what you two have been up to."

Aunt Margaret answered first. "We're fine, hon. Tell us about this treasure hunt. We saw a story about it on the news. It's the big story in South Florida right now. Well, after that waitress who saw Elvis in a plate of mashed potatoes."

"I think I've told you all about it, but I don't mind going over it again." While Morgan explained the details of the ship and hunt, Bob excused himself to check out the ladies' yard. He wanted to make sure the yard crew he hired was fertilizing and cutting the St. Augustine grass properly. He was pleasantly surprised to see that the yard looked great.

After a long chat, the ladies went inside to set out sandwich fixings for supper. Morgan missed this. The sound of others chattering and working as a group to set out a meal. She didn't realize how quiet her home was until she got around others. And this was only two others. How blessed people are to have large families. Lucy's parents hosted all the children and grandchildren, plus a few neighbors, each year. If everyone showed, they would have twenty-six people at their Thanksgiving dinner. Lucy joked that she learned to eat fast just to survive. Large family gatherings were foreign to Morgan and Bob. But for now, the foursome eating sandwiches—complete with sour pickles—was perfect.

After supper, Bob and Morgan walked down to a nearby duck pond. They left the older ladies asleep in the living room. The afternoon had been just what Morgan needed. She felt her infertility most during the holidays. Being around her mom reminded her that she did have roots. She just didn't have as many roots as others.

"You seem peaceful today," Bob remarked. "You probably would never admit this, but you are so much like your mom. It's good to see you two together."

"I miss her around the holidays. We have such a great life, but I still feel that someone is missing. I miss our daughter. With her big hairbows and sullen attitude. Or our son. Someone for you to toss a football to in the back yard. We missed out on an entire chapter that most people probably take for granted."

"I doubt that many people take their children for granted. But I know what you mean. Tom's son is starting to get scholarship offers. I'm happy for him and enjoy hearing the details. But I can't help but think what our son or daughter would be like. We must trust in God's plan. He knows what He's doing. We have a great life."

"You're right. I have so many blessings. My mom and Aunt Margaret are two of them. They love us so much. Mom mentioned something about getting out of West Palm for a few days. I think the surprise trip to the Ark Encounter will be a great Christmas gift. They will be thrilled to hear that we've made plans for the four of us to go in February. Maybe we will even see snow."

The two sat on a bench for a while enjoying the scenery. A couple walked by with a toddler in a stroller and a preschooler riding a bike. The bike had training wheels, but the boy was maneuvering like a pro. Bob squeezed Morgan's hand. He knew her thoughts without hearing them. Before leaving the pond, Bob asked God for the miracle of a child or peace in a future without one.

On Wednesday, Sonja was busy with preparations for tomorrow's Thanksgiving dinner. Her parents would be joining the group for the meal, and her mom would bring old-fashioned cornbread dressing. The Barone family embraced the American tradition but would often add pasta and tomato dishes to the turkey and its accompanying sides. Before he left Miami, Luca ordered three types of pies to be delivered today. He hoped the desserts would lighten Sonja's baking load.

Marco suggested that the boys leave Sonja to her baking and kick around a soccer ball in their neighborhood park. Sonja thanked him for giving her a child-free kitchen for a few hours. She planned to put her feet up once the table was set and hors d'oeuvres were prepared.

Luca dressed in loose slacks and tennis shoes. He hadn't played soccer since his last visit in September. The boys agreed to take turns as papa's partner and began kicking the ball. Luca was amazed at their skills. Both boys had improved since the summer. He could not keep up and finally sat on a bench to watch the younger Barones challenge their dad.

After an hour of playing, the sweaty children asked for milkshakes. Marco declared that today was a special occasion and gave in to the request. The foursome went to a nearby restaurant and ate oversize cheeseburgers, greasy French fries, and chocolate milkshakes. Luca listened to the chatter of the boys. *You should be here, Dahna. They have your spirited nature.*

After the meal, the men returned home to find Sonja asleep on the couch. Marco insisted that she continue to rest, and he took Luca to the backyard to show him his winter garden.

"Your mother would be proud. She loved to cook with spinach." Luca walked around the vegetables and admired the neat rows.

"I remember. Sonja makes spinach and cabbage soup that is as good as Mama's. I miss her. How are you doing? Is the work too much?"

"I am fine, son. God is giving me the strength I need," Luca confessed.

Marco's eyes widened. This was the first time his father had mentioned God since his mama's funeral. He and Sonja were members of a nearby church and invited Luca to join them when he visited. But he usually found an excuse to avoid attending. The loss of his mom shook Marco but changed Luca. He didn't have the sparkle in his eyes anymore. Perhaps the captain was no longer angry at God. That would be a Thanksgiving blessing.

The boys treated Sonja to dinner tonight. She had been cooking for most of the day. Paolo suggested peanut butter and jelly sandwiches. Marco was hesitant but finally agreed. Luca heated up chicken noodle soup while the others gathered the sandwich supplies. This simple meal was hardly equal to some of the fine dining found on cruise ships, but it was certainly more special. The family ate sandwiches and chips on paper plates and laughed at Anthony's stories about his best friend's pet tarantula. Family time is *spendido.*

At bedtime, the boys asked their papa to tell stories about the sea. Those were their favorites. He sat in a comfortable chair and shared tales about unexpected storms and mechanical malfunctions. He told the boys about the time he saw a pod of whales near Bermuda as they were migrating to Canada. Eventually, Paolo asked about *Golden Fortune*. Luca gave details about the décor and the pool deck. He also shared the layout of each of the islands he would visit and showed a picture of the large slide on Mermaid Cove from his phone. Everyone in the house slept well on Thanksgiving Eve.

CHAPTER THIRTEEN

November 28, Thanksgiving Day

Thanksgiving was nearly flawless. The early weather was ideal for a walk, so Bob and Morgan took a brisk stroll around the neighborhood. Helen and Aunt Margaret worked together on the side dishes with the Macy's Thanksgiving Day Parade playing on the TV in the background. When they returned, Bob and Morgan set the table and helped in the kitchen. Aunt Margaret questioned Bob three times about the turkey. "What time will it be delivered?"

"It will be here at noon. The website had a variety of options, but I thought noon would be best. The bird should be cooked and loaded with chestnut stuffing. I'm happy to do the carving."

Helen laughed. "You better do the carving. I'm not allowed to tell you what happened the last time Margaret carved a roast." Aunt Margaret swatted Helen with an oven mitt. Morgan could tell that the ladies were speaking in jest, but she had a slight concern that something dangerous might have happened. She made a mental note to ask her mom about the incident after the cruise.

"I think everything is ready," Aunt Margaret added. "We just need the bird."

Right on cue, the doorbell rang. Bob rubbed his hand together and darted to the door. "I can smell that bird already." He opened the door to find a teenage boy holding a cardboard box.

"Delivery for Stevens."

"That's us." As Bob was reaching into his pocket for tip money, the boy called out the order.

"That's a twenty-six-pound Tom. Cajun-spiced. Extra spicy. Crawfish stuffing."

Bob exchanged the bills for the box. "Wait? Say that again."

"Stevens family. One twenty-six-pound Tom turkey. Extra Cajun spice. And crawfish stuffing."

Bob tried to hand the box back, but the boy turned away. "This isn't what I ordered. We should be getting a twelve-pound baked turkey with chestnut stuffing."

The boy showed Bob the order ticket. "I'm sorry, sir. You ordered the Cajun turkey with double-extra spice. We wouldn't make a mistake about that. You can call the number on the box, but the office won't be open until Saturday." The deliverer walked back to his car.

As he looked at the box, Bob's eyes started to water. The extra spice was kicking in. Not sure what to do, he walked to the kitchen in placed the box on a counter

"Good grief, Bob. What is in there?" Margaret's eyes were also watering.

"Looks like there was a mix-up, and we got an extra spicy Cajun turkey instead." Bob wanted to laugh but couldn't.

"That won't go well with my diverticulitis," Margaret warned. "And I'm having trouble breathing."

"It's not that bad, Margaret," Helen insisted. "Let's look at it." She opened the top of the box and jumped back. "My gracious. That was cooked with tear gas. We can't eat that. The coroner wouldn't be able to get to our bodies for days. Take that outside, Bob."

Morgan eyed Bob, and he picked up the box. "We can't leave this hot turkey outside. It will attract animals."

The ladies laughed, and Margaret spoke for the three of them. "Can't think of one animal that would get near this fiery bird. My concern is that it combusts on the patio. Put a pail of water near it just to be safe. I need some water too. My lungs are on fire." Bob moved the flammable turkey to the table on the patio. Tears were coming out of his eyes now. How could someone eat this? Are there families in Louisiana sitting around a table crying over their Cajun turkey? Is the father carving it with a bucket of water nearby? And what in the world is crawfish stuffing?

Helen took turkey lunch meat out of the refrigerator and placed three slices on each plate. "That's all the turkey we have in the house. It will have to do. The rest of the meal is fine. After we eat, we can hose down Sparky out there and apologize to the neighbors."

"I wish we had some Cajun neighbors. We can't waste such a huge bird." Bob agreed but added that the catering company created the waste when they added the irritant spices.

Even with limited tryptophan, the group later fell into a food coma in the living room after their meal. With the Dallas Cowboys playing in the background, Morgan spoke to God. "I'm sorry for ever being ungrateful. My life is full, and I thank you for everything. Absolutely everything."

Thanksgiving morning brought freezing temperatures to Atlanta. The weather seemed fitting for a holiday meal. Marco started a fire in the fireplace, and Sonja had coffee and cinnamon rolls out for a light breakfast. The family would eat their meal at noon, so Luca could make his 6:14 evening flight back to Miami.

"Can I help you with anything?" Luca asked. He estimated that Sonja started cooking the turkey at 6:00 a.m.

"No thank you, Papa. I've got everything covered. Please, sit down and rest. You won't get a break for ten more weeks. Did Marco ask you about visiting in February? We would love to have you."

"Yes, he did mention it. My schedule is free, so I can probably come for a week in February. I'm visiting Gio's family in early March, so February works well."

"Please send me pictures of Treasure Island if you can. I can't believe we will be there in April. The boys ask questions about pirates almost every day. Thank you so much for arranging this trip. I still can't believe we will be sailing on *Golden Fortune* with the legendary Luciano Barone. I'm ready to start packing now." Sonja excused herself to the kitchen while Luca sat near the fireplace. He wouldn't see weather this cold for at least two months. And he hoped he wouldn't smell burning wood in that time either.

Sonja's parents arrived with a huge pan of chestnut dressing and plenty of hugs for the children. Luca greeted her dad with a handshake, and the older men moved to the living room. The women were placing food on the dining room table, and Marco was carving the massive turkey.

"How are you doing, Pete?"

"I'm great, Luca. Or should I say, *Captain Barone*? I saw the press conference for your cruise. That treasure hunt is causing quite a stir around here. I heard two guys talking about it at the gym last week. Do you know where the treasure will be hidden?"

"No. I won't know until twenty-four hours before each 'find.' The pursers will handle the clues and the locations of the treasure. They know the plans for the first twenty-five hunts. We've identified dozens of locations for clues, so there are enough combinations for this ship to create unique experiences for at least two decades."

Pete looked surprised. "I guess the pursers are sworn to secrecy. Everyone they know would be interested in the location of a chest filled with $50,000 of gold."

"Oh, there are several safety measures in place to keep the details secure. My concern is more with the passengers. As you said, everyone is interested in the gold. I hope we don't have fights breaking out or hunters dangling from balconies. We have extra security guards and cameras in place to prevent those types of dangerous activities."

"I hadn't thought about that. *Golden Jewel* is fortunate to have you at the helm. No pun intended."

"Thanks, Pete. I'm ready for the job. It should be fun." The men were called to dinner and found a feast on the table. Marco thanked God for another year of blessings. And for special protection of their papa as he sails in the Caribbean. The meal was filled with good food, laughter, and turkey place cards that Paulo made from pinecones. Luca thought the turkey was a little bland but would never tell Sonja. The woman prepared a delicious meal for the family without one complaint. He remembered the spicy turkey that Dahna prepared their first Thanksgiving as a married couple. She added too much of everything and apologized for two hours. His eyes watered as he ate it, but he never complained. His wife was his greatest blessing, and he never wanted to hurt her delicate feelings.

After lunch, Marco, Sonja, and the boys drove Luca to the airport before he fell asleep on the couch. He hugged everyone twice and promised to do his best to visit in February. During the flight, he once again saw the advertisement for *Golden Fortune* and cringed slightly at the clip of his press conference. He wondered if any of the travelers would be passengers on the ship. With only three days to sailing and a holiday weekend, some passengers were surely on their way.

Back in his apartment, Luca texted Marco and his brother Gio to let them know he made it home safely. He unpacked his bags and washed a load of laundry. After a light supper, he gathered his notebooks and data charts to look them over one last time. He would move into the Captain's Quarters tomorrow and had already arranged for a large Uber vehicle to transport him and his belongings. Finally, he fell asleep on the couch while watching the Detroit Lions and the Green Bay Packers battle on the American football field. When he awoke, the big adventure would begin.

CHAPTER FOURTEEN

November 30, Saturday

Morgan decided to skip Black Friday shopping this year. She didn't want to leave any gifts in their car while they were on the cruise. Instead, she helped her mom work on a thousand-piece jigsaw puzzle. The picture of fifty cats was a little unnerving, but the time with her mom was a real-time treasure. They had completed over half of the puzzle yesterday and would attempt to finish it tonight.

Bob left the house early to help clean at the local food bank. He had taken a chance after Thanksgiving dinner and brought the tear-gas turkey to the Palm Beach food bank. A dozen people were in a line outside of the building, and Bob knew instantly that the turkey would not be wasted. The volunteers were grateful, and Bob offered to come back the next day to help. On the way home, he stopped at Publix to get a cooked chicken. Thanksgiving leftovers weren't appealing without some sort of poultry.

Morgan's pew neighbor, Cindy Foster, texted an update on her mom. Apparently, a Walmart greeter had his eye on her mom recently and asked her on a coffee date in front of nearby shoppers. They hit it off immediately, and Cindy's mom brought him to Thanksgiving dinner. Cindy added that she was relieved that her mom was dating someone her own age and added that her mom walked in with a mum the size of a dinner plate pinned to her shirt. "She had trouble eating around that huge flower but beamed with pride that her guy had been so thoughtful." Morgan added her delight in the budding romance and thanked God for late-in-life relationships.

When Bob returned, he fell asleep on the couch while watching college football. The ladies drank lemonade on the porch, and all three agreed that they could still smell the Cajun spices. Morgan brought up their Christmas plans. "Are you sure you can drive yourselves to our house? I-95 will be nuts at Christmastime."

"We can do it, sweetie," Aunt Margaret replied. "We will travel early on Monday morning and get there right after lunch."

"I'm a little uneasy about that, but we can think about it some more. Bob and I can come get you on Sunday. Or I can even book you flights to Jacksonville. Don't take any risks."

"We appreciate your concern, Morgan," Helen added, "but we will be fine. And we want to try out Buc-ee's. Lillian Vonover says that they have the best biscuits. And some sort of nuggets."

Morgan nodded. "Yep. The biscuits are worth the stop. And you will love the bathrooms. Cleanest public restrooms I've ever seen." Bob appeared at the screen door and asked if any of the ladies would like to drive to Deerfield Pier. Morgan jumped at the chance, but Helen and Margaret declined. They would work on the puzzle and catch some football. Both agreed they missed that "cutie patootie" Coach Nick Saban.

On the drive to the pier, Morgan asked Bob's thoughts on her mom driving to their house for Christmas. She added that the highway was getting busier and busier. Bob suggested the ladies fly to Jacksonville, but Morgan shared they were looking forward to Buc-ee's.

"I can't believe we are making Christmas plans around a fictional beaver," Bob joked.

"It's not the beaver they want. It's the biscuits."

"Why don't we come down on Saturday, stay a night, and drive them to our house? They can fly home."

Morgan squeezed Bob's hand. "Thank you for loving my mom like that. I so appreciate it. That would be perfect. And we won't be seeing your family at all."

"That's okay. We saw them in June for Jessica's recital. And they don't seem to want to go on a vacation with us with Jess so busy right now. I'm fine with it. We'll see them again next June. Maybe they will consider a *Golden Fortune* cruise if we send them lots of pictures. They have to have some free time somewhere."

Bob found a metered parking space near the pier and walked with Morgan on the boardwalk. The beach was full of families on blankets and teenagers playing volleyball. As they strolled, Bob looked at his watch. "We will be searching for treasure this time tomorrow. It's getting real now."

"Gosh, it is. This is so exciting. I'm going to take pictures of everything and write it all down when I get back to my office. We are expecting a rush on *Golden Fortune* cruises this month. As soon as word gets out about the first treasure, people will want to join the fun. I can't believe we get to go on the first one. This is a trip of a lifetime."

Bob agreed and suggested they eat at Whale's Rib. It was one of his all-time favorite restaurants, so Morgan had anticipated that they would eat there. The wait was about twenty minutes, and the food was great as usual. While they were eating, Lucy texted that she and Earl had checked into their Miami hotel. They were going find a restaurant with an ocean view and get to bed early. The women agreed to meet at check-in, if possible.

When they returned to her mom's house, Bob and Morgan found the house quiet. Helen and Aunt Margaret had gone to bed.

Morgan also noticed that the cat puzzle was complete. She knew they should get to sleep early but decided to watch football and finish the night with pumpkin pie and extra whipped cream.

"Can you bring this much on a ship, sir?" The Uber driver was helping Luca load up his clothing, toiletries, desk supplies, and notebooks.

"I am the captain of *Golden Fortune*, so I will be living on the ship for an extended time."

"Whoa! Are you serious? Do you know where the treasure is hidden?"

"No, son. I'm not that important. I just move the ship from island to island and back to Miami each week."

"That's so cool! Can I take a selfie with you?" Luca agreed. He smiled extra wide—not for the picture but for the joy he had been feeling since the church service in Freeport. What a fool he was to reject God for so many years. His heart was still broken, and he missed dear Dahna every day, but the bitterness was slowly being released. Her illness was not God's fault. Luca knew that he would hug her again and tell her all about their beautiful family.

At the Jewel Cruise Line port, Luca arranged for porters to deliver his boxes to his cabin. Being the captain meant a lot of responsibility, but it also came with some perks. His cabin was the size of three regular cabins and had room for a mahogany desk. His meals were free, and he had unlimited laundry and housekeeping services. To avoid gaining extra pounds from the late-night pizza, Luca visited the ship's gym and running track three or four times per week. Best of all, he was able to bring his family on board for a free cruise once each year.

For the remainder of the morning, Luca attended meetings on the bridge. After a quick lunch of sandwiches, he dressed in his bright white uniform and secured epaulettes on his shoulders. His badges had four golden stripes, indicating his position as the highest-ranking crew member on the ship. The afternoon would involve final interviews with the press. The line had arranged for major news outlets to have thirty-minute slots with Luca.

As he walked down the hallway, or passageway in sailor jargon, Luca paid extra attention to the details. Even the carpet looked like it belonged on a pirate ship. He marveled at the talent of the design team and wondered to himself if the line hadn't gone overboard with the theming—pun intended.

The first scheduled interview was with a reporter from a local television station. Expecting to field questions about the treasure, Luca was surprised when she opened with the makeup of the "preview" cruise. "Thank you for meeting with me today, Captain. Would you please explain to our viewers what makes this 'preview' cruise different from the others?"

"Thank you for your interest. As you mentioned, tomorrow's cruise will be a preview cruise. Travel agents and journalists from around the world will be able to see firsthand the unique adventure vacation *Golden Fortune* has to offer. They can travel at a discounted rate and bring family members with them in their one allotted cabin. Jewel Cruise Line is eager to share with the world the excitement of the first-ever adventure cruise, and we expect the travel agents and reporters to spread the news." The "preview" cruise would involve daily seminars for those interested in behind-the-scenes details but would run as a normal trip otherwise. Most cruises of this type run for two or three days to give the media a glimpse of the surroundings, but this one would run the full week so the special passengers would get the full effect of the treasure hunt.

The reporter wrote a few words in her notebook before asking Luca about the younger passengers. "Is it true that local foster children have been invited on this cruise as well?" The media team for Jewel had downplayed the presence of the children to avoid unwanted attention, but Luca took the opportunity to praise the line for its charitable efforts.

"Yes. Jewel Cruise Line has reserved one hundred cabins for foster children in the Miami area and their guardian families. The children will get to experience an adventure of a lifetime, and the cruise line will get to test out their facilities with the eager youngsters." Luca praised executives when they announced the plan to include the foster children. Each child had to receive special permission from a judge to leave the country, and county officials merged their efforts to make the trip happen. It was decided jointly that only children above the age of eight would be included for legal and practical reasons.

"Would you share with our viewers the precautions taken to keep these children safe?" The reporter had done her homework. He hadn't been asked about the generous act yet, as the line was not advertising the inclusion of the children. Luca wondered to himself if she had been personally involved in the foster system somehow.

Happy to discuss the special visitors, Luca continued. "As you may know, foster children may not be photographed for media outlets and must always be supervised by their legal guardians. Each received special permission from a Dade County judge to leave the country. I believe that several members of our youth staff received special clearance to be able to assist with the children in any unforeseen circumstances. I will also be meeting with the families in a special ice cream party on day three."

"I can't tell you how impressed I am with *Golden Fortune* opening its doors to foster families. I have a personal connection to the foster system and want to thank you on behalf of myself and our viewers."

Luca's busy day was brightened by this young woman's questioning. The rest of the interviews went as expected. "Where is the treasure hidden?" "Have you ever experienced real pirates?" "How do you stop a ship this size?" The captain answered them expertly and was relieved when the interrogations were over.

Later, the officers of the ship and heads of departments ate dinner together. It was the last night before the inaugural cruise, and spirits were high. Over the years, Luca had found cruise ship lasagna more than edible. It wasn't nearly as good as Dahna's dish, but still worth eating. The lasagna on *Golden Fortune* was no exception. He enjoyed his meal and ordered two desserts before walking up to the bridge.

Luca found engineers replacing two instrument lamp bulbs that had begun blinking earlier in the day. Luca sat nearby and watched crew members entering and exiting the platform. As the nerve center of the ship, the bridge was continually manned, and its upkeep was a high priority. Luca trusted the crew around him to keep the navigation instruments working efficiently. He organized his notebooks and looked over the most recent weather reports.

While the bridge was buzzing with activity, Franny walked in and called for attention. "Excuse me. I would like to pray for everyone tonight." The room grew quiet, and all eyes turned to the cruise director. "I am honored to work with all of you this year. The adventure cruises will be so much fun and will give me a chance to push my abilities. Would you please pray with me?"

This was the first time a crew member had offered to pray for him on the bridge. Dahna had prayed over him numerous times, but his coworkers usually kept their faith, or lack of faith, private. He spoke for the group. "Thank you, Franny. I would appreciate your prayer."

Franny smiled and bowed her head. "Father, I thank You for the people gathered here and for every crew member serving *Golden Fortune*. We pray that You give us wisdom and safety as we complete our jobs. Please protect our passengers as they travel to our ship and on our ship. Thank You for the technology that enables us to sail the marvelous seas You created. We dedicate our efforts to You. In Your holy name we pray. Amen."

Soft "thank yous" filled the area as Franny finished. Her prayer covered the room in a blanket of peace that all could feel. Slowly, each person resumed his or her assignment, and the room became filled with a buzz of conversation and activity. The atmosphere felt familiar to Luca, and he went back to reviewing the weather data. Winds were expected to be calm for the next ten days.

PART TWO
High Seas

" Delight yourself in the Lord,
and He will give you the desires of your heart."
Psalm 37:4

CHAPTER FIFTEEN

December 1, Embarkation Day!

When Morgan's phone alarm sounded, she instinctively reached out for Bob. His side of the bed was empty. As usual, he was up early on travel day. As she gathered her things for the shower, she could smell fresh coffee and hear Bob talking with her mom. They were discussing the foliage in her backyard.

Morgan showered and dressed in comfortable joggers and a T-shirt. Embarkation day involved a lot of walking, especially for a preview cruise. She and Bob would walk from the parking lot to the ship, through check-in, and over each deck of the new vessel. She usually logged over fifteen thousand steps on the first day of a cruise.

As she sat at the kitchen table, Morgan heard her mom telling Bob about her pickleball adventures. He was patiently listening to the details, despite his eagerness to get on the road and drive to Miami. Morgan heard words like *kitchen*, *lob*, and *dink*. And her mom seemed excited to share her knowledge with Bob. He, on the other hand, was simply listening out of kindness. Morgan made mental plans to arrange a game with Bob, her mom, and Aunt Margaret.

Morgan interrupted. "Mom, bring your paddles, or whatever you call them when you visit for Christmas. Bob and I will challenge you and Aunt Margaret in pickleball."

"Aw, you don't want to play with two old ladies. You'll need chairs to sit on while you wait on our serves."

"I'm serious. Bring the paddles." Bob directed a slight eye roll at Margaret, and she knew he was teasing. The group would have fun playing on the new courts in the city's tennis complex, even if it was painfully slow. And Morgan had a feeling that the games wouldn't be that slow.

Helen left to tell Margaret about the challenge. Bob side-hugged Morgan. "You just woke up, and you have us in a death match with the sisters."

"Ha! You know they will be talking about this for weeks. We should have offered to play yesterday." Morgan sipped on her coffee and eyed the leftover pumpkin pie. She and Bob would eat lunch shortly after they boarded the ship, but she didn't want to take any chances. She needed her strength for the day and sliced herself some pie. As she was searching the fridge for whipped topping, she heard the ladies walk in.

"Ahoy, mates!" Aunt Margaret was grinning from ear to ear. She and Helen were wearing pirate eye patches. "You've been captured by Captain Mags and her first mate. Now you must walk the plank." The ladies doubled over in laughter.

"Wow, Margaret. You scared me there." Bob was also laughing. Morgan could only smile as she finished her pie. Yes, God had given her a beautiful family. Tiny, but beautiful. She found her phone and snapped a few pictures of the geriatric pirates.

"It's never a dull moment with you two," Morgan added. "We will send you lots of pictures."

"Please do. You've been so kind to pester us about going on one of these cruises with you. But you know we couldn't keep up. We'd sleep the entire time and miss all the fun."

"I seriously doubt that, Mom. We'll keep pestering." Morgan put her dishes in the dishwasher and went to the guest room to finish packing. As usual, Bob had his suitcase by the door. He was sitting in the living room looking for a weather update on TV. Morgan decided on a quick walk around the backyard before she packed. They had plenty of time before they needed to start the ninety-minute drive to the cruise port.

After dressing and closing her bags, Morgan placed her packed suitcase next to Bob's and walked into the kitchen where her mom and Aunt Margaret were giggling with Bob. Aunt Margaret spoke up. "Watch out for this one, Morgan. He likes his poultry spicy."

"Yep, Aunt Margaret. He thought he could get away with that tear-gas turkey. But we caught on right away."

"Slow down, ladies." Bob had his hands in the air to surrender. "I would never order a deadly turkey like that. It will take a month for the acidic smell on the patio to clear out. Don't pin this one on me."

"Okay," Helen declared. "You are off the hook, even though you are the one who ordered Sparky." She held her arms out to hug Bob. "We are going to miss you two. This Thanksgiving was one for the books. And we can't wait to hear all about your adventures."

The four shared a group hug, and Morgan promised to send regular updates. Bob loaded the car, and the ladies waved as the couple drove away. Morgan was chuckling as she watched her mom and Aunt Margaret waving goodbye with their eye patches. To be that alert and content at their age was one of her life goals. "I hope they don't wear those to church."

"Ha! I wouldn't put it past them," Bob added.

The plan was to leave at 9:00 a.m. so they would arrive at the cruise terminal thirty minutes before their 11:00 check-in. Fortunately, Bob insisted that they leave thirty minutes earlier. Traffic on I-95 was heavy for a Sunday morning. And it came to a complete standstill ten miles outside of Miami. Bob was unusually calm for the dense traffic. Morgan figured that the extra cushion of time eased Bob's concern about being late.

"I see lots of minivans this morning," Morgan noted. "I bet we see a lot of them turn off at the port exit. I believe there are six ships departing from Miami this morning. Should be plenty of people vying for those coveted parking spots.

Bob nodded. "I think we'll be okay. The new Jewel parking lot was built with three ships in mind. Since they only have one running for now, it shouldn't be even half full. At least, I hope not." Bob inched their car along. He expected holiday traffic but was surprised to see so many cars heading south this morning. The cold front was easing, so families were probably taking advantage of a beautiful day. And six ships of people would mean lots of extra cars on the highway.

Morgan's phone rang. As expected, Lucy's face popped on the screen. "Hey, Lucy! Where are you?"

"We just parked, and Earl is getting our bags out of the van. Where are you?"

"We are near Exit 7. Not too far away."

"We parked on the second level, so you shouldn't have any trouble finding a spot. The garage has seven or eight levels. There is a cute sign at the entrance of the parking lot that reads, 'Entering Davey Jones' locker.' That did it for me. It feels like a treasure hunt now. Wait until you see the Jewel employees. Their uniforms are so cute."

"This is exciting. Don't wait for us. You will lose valuable time. We'll look for you at the buffet. If we are late, we'll meet up by the pool sometime. Does that work?"

"Heave ho! Goodness, does that even make sense? Sounds good. I'm telling you it will take us a week to get back to sounding like landlubbers again. Talk about immersive experiences. They haven't missed a single detail."

"I can't wait to see it. Tell Earl we say hi. See you soon."

"Will do. Take care."

Morgan ended the call and looked over at Bob. "Can you imagine what it would be like to go on this cruise with small children? It might be overwhelming for the kids to have so much fun in one week."

"The theming might go over their heads, but spending so much uninterrupted time with their parents and being surrounded by pirates and mermaids . . . I imagine those kids will never forget this. Heck, I don't think I will ever forget this."

"Same here. It will be good to get away for a week. Completely get away. Like to another point in time."

Bob thought for a minute. "Do you think your mom could manage a week-long cruise? Like, really manage it?"

"Yes, she could do it. We would just have to take things slow. Let's see how the week goes. Maybe we can convince them over Christmas."

Luca woke early in the captain's quarters and dressed quickly. His cabin was unusually large for a cruise ship. It was really a suite. He had two large closets for his clothes and a separate room that served as an office. Near the back of his office was a small kitchenette that Luca would rarely use. He was happy to eat at one of the many dining venues on the ship instead. The quarters felt homey to Luca. He even had family photos hanging on one of the metallic walls and a wooden carving of a ship that his grandson Anthony created.

The captain skipped his usual exercise routine and went straight to the executive entrance to the bridge on Deck 12. General passengers couldn't access this entrance. Along the way, he passed crew members setting up displays, wiping down railings, and mopping floors. Passengers would be boarding in three hours. He would go over his master checklist and then trust his team to provide a top-notch experience.

A small display of breakfast was set up near the control room. Luca chose coffee and two cinnamon rolls. It reminded him of Thanksgiving morning. He missed his family already. But the next few weeks would be busy enough to keep his mind occupied. He would enjoy the boys on the ship in April. And he would offer them plenty of cinnamon rolls.

Walking around the area, Luca felt confident in the crew's preparations. He checked the weather forecast and moved to the small conference room adjacent to the bridge. He would meet with Jenny Lu, the staff captain, and the department heads. This is when major issues could arise without warning. Luca asked God to protect the ship from problems and to give him wisdom if problems did occur. God always gave him the wisdom he needed right when he needed it. He just hoped he wouldn't need too much today.

As he finished his breakfast, Luca welcomed the crew members. The excitement of a new ship was noticeable, and Luca appreciated the opportunity to command a ship again. He felt alive and wondered if Dahna knew he was sailing. "Good morning. Let's go down the list and handle the issues in that order. Unless there is anything pressing."

The staff captain spoke first. "I'm sorry to bring the first issue, but we have a family of ducks swimming in the main pool. They've been there since late last night."

"That's fine," Luca said. "They will fly off once we start sailing." Local fowl were common visitors on cruise ships. One time, two birds flew into a passenger cabin and tried to make a home in their shower.

"No. These are Muscovy ducks. They are protected. We can't move them. The ship can't move with them on board. The Coast Guard is completing their inspection. That looks good, but they said we must follow Florida statutes with the ducks. We are working with a professional trapper. He is on his way. But we can't sail until they are properly removed.

"Are you serious?" Barry Manning, the hotel director, asked. "We have been literally running to get everything ready in the cabins and dining venues, and we may be halted by ducks? That beats all!"

"Yes," Luca replied. "That is a little bizarre. But we must follow policies. There is no other option. Jenny, would you please follow up on this and keep everyone in this room updated?"

"Yes, sir." As staff captain, Jenny was Luca's direct connection to all the department heads.

Luca began at the top of his list with the chief engineer. "Have we corrected the issue with the elevator buttons?"

"Yes. And no. The buttons on Elevator 8 light properly, but we now have a problem with Elevator 3. The lights flicked when the car traveled upward. Once again, the issue does not pose a safety hazard. But it does may cause uneasiness in some of the passengers. I tried it, and it is a weird effect. We are working with the manufacturers to fix the light."

"Okay. If it isn't fixed by 10:30, mark that car as closed. We don't want any reporters filming the uneasy effect." Next, Luca addressed the customer services director. Strangely, the large Christmas tree on Shipwreck Boulevard was also flickering. Electricians on board were working on the problem and hoped to have it resolved before embarkation.

The human resources manager reported the numbers of crew that were officially working. Hiring so many new workers and transporting them to the ship was a monumental task. A few dozen were still awaiting work visas and would join the crew in a week or two. But the vast majority were on board and working full time. Uniforms were on time, and schedules were set.

Next, Barry spoke about the accommodations for the upcoming cruise. "We have two problems, Captain. And I have a work-around for both. First, we just found out that more than half of the room stewards have no idea how to create towel animals to leave in the cabins after the nightly service. That may seem minor to you, but passengers expect them. Trust me. We see plenty of comments about those popular towel animals. We have scheduled two training classes for late in the week. But in the meantime, we prepared some 'make us a towel animal' cards. We will place these on the beds with two hand towels. Hopefully, the guests will think we planned it that way."

Luca thought for a minute. "Clever."

Barry continued. "Now, for the doozy. The cabin supplier sent us only child-size coat hangers for the closets in all the cabins. They are small and were placed in the closets before we noticed it. We tossed around some ideas to make the hangers seem like part of the treasure hunt, but they just didn't work. I suggest that we place 'Oops!' notes on the desks and admit the problem. We have regular-size hangers waiting for us when we return to Miami, so this is a one-time issue."

"Okay," Luca said. "We could receive some complaints for this. But I expect people traveling with expensive suits and dresses will have hangers. Don't put out oops notes. Just go with the hangers and replace them next week. Please warn guest services and the room stewards of the issue. If there are any complaints, they will be the ones to hear them. What's next?"

The food and beverage manager spoke up. "I can't believe I'm saying this, but we have no issues. Everything is stocked and inventoried. We have crew ready to serve. And the new equipment is working beautifully. Vendors are ready in Miami for the restocks on Sunday. We also addressed the first clue. Nothing to report, Captain."

"Great news! What about you, Franny?"

"We are good, Captain," the cruise director said. "The only issue we have is with the movie screen on Parrot Perch. We did a test run, and smoke came out of it when we turned it on. The smoke went away, so I think the problem is solved. But one of the electricians is looking at it now. That's all I have for now."

"That leaves me, Captain Stubing." Doc got a laugh from the quiet group. "We are good to go. I'm ready to treat sunburn all week. Seriously, the facilities are great. And I trust my team. The passengers needing help will be treated well."

"Good to hear, Doc. I am pleased with the efforts you have put in these past few weeks. Thank you, everyone. Please keep me updated on the duck situation. And *buon viaggio*." After some quick greetings, the group parted for their individual posts. Luca made notes from the meeting and double-checked his master list.

Luca, Franny, and Jenny were expected to meet guests as they entered the ship on Shipwreck Boulevard. Luca always dreaded these encounters at first but ended up enjoying the greetings. He was isolated from the excitement of the passengers when working on the bridge. Spending two hours of individual time with people from around the world was one of the best parts of his job.

Of course, speeding two hours greeting passengers was also tiring, so Luca stopped at the ship's buffet for coffee. He snuck a piece of cake as well. From his seat in the empty restaurant, Luca could see through a tall window the top of the parking deck. Cars were filing in, and people were entering the cruise terminal. The world's first adventure cruise was about to begin. Luca quickly decided that a second cup of coffee was in order.

Bob pulled into the Jewel parking deck with plenty of time to spare. Traffic in the port area was heavy, but also somewhat organized. He followed the signs to the new terminal and found the entrance with ease. Morgan cheered when they saw the sign welcoming them to Davy Jones' Locker.

With two suitcases and a duffel bag in hand, the couple walked to the nearest elevator. A family of four was already waiting for the doors to open. Their two little girls were wearing smocked dresses with tropical prints. Morgan felt a second of sadness before she addressed the girls. "You look like you are ready for a pirate adventure." The girls looked up but said nothing.

Their mom spoke up. "We sure are. None of us could sleep last night." Morgan introduced herself and Bob. She learned that the father was a travel agent from the Tampa area. He made a comment about the heavy duffel bag that Bob was toting and was surprised to learn that it was full of treasure hunting supplies. The family was obviously unprepared. But those girls probably had no worry about that at all.

The passengers made their way into the new terminal building and found the line for check-in. The attendants, who were employees of the City of Miami and not the cruise line, were wearing black-and-white striped shirts and black pants. They cleverly added to the pirate ambiance.

"Ahoy! Welcome to *Golden Fortune*. May I see your travel documents?" The sweet older lady looked at Morgan with excitement.

"Of course." Morgan opened her ever-present fanny pack and handed the grandmotherly pirate their passports and confirmation passes. The woman scanned the documents and handed them back. After taking quick photos of Morgan and Bob, she welcomed them to the adventure and directed them to the appropriate waiting area. The Stevens party would be called to embark in order of arrival.

Bob walked toward two empty seats when a boy of four or five years ran right into him.

"No! I'm not going! Get me out of here." It seemed a little early for the boy to be grumpy, but he managed. His mom apologized before chasing after the child. The entire waiting area became quiet and watched the chase unfold.

"Stevie, stop!" The mom was losing ground. The boy ran into an advertising board and knocked it to the ground. Shortly after the mishap, a pirate-clad employee attempted to halt the scallywag, but the man only made Stevie more upset as he continued to run. He was eventually stopped by the entrance door, which would not open, and scooped up by his mom.

"No! I'm not going. Let me go!" Officials from the line discretely steered Stevie's family into a side room and mentioned something about a green bird. The trick must have worked because the screaming stopped.

"Whew!" Morgan exclaimed. "That was close." But she had spoken too soon. In the waiting area, two dozen children suddenly started to cry. Most were clinging to their parents, but some were lying prone on the carpet. Stevie had caused a chain reaction of panic amongst passengers under the age of six. In an expert response, a pirate-themed clown emerged from a side room and began singing a catchy tune.

> *Here we go now. Here we go now.*
> *On the sea. On the sea.*
> *Pirates, gold, and pizza. Pirates, gold, and pizza.*
> *Follow me. Follow me.*

Almost all the kids immediately stopped crying. They stood at attention and watched the clown before joining in the song. Soon, parents began singing and order was restored. The clown started walking around, shaking hands with the passengers. Crisis number one averted.

"Wow. They thought of everything." Bob was impressed. "As someone responsible for putting out fires every day, I hadn't thought of singing a catchy tune. But I guarantee that I will write one for the Allen brothers if they give me any trouble."

Morgan swatted him on the shoulder. "Please record that if you do."

About ten minutes later, the section in which Morgan and Bob were sitting was called to board. The two adults were as excited as the children. "Here we go," Bob said as he stood. He lifted the supply bag over his shoulder and pulled his suitcase. Morgan was in front of him, pulling her suitcase.

As the two approached the final check-in kiosk, Bob noticed another man with a large duffel bag on his shoulder. The two locked eyes and nodded. The hunt was about to begin.

As their boarding passes were scanned, a robust man welcomed them aboard. Morgan and Bob followed the cue over the gangway and onto the ship. They stepped through an entranceway and were immediately immersed in a pirate adventure. From the wall coverings to the lighting to the uniforms, the theme was authentic and intense.

As the guests entered the ship at Shipwreck Boulevard at the center of the vessel, costumed employees were welcoming guests. Jaunty music with simple chords was piped through the sound systems, and members of the entertainment team were handing out colorful brochures with important information for the incoming travel agents and reporters. Near the center of the area was a massive twinkling Christmas tree.

Crew members were greeting guests as they embarked on the ship. At the end of the welcome line was the ship's captain, Luciano Barone. He looked more regal than Morgan expected. With short-cropped white hair and chestnut-brown eyes, the captain stood tall while shaking hands with the entering passengers. Morgan and Bob appreciated the early opportunity to meet the highest-ranking official on the ship.

Next to the captain were two officers and Franny Meyers, the ship's cruise director. Morgan and Bob had sailed on two previous cruises with Franny and knew that she was a favorite of families with children. They shook hands with the crew members and shared their excitement for the upcoming adventure. After greeting the captain, they continued walking to the rear elevators. Since this was the maiden voyage of the ship, cabins were ready for passengers to enter.

"Hurry! Let's read our first clue." Morgan pulled Bob toward an opening elevator.

"I'm coming. Let the adventure begin."

The first hour of welcoming guests flew by. Luca enjoyed meeting the excited guests. The children of the travel agents and reporters were surprisingly wary of the whole experience. Luca especially enjoyed greeting many of the foster children and their families. Passengers of all ages were eager to see the new ship and read the first clue.

Periodically, Jenny would update him on the duck situation. Apparently, the ducks were not Muscovy ducks. But they had to be removed before the ship could sail. Luca silently prayed about the situation and left the chief engineer to handle the problem. The Coast Guard had cleared the ship, pending the removal of the ducks. A trapper was humanely capturing the animals and would be discretely removing them soon. In the meantime, the pool deck was off limits to all passengers.

"Luca Barone!!" Luca was startled to see a woman in her seventies rolling toward him on a motorized scooter. She would have crashed into him if he hadn't pirouetted out of the way. "I can't believe it. It's really you." The woman spoke with the heaviest Southern drawl Luca had ever heard. Was she faking it? Surely she didn't speak with that drawl every day.

"*Bonjorno, madame.*" The woman was clearly delighted to meet the captain, but he had no recollection of ever meeting her.

"I'm Abilene Jackson, a travel agent from Savannah, Georgia. My friends call me Daisy. And you can call me for dinner. Ha ha!" Daisy stood up and gave Luca a bear hug. She was wearing a navy T-shirt that read "Ship Shape." She wore a rhinestone-studded lanyard around her neck, ready to be used for a room key card. *Golden Fortune* used bracelets as room keys, but Luca guessed that the woman would wear the lanyard even if empty. On her ears hung colorful parrot earrings. And around her waist was a gold fanny pack the size of a toaster.

Daisy gave Luca a bear hug. "Goodness, sugar! You feel stronger than a polecat before mating season. Let me rub your back. Oooh . . . This uniform is slicker than a banana peel. Who's driving the boat while you're down here?"

Luca smiled and looked toward Franny for relief. Thankfully, she put her arm around Daisy and helped her back onto the scooter.

"I'll best be goin' now. But expect to see a lot of me, dahlin. I'm your biggest fan. Save a seat at your table for Daisy, you hear?"

By now, Luca's face had turned three shades of red. He was used to being a low-level celebrity on his ships. But Daisy was the first to yell his name at first sight. She was innocent but could become a nuisance if the overbearing attention continued. As he was shaking the hands of a middle-age couple, he could hear Daisy calling for the elevator to be held. She was about to fit her scooter in the car "tighter than a June bug in molasses flip-flops."

The second hour was uneventful, and the officers rushed to the bridge as soon as they were free. Luca found a table with finger foods near the entrance and made a small plate for lunch. He was quickly told that the ducks had been removed from the ship. They put up a fight but were taken safely.

For the next hour, Luca and the senior officers monitored the conditions of the Miami port and its traffic. They continued the checks and procedures necessary to sail. The air and oil systems had been started earlier, and all pressure levels were correct. After the water-cooling mechanism was employed, the engine was turned to its correct position. Fuel levels were full, and safety systems were engaged. Luca remembered when most of these functions were done by hand. Today's technology was truly a marvel.

Morgan and Bob found their "Scallywag" cabin on Deck 9 aft, or rear. Cabin number 9289. They found rubber bracelets with embedded technology on the handle and opened the heavy door. The cabin was basic with a small bathroom, king-size bed, and adequate closet. Past the bed was a sitting area with a modest sofa and desk that also served as a dressing table. At the end of the cabin were sliding doors that led to an outdoor balcony. Bob insisted on booking a balcony cabin so he could watch the stars at night. Morgan felt uneasy on a balcony in the dark but would enjoy sitting outside in the mornings.

While the layout of the cabin was simple, the décor was not. Decorated in yellows and reds, the space looked like a "working" pirate's cabin. Over the sofa was painted a large treasure map with a red *X* near the bottom. Morgan wondered if the map held a clue. Also on the walls were a nautical rope display and a pirate's flag. The darkening curtains covering the balcony door were a soft brown color, giving the appearance of faded wood.

On the desk, the couple found two pirate eye patches and a yellow envelope with "Clue #1" printed on the outside. Bob stored the tool bag in the closet and set the suitcases on the sofa to be unpacked.

"Open it!" Morgan said. "It's our first clue."

"Already? We haven't even unpacked."

"Open it! I'm too excited. We may have to beat others to a certain location."

"Okay. Let's see." Bob exaggerated the time it took to open an envelope just to annoy Morgan. She attempted to snatch it from him before he got serious. "Calm down. I'll open it."

Bob found a small white card inside the cover and held it up. "Here we go. The adventure begins now." Morgan clapped as he began to read the clue.

Welcome aboard from the Captain, Doctor, and Chef. To find the treasure, look under the *F*.

"Under the *F*?" Morgan sat down. "What could that mean?"

"I'm not sure, but we better unpack. If we hurry, we can beat the rush to the lunch buffet."

Morgan gasped. "I forgot about lunch. We should go now and unpack later. If we wait too long, we will face a longer line. Lucy and

Earl were going to wait on us, if possible." Bob agreed, and the couple left their cabin quickly.

Blackbeard's Fortress was the ship's only buffet-style eating area. It served breakfast, lunch, dinner, and late-night pizza to all passengers. The walls were covered in faux concrete blocks to simulate the inside of a castle. At the entrance was a seven-foot statue of three pirates standing together in victory.

The crowd was heavy, but a line had not yet formed. Bob and Morgan separated to gather their lunch and agreed to meet on the starboard, or right side of the boat. Morgan found the salad area and created a healthy plate. She knew without looking that Bob would go straight for the meat and potatoes section. As she was scanning the dessert options, Morgan heard her name. Lucy was calling her from a table near a starboard window.

"You made it!" Lucy delighted.

"We did. And we almost forgot to eat lunch."

"Ha! Earl would never let us forget lunch. He just went back for more seafood bisque. It's already his favorite dish on the ship." The Bonds were sitting at a table for four, so Morgan set her salad next to Lucy's dishes and went back for dessert. She couldn't choose one and decided on chocolate pudding and a lemon tart with lots of powdered sugar. Bob joined them, and the four took a moment to embrace the upcoming fun.

Morgan was about to say a silent prayer when Lucy interrupted. "Earl and I do 'buffet prayers' on our trips. We each pray on our own, if that is okay."

"Sounds like a good idea. We do something similar." The group ate in silence for a minute before Earl spoke up.

"*F*? Do you think it's a literal *F*? Or does the *F* represent something?"

Lucy rolled her eyes. "There goes lunch." The group spent the next twenty minutes speculating on the first clue. Bob noticed that the crowd was building and suggested that they begin exploring the ship and give another group their table. They decided to cover the decks from the top down and started by walking up one flight of stairs to the pool deck.

On the way up the stairs, Earl noticed the name of the ship spelled out on each landing. "Do you know how many times we will see *Golden Fortune* written on this boat? We can't check every single *F*."

"Or can we?" Lucy went back down a flight and checked the large *F* on the wall. "Nope. Nothing under there."

"This will be maddening," Bob added. "We could spend days looking for *F*s."

"It shouldn't take that long. And act natural if we find something. We want the head start if we do see the clue." Lucy had a big smile on her face. She loved puzzles.

Work continued on the bridge smoothly. Luca was comforted by the expertise and experience of the engineers around him. He trusted the crew to command the ship safely when he was off-duty and away from the instruments. Jewel Cruise Line had put together a top-notch crew, and Luca was grateful.

During a moment of quiet, Barry Manning appeared. "Good news to report."

"So soon? Please, go on."

"The room stewards are reporting that guests think the small coat hangers are intentional. They assume it's authentic pirate gear. I say we leave them as they are and handle individual complaints when the arise."

"Sounds good, Barry. Thank you for letting me know. Anything else?"

Barry smiled. "One more thing. We scrapped the make-your-own towel animal idea as you suggested. We think the guests will see through it. The team decided to skip them tonight since each room will have eye patches and a clue. The stewards are making enough to use tomorrow night, and training will occur on Tuesday. Oh, we also had a scare with the toiletry dispensers. The shampoo and conditioners were added to the wrong containers. But the labels are easily interchanged, and we fixed them before anyone embarked. Whew! The earth-shattering crises I must manage every day."

"Ha! I'm glad we have you, Barry. Our passengers deserve the very best, and you are providing it."

"Back at you, boss!"

Luca remembered that same expression being said at *Golden Fortune*'s naming ceremony in October. The tradition of formally naming ships goes back many centuries. A bottle of champagne is usually broken on the ship's hull for good luck on the seas. Today, many cruise ships are assigned godmothers also to bring good luck. These celebrities bless the ship and act as an informal sponsor.

Golden Fortune's godmother is the widow of a real-life treasure hunter. Her husband discovered twelve shipwrecks worth over $500 million combined. He is considered the most famous treasure hunter of modern times. When Luca thanked the woman for blessing his ship, she answered, "Back at you, boss!"

As Luca was looking out at the sea, Barry returned. He was holding a massive towel creation. "This is for you, boss. One of the stewards made this enormous whale for you. Would you like me to leave it here?"

"Wow! That is interesting. Would you mind placing it in my cabin? I don't think we have room for that up here. And please thank the steward. Thank all of them. They work so hard making each person feel special."

"I'll be sure to thank them. Enjoy the whale, boss."

After lunch, the couples explored the ship from top to bottom as planned. Deck 14 held the main swimming area, which consisted of a large swimming pool and a kiddie splash area. On each corner of the pool was an oversized hot tub with LED underwater lighting. The remainder of the deck area was filled with hundreds of lounge chairs. Most chairs were facing the pool, but the outer row of chairs was facing outward to the ocean. Morgan noticed small feathers on the port side of the pool. She was surprised to see them on a brand-new ship and figured that a flock of birds must have flown closely over the pool.

On the starboard side of the ship was the Walk the Plank attraction. The twelve-foot platform extended out from the ship. It had a translucent floor and was surrounded by chest-high railing. Passengers could walk onto the four-feet-wide area and literally see the ocean below them. Not for the fearful, the "bottomless plank" would lure the adventurous to sail over the ocean from a different perspective.

Bob spoke first. "This is a nice setup. The entire area is simple. Not too complicated. Children won't get lost in this section."

Morgan pulled out a notebook from her fanny pack. "Good point. I'm going to write that down." She planned to keep notes throughout the week and use them when she returned home to prepare an extensive "Frequently Asked Questions" bulletin for her clients. She wrote a few details and took some pictures with her phone.

Lucy agreed. "It is laid out nicely. And I see two soft-serve ice cream machines over there. This section will be popular on sea days. Let's check out the slides." The group headed to the back of the ship, or aftward.

The rear third of *Golden Fortune*'s top deck was the "fun zone." On one corner were three slides in increasing level of thrill. The smallest was about ten feet tall and sent its riders straight into a splash pool. The remaining slides started about thirty feet up. One was open to the sky and contained multiple twists and turns. The most exhilarating slide was entirely enclosed, making the riders speed to the end in the dark. A dozen children were already zipping down the middle slide while four sets of parents watched. They must have packed swimsuits for the youngsters in their carry-on bags.

Next to the slides were a miniature golf course filled with pirate theming and an enclosed basketball court. Bob pointed at the court. "I believe those are pickleball lines. We will have to look at the schedule and catch a match. Your mom and Aunt Margaret would love to hear about pickleball at sea."

Morgan laughed. "Oh, they would."

On the remaining corner was the Parrot Perch, an outdoor dining venue. It served hamburgers, hot dogs, and tacos, as well as French fries and chocolate chip cookies. Families could eat poolside without leaving the fun. The area had brightly colored tables and chairs and another soft-serve ice cream machine. Lucy filmed the entire area with her phone's camera.

Morgan turned to the others. "Boy, those burgers smell good. And did you see the cute pudding cups that look like beach sand?"

Earl agreed. "Those will be hard to resist. But more importantly, do you see any *F*s?"

"I've been looking. '*Golden Fortune*' is painted on the railing over there and the life preserver here, but there isn't anything below them," Bob said. "Maybe it's a figurative *F*."

Lucy spoke up. "Why don't we finish our tour, then start to hunt? I'd like to check on our luggage and unpack after we explore. Plus, I promised the kids that we would call before we leave the port. My mom has texted me three times already."

Morgan agreed. "Sounds good. Let's finish our walk-around. But I won't be able to resist checking out any *F*s we see."

At the front of the top deck was large seating area with assorted chairs and benches facing a jumbo-size video screen. A welcome video from the captain was running and a few families were already relaxing in the chairs. The area would be a central entertainment area with a spectacular ocean view.

Morgan snapped some pictures of the movie area and made some notes. "This is practical. The line can show movies or play games or hold media events. Just sitting here with the sea breeze would make any occasion seem more fun."

The group took the stairs down to Deck 12, which was the next level. Just as most hotels skip Floor 13, most cruise ships avoid Deck 13. The superstition affects ship builders and crew members as well as passengers. Not only are they afraid of staying on the thirteenth floor, but they are also scared to even push button 13 on the elevators' floor selection panels.

The foursome arrived at the entrance of the Ahoy Kids' Club at the bottom of the stairs. With the cruise marketed toward families, the cruise line anticipated an uncommonly large number of children on board each week. The kids' club offered activities for children during the day and supervised care in the afternoon and evening. Parents could leave their children at the club confident that they would be safe as well as entertained. Many children looked forward to time playing with new friends there.

The section for babies and toddlers was near the front of the club and held numerous cribs, tables, and tiny chairs. Age-appropriate toys were found in cabinets near colorful carpets. Farther back, larger tables and chairs were available for older children to play and learn. The teen section consisted mostly of Ping-Pong tables. Stylish seating areas, including bean bag chairs and high-top tables, were placed around the game tables. The area had high-tech lighting and plenty of phone charging stations.

The central feature of the Ahoy Kids' Club was a mock pirate ship for youngsters to climb over. They could pretend to be pirates as they stood on the deck, looked through mounted spyglasses, or walked the child-size plank. At the end of the plank was a large ball pit that children could intentionally fall into. The ship also had a net feature that preschool children could climb and a maze of treasure chests below the pretend deck. One of the chests could be opened and closed safely by the young pirates.

Surrounding the pirate ship were six activity stations that were closely monitored by trained crew members. Morgan took pictures of each station. "Can you believe this? A science lab, an art studio, a dance floor, a book loft, a dress-up area, and a cooking station. What kid wouldn't love this? I would love this."

"Oh, I totally agree," Lucy added. "The colors are great. I read that Franny Meyers came up with the initial concept. Her team designed the spaces. And the crew members in this area receive special certification before they are even allowed to enter."

"There are security cameras everywhere." Bob was pointing to a few of the many cameras placed in the club. "This place will fill up quickly."

As the group was leaving the kids' club, they noticed a group swarmed around the entrance. The people were commenting on an *F* in the word *Fun* just below the large letters spelling "Ahoy Kids' Club." Under the letters was a large design of a palm tree with children dancing around it. Directly under the *F* was a coconut attached to the tree.

"What are they looking at?" Earl noticed the frenzy first.

"I hear *coconut*." Morgan moved closer to the group and took a quick picture of the letters. "There is a coconut directly under the letter *F* in *Fun*. I wouldn't have even noticed that if there weren't such a buzz around it."

Lucy agreed. "Do you think this is the next clue?"

Morgan answered first. "It must be. Notice how the coconut is directly under the letter. That had to be intentional."

Earl wasn't so sure. "The entire tree is under the letters. It could have something to do with a coconut tree."

"No," Morgan added. "I don't think it's the tree. It must be the individual coconut. Let me try to get a better picture."

After Morgan and Lucy took pictures of the clue, Bob spoke up. "It's the only clue we have, so we must go with it. Let's continue our tour and look for anything related to coconuts." All agreed and left the kids' club area. They headed toward the back of the ship and the buffet area.

The line to Blackbeard's Fortress buffet was building but still manageable. As more passengers boarded, the dining facilities would continue to fill up. Morgan was pleased to see that there seemed to be sufficient seating to handle the crowd. And Earl was pleased to see that there was plenty of seafood bisque remaining.

The group took the stairs down once again. At the rear of Deck 11 were luxurious suites with oversize balconies and full-size bathtubs. These suites were designed for couples, as well as families. With high-end décor and amenities, they provided the ultimate lavishness for passengers. Most were found aft on Decks 11, 10, and 9. Ahead of the suites on these floors were interior, window, and balcony cabins.

The front half of the deck contained the ship's Wellness Center. With a 7,500 square foot gym, the center would allow passengers to continue their exercise routines while at sea. The area was equipped with modern training equipment and included two spaces for fitness classes. The views of the sea made Heave Ho Gym something spectacular.

As the group walked through the gym, they looked for anything coconut related. Several people were already running on treadmills. One beefy man was squatting a large amount of weight and grunting every time he stood up. Morgan wondered what kind of dedication a person must have to work out like that as soon as he boarded the ship.

Seeing no coconuts, the group continued walking. Beyond the gym was a full-service spa. Passengers could be pampered with massages, facials, and pedicures while overlooking the turquoise waters. Of course, the services came at a hefty expense. But the experiences were top-notch, and plenty of passengers would use their vacation as a time to splurge on such extravagances.

Since decks 9 and 10 only held passenger cabins, the foursome next took an elevator down to Deck 8. When the doors opened, the smell of pizza immediately filled the elevator. Bob smiled. "We have found the pizza parlor—my favorite." He led the rest toward the tomato-y smell.

The front of Deck 8 hosted a popular area for all passengers. Designed as an old-fashioned soda shop, the open area had a large pizza counter to the left, or port. Named Oro, or "gold" in Spanish, the quick-serve area was open twenty-four hours per day. Children and adults could eat pizza at white metal tables and chairs. At the back of the area was a fifties-style jukebox that offered classic songs for a quarter. To the right of the eating area was a game room containing arcade machines, Skee-ball lanes, and three billiard tables. The area was open and spilled into Oro.

Bob spoke over the music. "This is awesome! But would you believe that I don't see a single coconut in the entire area? I do see pineapple, Morgan. You can ruin pizza with it all week."

Earl laughed and shook his head. "I agree that this is great, but I don't think I could handle the noise for too long. I sure hope the crew members get frequent breaks with peace and quiet."

"This is exactly what our clients with children sign up for when they book a cruise. Everyone likes pizza. And the parents can lounge while the children burn off some energy playing games." Lucy walked around the area, taking pictures along with Morgan. "Should we?"

"I'm in!" Earl herded the others to the pizza line. "Everyone, grab a slice. We will need them for the rest of the tour." The group joined the line and ordered a slice of pizza and a drink. They sat at a table near the jukebox. The area was empty but would likely be active for the rest of the cruise.

"This is exactly why I like cruising," Bob added when he was seated. "They're practically forcing you to eat yummy food all day long."

"I don't know about forcing," Morgan countered. "But the temptation is awfully strong." After the pizza fuel, Morgan led the group toward the back of the ship where they would find the expansive ice-skating rink. They passed two dozen cabins as they made their way back. All agreed that staying that close to the pizza parlor would be a blessing and a curse.

The ship's ice-skating facility was state-of-the-art. The rink was oval-shaped to allow the skaters to speed around the ice without crashing into walls. The audience would be seated around the ice in comfortable chairs. Above the ice was an array of lights that could project scenery onto the ice and spotlight the performers. The *Bumbling Treasure Hunters* show would run on three different nights and one afternoon. Time was also allotted for passengers to enjoy skating on the ice themselves.

Morgan and Lucy took pictures of the entire area. An image of the show's logo was projected onto the ice to advertise the upcoming fun. Bob walked closer to the ice and inspected the picture. "Is that a coconut?"

The rest of the group joined him and inspected the projected image. Lucy spoke first. "That does look like a coconut in the sand near the treasure box. But only half of it is showing."

Morgan added that the coconut was sitting in sand. "The image shows sand below the coconut. But there is real ice below it. We can't go out there and dig up the ice, can we? That would damage the floor. And we left our tools in the cabin."

Bob needed to be sure. "I'm going to go out there and check."

Morgan grabbed his arm. "You can't go out there. We'll get in trouble. And you're wearing flip-flops."

"I'll go quickly. There's no one here. This is perfect." Morgan sighed and turned around. She didn't want to watch. Bob found a gate that led to the ice. Earl stood watch while the women covered their eyes and waited quietly at the top of the seating area.

Bob slid onto the ice and moved slowly toward the center. He crouched low to keep his balance. He approached the projected coconut and slipped onto his knees. Earl encouraged him to get up and move quickly. Just as Bob found the area where the half-coconut was displayed, two families walked into the arena. One of the children spotted Bob and ran to the ice.

"It's a clue, Mom. An *F*!" At once, four children slid past Earl and onto the ice. They crashed into Bob, sending him sliding a few feet away. The children were yelling and drew attention from people walking nearby. Soon, a dozen people were scrambling around the ice."

"*Bumbling Treasure Hunters* Ice-Skating Show doesn't have an *F*."

"No. We're looking for a coconut now. There is a coconut below an *F* at the kids' club."

"Are you sure? We haven't heard anything about a coconut."

Bob scooted quietly toward the entrance and heaved himself off the ice. As he was telling Earl that there was nothing on the ice, he heard a soft whistle blow.

"Did anyone see the signs that say, 'Keep out?' Please exit the ice now." A crew member who looked like an important officer seemed astonished to see so many passengers flopping around on the ice. "We appreciate your exuberance about the treasure hunt, but the clues will not involve breaking any rules. Please stay off the ice. You are welcome to enjoy fresh pizza at the fore of the ship."

Bob and Earl hung their heads and walked toward their wives. Morgan and Lucy were sitting down, laughing together. Morgan stood up and hugged Bob. "It's a good thing you didn't have your tools. We might have been thrown off the ship. Any longer and you would have caused a full-blown riot."

Bob rolled his eyes and walked toward the exit. "What's next?"

"Shipwreck Boulevard! Let's go!" Morgan took Bob's hand and led him toward the stairs. The group went down one flight to Deck 7. The rear and center of this deck was laid out as a shopping mall. Complete with specialty stores, boutique restaurants, and live music, the Boulevard was the central activity hub of the ship. At the center of the open space was a food court. Young passengers could snack on warm cookies, popcorn, and "pirate" nuggets. Adults could enjoy fancy coffees, finger sandwiches, and hot wings.

Near the center of the ship was a dance floor with room for a live band. Today, a cheerful keyboardist was playing popular chart toppers. A few children and adults were already dancing away to celebrate the beginning of their voyage. Behind the musician was an oversize Christmas tree decorated with nautical ornaments and bright multicolored lights.

"This is almost too much to take in," Lucy piped. "This is brilliant marketing because passengers of all ages will flock to this area. They won't want to be left out of the excitement. And there are plenty of places to part with their money, including the cool Cutlass drinks. I didn't notice all these details when we boarded."

Morgan nodded. "This is a great place to hang out, especially when one has run out of energy. I really like how the ship has invested in 'hang-out' spots. It helps multigenerational groups. The younger people can dance and play while the older ones can eat and relax."

"I feel like we should eat again, but I would explode," Bob added. The rest agreed that the food court looked enticing, but they couldn't possibly eat a third lunch. As they continued toward the back of the ship, they entered an area with multiple pathways. Each featured different foliage and several benches and café tables. The peaceful strolls were a stark contrast from the lively Shipwreck Boulevard.

At the end of each "garden path" was the lobby before the Swashbuckler Theater. The theater encompassed Decks 6 and 7, with a balcony area on the upper level. Morgan snapped photos as the group entered the higher tier. She made notes about the comfortable seating and the eighteen-foot LED screen.

Dozens of people were sitting in the lower level of the theater listening as members of the entertainment staff provided an overview of the ship and the treasure hunt. The informational sessions were being given every half-hour until 8:00 p.m. After that, a comedian was scheduled to perform at 9:00 and 10:30 that night.

"Should we go down and listen?" Morgan asked. She had a good feel of the ship but would be interested in hearing what the staff had to say. These are the details she was hoping to obtain on this preview cruise.

The group agreed to catch the remainder of the session and walked down the stairs leading to the lower deck. They discovered that the Jenny Lu, the staff captain, was leading the sessions. She was joined by Shawna Thames, the assistant cruise director. Dressed in killer high heels, Jenny Lu was going through photographs of prominent areas on the ship. These photos were projected onto the theater's massive screen. Morgan had seen most of the areas, but listened for any details she might have missed.

"Now, about the treasure hunt," Jenny started. "I'm sure you are aware that the chance to win $50,000 is our marketing strategy. We've designed every space to ensure that passengers feel like they are on a real treasure hunt. We have solid plans for the first twenty-five weeks and loose plans for the remainder of the year. Please reassure your clients that every clue will be able to be completed by a child and will involve safe conditions. No one should be dangling off the ship or tearing down walls." That comment received chuckles throughout the crowd.

"We would like for you to sell this as an adventure for cruisers of all ages. The hunts will change each week, so return visitors won't know what to expect. Shawna and I would be happy to answer any questions you may have at this time."

A few hands shot up. "Yes, you in the white shirt. What would you like to know?"

"Where is the treasure?"

"Ha! We get that a lot. And I do not know. Only the purser's office knows that. What else?" The remaining questions included probes about the plans for bad weather, holiday cruises, and the next cruise ship, *Plunder*. Jenny and Shawna answered knowledgably and cheerfully. When time was up, the theater emptied, and another group of professionals entered.

Morgan looked at her watch. "We better get moving if we are going to have any time to unpack before our 7:30 dinner reservation. Let's see the dining rooms." Heading toward the rear of the ship again, the group passed a lively looking dance hall and two specialty restaurants before finding the top level of the galley dining room.

"Wow! This is so elegant." Lucy spread out her arms. "I was not expecting the dining room to be so fancy." She walked toward the tables decorated with shimmering tablecloths and sparkling tableware. Bob and Earl rolled their eyes at each other. The ladies laughed.

Just as Lucy turned around, the captain made an announcement over the loudspeaker. "Welcome aboard *Golden Fortune*, the world's first adventure cruise ship. We are happy to have you joining us. Remember that informational sessions are running every thirty minutes at the Swashbuckler Theater, and Blackbeard's Fortress is still serving lunch.

"Important! The muster check-in stations are now open. Each passenger must report to his or her station within the next two hours. Bring your cabin bracelet with you. The location of your muster station is listed in your cabin and on the app. Everyone must attend the briefings. We do not anticipate any emergencies but want to ensure the safety of all on board. *Buon vento!*"

Morgan held up her phone and checked the app for their muster station. "We're at the theater. What about you?"

"The Italian restaurant near the theater. We can head there now. Earl and I need to get back to our cabin and call the kids. Are you going up for the sail away?"

"I don't think so. I'd like to see Deck 5 and go back to our cabin. We will watch the sail away from our balcony, if Bob doesn't mind. Meet back here at 7:15?"

"Sounds good." The four walked back toward the theater. Lucy and Earl stopped at the Italian specialty restaurant to hear the safety instructions and have their bracelets scanned. Morgan and Bob continued to the entrance of Swashbuckler Theater.

Crew members were waiting with handheld scanners at the theater. Morgan and Bob approached one named Shabbi. "Here are our arms."

"Welcome aboard. Before I scan you, I must go over our safety procedures." Shabbi pointed to a posterboard standing on an easel. "If you hear the evacuation signal, report here immediately. That would be seven short blasts and one long blast. Make sure you know how to get to the theater via the stairs. We will distribute life jackets and assist you into a lifeboat. If we must travel through bad weather, a crew member will make announcements about any venue closings or safety issues."

"Are you listening?" Morgan elbowed Bob with a smile.

"Yes, report to the theater. Got it. Let's hope we don't hear the signal."

"In the event of a passenger going overboard," Shabbi continued, "we will announce 'Oscar.' Do not try to rescue the person. If possible, throw out all in the nearby life preservers and keep an eye on the person's location. It is impossible to stop a ship of this size quickly, so we will deploy a TorpedoX lifeboat to the area. Are there any questions?"

"What is a TorpedoX lifeboat? I would like to share this technology with my clients." Morgan took out her notebook and began writing.

"Jewel Cruise Line has utilized advanced technology to develop the newest concept in cruise safety. The TorpedoX lifeboats are collapsed into a missile shape and are loaded in six launch spots around the hull of the ship. In an Oscar emergency, an officer on the bridge can release one or more of them to race directly toward the person in the water. The boats will inflate instantly and are equipped with rope ladders to assist victims in entering the boat."

"That is amazing. I hope you never need them."

Shabbi nodded. "I agree. We do test them every three months, and I have been able to see one deploy. They are quite effective."

"Wonderful. Thank you for the information. Have a nice day."

"Have a great cruise!" Shabbi's nametag indicated that he was originally from India. Morgan and Bob took the stairs down one last time. They would view Deck 5 before returning to their cabin to get ready for dinner.

Immediately behind the elevator bank were the medical facilities for the ship. Morgan walked toward the area and was greeted by a crew member walking out one of the doors.

"Hi, there! I'm Doc. Are you media or travel?"

"I'm a travel agent from Jacksonville, Florida," Morgan responded. "It's nice to meet you. Have you been doing this long?"

"Nice to meet you too. I've been working in the cruise industry for eight years. Before that I was a corpsman in the Navy. Please let your clients know that we take their health very seriously. We have two general examining rooms and a working pharmacy. We also have surgical facilities in case of an emergency."

"That's great to know. May I take a few pictures?"

"Sure. I'll show you an examining room." Doc opened the nearest door and invited Morgan and Bob to view it. The room looked very much like a regular treatment room on land. But Morgan noticed that items seemed to be secured so they didn't move if the ship hit stormy seas. A rocking ship could cause a lot of problems throughout these facilities.

Doc then led the couple through a door in the back of the room to a modest operating room. The area seemed to have modern equipment, but the entire area was smaller than Morgan expected. A nurse walked in and asked to speak with the doctor, so Morgan and Bob excused themselves.

Bob shook Doc's hand as they were leaving. "Tell Isaac and Gopher we said hi."

"Ahh, that never gets old."

Morgan and Bob continued toward the front of the ship. At the center were interior cabins, and at the back were more specialty dining restaurants. They spotted three of the TorpedoX launch sites on the port side of the vessel. They were labeled clearly but were completely enclosed by a secure door.

With the top-to-bottom tour of the *Golden Fortune* complete, Morgan and Bob found an elevator to take them back to Deck 9. Both were eager to unpack and rest a little before getting ready for dinner. As the doors to the elevator opened, the couple was greeted by the family from Tampa they met on the parking garage elevator. The girls were still wearing their tropical smocked dresses and were smiling excitedly.

Morgan clapped as she entered the elevator. "We must be elevator friends. Are you having fun?"

Once again, the girls did not speak, but this time they nodded. Their mom nodded also. "Oh yes. We've already eaten pizza in Oro."

Bob laughed. "We have too. Couldn't pass it up after we caught the smell."

The mom agreed. Morgan and Bob exited the elevator on Deck 9 and wished the family a *bon voyage*. They walked the long passageway to their cabin. Both noted that the medical facilities were impressive, but they would prefer to not see them again. "Now the pizza parlor." Bob laughed. "I'm fine if we see that every day."

Luca was in contact with the port authorities and the Coast Guard as he prepared the ship to go underway. Modern vessels were generally self-assisted when at sea but leaving and entering the ports involved delicate maneuvering. *Golden Fortune* ran primarily on LNG, or liquified natural gas. The fuel was currently more friendly to the environment and cheaper than traditional fuel oil. The engine department monitored the propulsion system around the clock. They were responsible for the maintenance and repair of the ship's engines, and everything related to them.

A local harbor pilot entered the bridge and walked toward the chief engineer. The two began discussing the departure from the port, and Luca joined them. At five hundred feet wide, the port of Miami was relatively complex to enter and depart. The officers of *Golden Fortune* must also follow the tight port schedule. With other cruise ships, as well as cargo ships and pleasure boats maneuvering, the channel was delicate to navigate.

As the bridge crew was completing their checklist, Luca's phone buzzed. He saw Marco's name on the screen. There was time for a quick call before the critical maneuvering began. "*Ciao*, son."

"Hi, Dad. I know you are busy. But I just wanted to let you know that we are all very proud of you. Our Sunday school class prayed for you and all the passengers this morning. The boys told everyone at school on Friday to watch the sailing on the webcam. We are watching it right now. I hope you are having fun. God has given you more days on the sea."

"Please tell everyone thank you and that I love them. I can feel God's peace about this assignment. The boys will love the ship. Tell Sonja that I miss her cinnamon rolls already. I'll call in a few days. *Arrivederci.*"

"Goodbye, Dad. We love you." Marco hung up, and Luca stayed quiet for a minute. God had given him so many blessings. He would see his precious family in a few weeks. For now, he had a floating pirate adventure to lead. Thousands of treasure-seekers were counting on him.

The bridge crew had a 270-degree view of the front and sides of the ship thanks to large wings that extend from each side. Originally, the officers served on a literal bridge built over the top of the deck. Today, modern bridges were now enclosed command centers with modern technology. The navigation area housed GPS tracking systems, and the communication area featured reliable connections to all areas of the ship and some land-based facilities. The engine monitors provided real-time information about the throttle and steering mechanisms. Above all the operations was the command center where the captain could observe and direct all aspects of the sailing. As many as two dozen people might be working on the bridge at a time.

"We've received our go, Captain. We are clear," said the first helmsman who was responsible for managing the ship's steering.

"Sound the horn in twelve minutes. *Golden Fortune* is ready to sail. Godspeed."

Luca said a silent prayer for the ship and the millions of people it would house over the next decade. In just a few minutes, it would make its first push out to sea with passengers. The families on board would have stories to share at Christmas dinners and family reunions. Luca was honored to play a part in their adventures.

Jenny Lu sounded the horn to let the passengers know they were about to sail. Luca reviewed the pre-sail checklist and began to move the vessel sideways away from the pier. The bridge crew briefly applauded for the first sailing of *Golden Fortune*. Slowly, the ship was turned 180 degrees to face the opening of the port and moved forward. As it passed a docked ship, passengers on both ships waved at each other from balconies and the top deck.

Back in their cabin, Morgan and Bob plopped down on the bed. Bob spoke first. "I guess we're the first people to use this bed."

"Yep. We're the first people to use everything in here. I'm already tired. How will we survive the week."

"We always do. Things will slow down . . . I think. Let's watch the sail-away, then get unpacked and rest. We don't have to leave the cabin until 7:00."

"Sounds good. I really need to get my things put away, but don't want to miss the very first sail-away." Morgan opened the door to their balcony. She found two chairs and a small table and sat at the farther one. Bob joined her, and they sat in silence for a few minutes. Their cabin was on the starboard side of the ship, so they could see the top of the terminal and people parking at a neighboring parking deck.

Bob began recapping the innovations on *Golden Fortune.* Morgan retrieved her notebook and added to her notes details she'd missed on their brisk tour. They also reviewed the two clues. Morgan felt that the coconut in the kids' club was a definite clue, but Bob did not. They agreed to look for *F*'s and coconuts going forward until they found another clue.

Morgan also reviewed the cruise line app on her phone and got excited about the calendar. "There is a 'gold' dance party on Tuesday night. I missed that. Did we pack anything golden to wear?"

"No, I don't think we did," Bob replied with a chuckle. "Of course, you brought enough clothes for three weeks. So I'm sure you have something shiny."

"I bet we can find something. I think I have something shimmery. We'll have to check that out. I've already reserved the major shows, but we need to plan for the smaller ones. There is a Meet the Captain event tomorrow afternoon in the theater. I'd like to attend that. I want to hear Captain Barone speak." Morgan went through the rest of the events and added the interesting ones to her app calendar.

Promptly at 4:30 the ship's horn sounded, and the mammoth vessel began to move. Morgan and Bob stood at the balcony railing as they slowly exited the port. *Golden Fortune* passed three other ships waiting to depart, and Morgan and Bob waved to their passengers. They saw tall palm trees on nearby islands and weekend boaters in the water. As they continued, the city of Miami became smaller and smaller. The world's first treasure cruise was now underway. Time to unpack.

The cabin had ample storage, and the couple found a place for all their things. Morgan found that the older she got, the more she appreciated order. In her younger days, she was fine with living out of her messy suitcase. But now, she wanted things in their place. She concluded that was the work of the Holy Spirit because Jesus demonstrated His appreciation of order on Earth. She placed her folded clothes in drawers and hanging clothes and shoes in the closet. The hangers in the closet were very tiny but worked. They must be European. She set up her toiletries in the narrow bathroom and put accessories like sunscreen and sunglasses on the shelves above the desk. As always, she attached magnetic hooks to the walls and ceiling to hang wet bathing suits and flyers. There were advantages to the metal walls of a cruise ship.

Once situated, Bob suggested that they take a one-hour nap before dinner. Morgan was surprised. "We never do that. If we fall asleep, we may never wake up. We've barely left Miami. Maybe we can get some coffee or something."

"Let's try. This may be a wonderful new tradition." Morgan yielded and collapsed on the bed. She had to admit that it felt great to stretch out and relax. She tried not to think of the thousands of people finding clues without her. What could be under an *F*?

It was a good thing that Morgan set the alarm on her phone, because she and Bob fell soundly asleep. She rose first and plugged in travel hot rollers to add some body to her weary hair. Bob decided on a quick shower as Morgan touched up her makeup. Getting ready for dinner was one of Morgan's favorite things about a cruise. The close quarters made the process seem more romantic.

Morgan selected a flowy, floral-print dress with beige sandals, and Bob selected a navy polo shirt with khaki slacks. They were joining Lucy and Earl tonight along with four other travel agents. The cruise line offered a group dining option for the first night to provide an opportunity for the reporters, vloggers, and travel community to meet colleagues at the start of the cruise. Morgan and Lucy selected an eight-person table and requested to be seated together. For the remainder of the cruise, the couples would eat dinner separately.

At 7:15, Morgan and Bob left their cabin to take an elevator to Deck 5. They were assigned to eat at the lower level of the galley dining room all week. When they exited the elevator, they were met by a crowd of people. It seemed that most of the passengers decided to eat at the main dining room tonight. Morgan found the end of the line and led Bob in that direction. On their way, they found Lucy and Earl near the middle of the line. Lucy was wearing a pale blue fitted dress that complemented her darker skin beautifully. Earl had on a light green, linen shirt. The couple looked elegant and tropical at the same time.

Lucy waved at Morgan. "The line is moving quickly. The staff is doing a wonderful job. We will see you at the table. Love that dress!"

"Thank you. See you in a few minutes." Morgan and Bob moved to the end of the line and were surprised at how quickly the guests were being seated. Morgan couldn't help gazing at the little girls in line wearing pastel dresses and tiny sandals. One girl had a hair bow nearly as big as her head. Morgan's heart ached for a minute before she chided herself for going down the infertility path. God had blessed her too much to feel sorry for herself—especially tonight.

When they made it to the host's booth, they were greeted and then seated by a petite woman named Jolly. The woman welcomed them with a magical smile, and Morgan followed her closely through the maze of tables and chairs. The dining room was full of chatter as passengers were enjoying their meals. The servers—male and female—were dressed in black-and-white short-sleeved shirts and black short-pants with red sash belts.

Morgan and Bob were the last to be seated at their table. Lucy and Earl were already speaking with two other couples. Morgan sat between Lucy and Bob. To the right of Bob was an older couple from Maryland. They introduced themselves as Helen and Charles of Happy Escapes Travel Agency. Next to them were Gina and Ryan, a much younger couple. Ryan was an employee of Davis Tour Company in Charleston, South Carolina.

Charles stood slightly as Morgan sat. "We were just talking about the ship. What are your first impressions?"

"I love it," Morgan replied. "We've certainly seen bigger and more elegant ships. But the adventure vibe is new. We are paying attention to more of the details, trying to figure out the clues. It's exciting."

"I agree," Lucy added. "My younger families will enjoy this." The conversation centered on the brilliant marketing of the Jewel Cruise Line. "They are offering a twist on a staple vacation venue. Some travelers seek rest and relaxation, while some seek culture and art. But another segment is looking for excitement and risk. There is a market for this environment."

The group ordered their drinks and reviewed the menu. Bob knew immediately what he would order. "I'm getting the lasagna. There is something about cruise ship lasagna."

Ryan agreed. "I'm with you, Bob. I always get the lasagna."

Morgan and Lucy chose one of the fish offerings, while the others went with the sirloin dish. The ladies then started a discussion on the desserts. All agreed that the cheesecake was a safe option, but the treasure pudding sounded too good to resist. Morgan elbowed Bob and teased that he always got vanilla ice cream.

He smirked. "You can't go wrong with vanilla ice cream. But I am interested in this puff pastry with a hidden and edible coin."

"Oooh!" Lucy spoke up. "I missed that. I'm getting the hidden-coin pastry. That sounds fun." A waiter took their orders and the couples shared details about their travel agencies. Helen and Charles seemed amazed that Lucy's company was faith-based. They asked questions about it until the food arrived.

Two servers walked up to the table with trays of food. The table guests oohed and aahed at their dishes. Charles offered to say a prayer before they ate. The group thanked him and bowed their heads. As Morgan dropped her head, she noticed Helen pick up the saltshaker. She closed her eyes as Charles thanked God for the delicious food and new friends. He also asked for the safety of each passenger and crew member.

When Charles finished, the tablemates noticed Helen holding the shaker. Earl spoke up. "Is that a Maryland tradition?"

Helen smiled. "Oh, no. I hold the saltshaker when Charles prays to remind myself that Jesus asks me to the salt and light of the Earth. It reminds me to bring hope to others and shine my light at

Jesus. Do you know Him?" She looked around the table as she asked her question.

"Yes, ma'am, I do," Earl said. "And you are shining your light beautifully. You have inspired me to try to shine my light this week."

Gina spoke quietly. "What does that mean?"

Helen spoke like a loving grandmother to Gina and Ryan. She shared that every person is born separated from God by sin and that God provided a way to reconcile through Jesus. She added that Jesus is the only way to be saved from an eternity of torment in hell. The only way. Shining her light is telling the others about Him and their need for Him.

Bob looked at Morgan, but she looked away. He knew that Morgan saw the light as arrogance. He knew that she had trouble with this concept. Helen did a beautiful job explaining our need to put the focus on the Savior of the world. He noticed that Charles listened intently to his wife. The love of the older couple also shone brightly to others.

"Thank you, Helen," Lucy commented. "That was beautiful. I will think of you every time I pick up a saltshaker."

"Oh, please don't do that," Helen said. "Think of Jesus. Now, let's eat."

The group began enjoying their food. Morgan delighted at the crispiness of her swordfish, and Bob bragged about the cheesiness of his lasagna. Everyone laughed when Earl asked Helen to pass the salt. Morgan was glad that she and Bob signed up for the group dinner option. The other couples were delightful.

"Has anyone booked a trip to Vietnam?" Ryan asked. "I have an older couple who wants to visit, but I am not sure where to start. I told them I would arrange everything as soon as I got home."

Morgan looked around. No one answered, so she tried to give a response. "No. I haven't had that request. I did arrange something to Malaysia recently. That's near Vietnam."

Ryan nodded. "Yep. I saw that. I think I have it worked out, but wanted to see if anyone had a good suggestion. We do a lot of bachelor parties and mountain retreats. Not many Asian getaways."

"That's interesting," Charles added. "We book a lot of fishing trips and New England getaways. I didn't realize how regional our jobs are."

Lucy pointed to their table. "But everyone likes a good treasure hunt."

"Yep," Charles said. "We have had constant interest in *Golden Fortune*. I can't wait to get back and tell some of our clients about this amazing ship. It's so different from the others." The group agreed that *Golden Fortune* was a unique experience that people of all sorts would enjoy.

As she cut another bite of her fish, Morgan noticed the beautiful design on the plates. She moved the food aside and gasped aloud when she noticed that on the center of the plate was a golden *F* decorated with ornate embellishments. The others looked at her.

"The plates have an *F*!"

Lucy gasped. "What?"

"Look at the plates. There is an *F* at the center." The rest of the group moved their food to locate the *F*. "I think there is a clue on the bottom of the plates."

Morgan looked around the dining room and noticed a man showing his wife the bottom of his plate.

"Morgan, we can't flip out plates over," Bob warned.

"Let's be discrete about it." She pulled Bob's plate closer and scraped the contents of her plate onto his. As she carefully turned her plate over, she found a shiny sticker attached to the bottom. "There is something here," she whispered. All at once, the others stealthily lifted their plates to search for the sticker.

Morgan removed the sticker and found a message typed on it.

Congratulations! You found the *F*.
Now find two *H*s and one *O*.

She didn't read it out loud but waited for the others to read their clues. A server came to refill their drink glasses and smiled. Morgan held her finger to her lips, asking him to keep their discovery secret. He nodded.

Slowly, each person at the table found their clue. Charles spoke first. "I think I know what this means."

"So do I," Earl said. "Let's keep quiet and eat our desserts. Then we can break off and work on the clues."

Lucy rolled her eyes. "Not a problem for us. Earl won't give up his dessert for a clue. Please go if you want to follow the clue."

"I'm not skipping dessert either," Bob agreed. The group agreed to enjoy the cheesecake and treasure pudding before investigating the hunt.

"Are any of you going to the ice-skating show tonight?" Charles asked.

"We are going to the 9:30 show. Will you be there?" Gina replied. Charles nodded. He and Helen would be attending the 9:30 show also.

"We are going tomorrow," Morgan said.

"Same with us," Lucy added. "That should be fun."

"And it may have something to do with our clue," Earl declared. All eyes turned to Earl. Ryan and Helen smiled. They knew what he was thinking.

"Okay. I'm behind," Morgan sighed. "Bob will have to clue me in when we leave. Should I try to change our reservations to tonight's show?"

"No," Bob responded. "That's just one of many options."

As the desserts were being served, Earl spoke. "Is the whole week going to be like this? Constantly trying to solve the mystery? We won't be able to rest if we are always following these clues."

Lucy patted his arm. "Good point. I think we need to set 'clue-seeking' times. I don't think we can keep this up."

"I'm loving this," Ryan added. "Finish your cheesecake, Gina. I think I know where the next clue is." The group laughed.

Charles commented that passengers in their twenties had the advantage of vitality. "But we older folks have the advantage of patience and wisdom."

"We'll see about that, hon," Helen commented. "Please be careful hunting. It has been wonderful dining with all of you. I can't wait to tell our grandchildren about Morgan finding a clue under her plate." Gina and Ryan said their goodbyes and left to find the next clue. The rest of the group decided to enjoy coffee before leaving. Morgan decided to keep their reservations to the ice-skating show for the next night. She and Bob would enjoy the soda shop area or dance hall tonight. Lucy and Earl agreed.

After coffee, the couples separated. Morgan and Bob walked toward the elevator area. They decided to take the nearby stairs up one flight to Deck 6 and then walk toward the dance hall. At the top of the stairs, Morgan could immediately hear the music coming from the hall. She and Bob walked through the circular-shaped entrance and found a seat to the left of the dance floor. The room had soft lighting, and a live band was playing classic rock tunes.

Bob stood. "Wanna try a Cutlass? Looks like they are quite popular. Especially with the older kids."

"Sure." When a waitress walked by, Bob ordered two of the special drinks. As the woman left, Morgan leaned close to Bob. "So, what do you think about the clue? I think we should go through all the venues and find one with exactly two *H*s and one *O*."

"I'm thinking something else."

"Hold on." Morgan was looking at the deck plans on the phone app. "The Heave Ho Gym. That's it! It has two *H*s and one *O*. The next clue is in the gym. Should we go look now? Or wait till morning?"

"I had another idea, but that does sound promising. I vote that we enjoy the evening and check out the gym before breakfast tomorrow." The waitress delivered their drinks in keepsake glass containers. The glasses had a frosty skull and crossbones image on two sides. Morgan quickly took a sip.

"Yum! This is good. It's like a cherry lime slushie from Sonic. But with pineapple."

"You and your pineapple. This is good though. We must be careful. They are $15 each."

"Yikes. I better enjoy this one extra." Morgan and Bob enjoyed a few songs from the band. They didn't dance but decided that they would come back for the 70s dance party on Wednesday. After a few more songs, they decided to walk about Shipwreck Boulevard on Deck 7. Morgan carefully placed their empty Cutlass glasses in her shoulder bag as they exited.

Shipwreck Boulevard was the social hub of the ship. The entire area was bustling with excitement as people of all ages were shopping, dancing, and eating. Morgan and Bob walked through the mall area and down the center garden path. The found a row of benches and sat on the last one. Couples and families walked by as they explored the area.

The garden area was filled with live plants and peaceful lighting. Morgan could hear soft, instrumental music playing in the background. "This is so nice. You can't even tell that there is mall madness underway one hundred feet away. This really is getting away from it all."

"Yep. We aren't in Jacksonville anymore. You should tell your clients that there is something for everyone on this ship. We ate at the buffet, the pizza shop, and the elegant dining room in half of a day. Then we enjoyed a dance hall, a mall, and a romantic garden after that. And this is only the first day. We better get plenty of sleep tonight. I have a feeling that clue-hunting will take some energy."

"Maybe not. The first clue was in our cabin. And the second one was under our plate. Not too taxing so far."

"That's true. I can't believe I got in trouble searching the ice rink."

"Oh, I can." Morgan laughed. "Let's go back to our cabin. It's been a long day."

"Aye, aye, Captain!"

Golden Fortune was cruising in open waters at twelve knots. It wasn't expected to dock at Cutter Cay for thirty-six hours, so the ship sailed at a slow speed and in a non-direct path. At 7:45, Luca was relieved of his bridge duties and expected at the captain's table for dinner. He ate with guests at a special table three nights per week. Luca was usually exhausted by dinnertime but enjoyed meeting passengers from around the world. Tonight was lasagna night, so he didn't want to be late.

As Luca turned the corner toward his table, he immediately heard the familiar Southern twang. "Where's Luciano? He's supposed to be here." Luca was tempted to turn around but knew that he couldn't shirk his responsibility. Especially on the first night of the inaugural sailing.

"Good evening, everyone. I apologize if I am late." The captain stood at the head of the table and greeted the nine others at the table. "Please introduce yourselves. I'm delighted to meet you."

The others kindly shared their names and hometowns. Daisy gave her full name and nick name again. "I'm so excited to be eating at the captain's table. My cousin's stepson's dog groomer wrote his friend from Instagram and arranged this. Ain't that the bee's knees?"

Luca couldn't help but laugh with the others. Daisy had a way of making everyone around her feel welcomed and at ease. She was most definitely different, but harmless.

Conversation around the table centered on the treasure hunt. Luca shared that he didn't know where it was hidden but knew that the purser's office had at least one clue released. An older woman at the end of the table joked that she would have to find that dear purser. Daisy added that in Savannah a *purser* was something on a restaurant table that you put in your purse without anyone noticing. The group let out a collective gasp and then laughed with honest Daisy.

After the requisite lasagna, Luca enjoyed cheesecake and coffee. For the first time today, he felt himself relax. The ship was handling perfectly, and the minor pre-sail issues had been managed. The others at the table were finishing their desserts when Daisy spoke up. "Well, I'm as full as a tick on a bloodhound. It's a good thing I wore my stretchy pants tonight. I'm saving my moo-moo dresses for the last days. That's when I'll go up two sizes." Luca could only smile at his new friend. Too bad he couldn't thank her cousin's stepson's dog groomer for the meeting.

After dinner Luca spent an hour on the bridge. Everything was running smoothly, so Luca finally retired to his stateroom. He took the long way so he could see firsthand the new venues in action. After two dozen photos with passengers, he found a table near Oro pizza and sat down with a cappuccino. He was exhausted and exhilarated at the same time. The very first day of the world's first treasure cruise. Luca would remember this day forever.

Little girls were dancing with their fathers, and boys were challenging their friends with pretend swords. Parents were speaking with other parents, and couples were sharing pizza at the café tables. Teenagers were awkwardly dancing near the jukebox. People were enjoying their time on the "high seas."

CHAPTER SIXTEEN

December 2, Day Two: Sea Day

Morgan woke first. She dressed to exercise and brought her laptop to the small couch. Thankfully, it came to life promptly. She checked her email and was surprised to see messages from five clients interested in *Golden Fortune*. The media must be putting out images already. She also had two emails from her mom. Apparently, her mom and Aunt Margaret had won their age group in a local pickleball tournament. They were awarded a gift certificate from the market that delivered the flammable turkey. Mom insisted that Morgan and Bob visit after Christmas to enjoy some "cold turkey."

Morgan's snicker at the turkey woke Bob. "Let's get to the gym!"

"Okay. Let's go." Bob dressed quickly, and the two grabbed bottles of water as they left the room. "It's only two flights up. We can take the stairs." Bob agreed and sped ahead of Morgan toward the stairs. He was wearing an old T-shirt from a St. Patrick's Day 5K he had run eight years earlier. Morgan smiled at his excitement and knew that it had nothing to do with fitness. He was eager to find the next clue.

When they entered the gym, Morgan and Bob were surprised to see the number of people exercising at 7:00 on the first morning of their vacation. Adults of all ages were stationed at weight machines or jogging on treadmills. The overall scene was somewhat tiring. Of course, Morgan knew that exercise would give them energy and endurance; they would need to enjoy their vacation throughout the week.

At the entrance of Heave Ho Gym was a welcome desk with plenty of towels folded into cylinders. Morgan reached for a towel, but Bob stopped and looked beneath the shelves and all over the front desk area. Morgan stood back and watched him thoroughly inspect the entire entrance of the gym. Thankfully, no one reacted to his bizarre behavior.

When satisfied that there was no clue at the entrance, Bob took a towel and walked over to Morgan. "This will be impossible. Do you see all those treadmills? Plus, the machines and racks of weights? A clue could be anywhere."

"Don't forget the classrooms. And even the restrooms. The spa has a different name, so I don't think we need to check there. What do you think?"

Bob thought for a few seconds. "Well, we are here. Why don't we get our exercise in and check out as much as we can. Keep an eye on any passengers looking suspicious. If we don't find anything, we can discuss plan B at breakfast. I have another idea."

"Good plan, Cap'n," Morgan said. "I see two treadmills open over there. Want to join me? You have the 5K shirt on."

"No. I want to do some strength work. I'll be over there near the weights. And I'll look for clues on this side. You check out the cardio area. Have fun!"

Morgan laughed. "Ha! You know I don't like treadmills. Running outdoors is so much better. But I can't skip running for two weeks, especially after that treasure pudding. It was like rocky road but with pudding. I hope I can have that again. See you in a few." She walked to the row of treadmills and slowly inspected the machines. She wasn't quite sure what the next clue would look like, so she looked up and down. A woman speed walking on a machine noticed Morgan looking at her feet.

"Is there something wrong?" the intense-looking woman asked.

"Oh, no. I'm sorry. I'm caught up in looking for clues."

"Why would you look at my shoes? They aren't wet." Morgan apologized again and walked to the farthest treadmill of the row. She was embarrassed and didn't look for clues. The awkwardness of the hunt was something she hadn't anticipated. But passengers should expect others to be looking for clues. She had done nothing wrong. And she didn't understand why she would have thought the woman's shoes were wet.

While Morgan did not enjoy running on a stationary machine, she did enjoy the magnificent view. The cardio equipment was lined up along the massive floor-to-ceiling windows in the area. The view today was over the calm seas of the Bahamas. The turquoise-blue water was beautiful, especially early in the morning. Morgan hoped to see dolphins leaping out of the water but knew that was rare.

As Morgan set her pace and began jogging, she thanked God for the experience she was sharing with Bob. The vacation getaways they took together not only strengthened their relationship, but also relieved a little stress from their busy careers. God was more than generous with the blessings He handed out to her, even without children.

Morgan marveled at the calm ocean. Would this be what the "sea of glass" mentioned in Revelation would look like? Does the floor in heaven look like the ocean? Morgan didn't understand John's vision, but she recognized the universal feeling of peace that a calm body of water provided to humans. For thirty minutes, she forgot about her job, her to-do list, and the treasure hunt. She escaped into the stillness of the water.

Bob surprised her when he blurted out, "I'm finished!" Morgan smiled and slowed to a walking pace. "Keep walking. I'm going to check out the men's dressing area. Maybe the clues are in both areas."

"Good idea. I'm going to cool down and come find you."

As they left the gym, they agreed that no clues were hidden in obvious places. If Heave Ho Gym held any secrets, they would have to come back in the afternoon. The couple took the stairs down to Deck 9 and collapsed onto the couch in their cabin before they showered and dressed in swimwear. Bob donned a Live It! Travel Agency T-shirt, and Morgan wore a navy cover-up dress over her swimsuit.

"It's still early. And I burned off enough calories to eat four cinnamon rolls," Bob remarked.

"Ha! You know you didn't burn that much. But I am looking forward to breakfast. That bacon is calling my name loudly."

"Mine too. Let's go." Bob rushed to the door while Morgan gathered a few things and stuffed them into her beach bag.

On their way to Blackbeard's Fortress buffet, Morgan and Bob planned out their morning. They agreed to find two lounge chairs on the pool deck and park in them until lunch. Morgan would enjoy a book, and Bob would make friends with passengers in the hot tub. They would make a point to attend the Meet the Captain event at 11:30 a.m. The ship's captain would be answering questions in the main theater for an hour, and Morgan planned to take plenty of notes.

The buffet was crowded, but Morgan and Bob found seating near the back of the room in a quieter section. Morgan tried to show discipline at all-you-can-eat buffets, but there was usually a weakness at each meal. Today's weakness was bacon. How could anyone resist unlimited, free bacon? Morgan added extra fruit to her plate to counteract the bacon—and the chocolate croissant.

That makes sense, doesn't it? she thought.

After filling their plates, Morgan and Bob found the juice selection and chose the Caribbean punch drink. After thanking God for their food, Bob dove into his omelet. "I don't think 'two *H*s and one *O*' is referring to the gym. Think about it. What has two *H*s and one O?"

"HOH? I'm stumped."

"You're not thinking. H-2-O. It's water! What did the clue say again?"

"It just said to go find two *H*s and one *O*. That's H_2O. You are right. How did I miss that? What do you think?"

Morgan worked on her bacon as Bob explained his thoughts. "It must be in water somewhere. I'm thinking that the ice rink could be a possibility, but I think the clue would have said something about the water being solid. So our best guess is liquid water. Let's list all the places with water on the ship."

"Good idea. I didn't bring my notebook, so we will have to keep the list in our minds. The pool is the largest amount. And there are four hot tubs near the pool. Plus, the kiddie splash area."

"That works well. After we eat, we can find some chairs and go look at the pools. What else is there?" Bob stood and refilled their glasses with punch. "I'm liking this fruit punch. Who knew?"

Morgan nodded. "Same here. Let's think about the ship. Where else is there water in public? I honestly can't think of another place."

"Well, every dining facility serves water. But that would be impossible. Hey. We put those water bottles in the recycling bins this morning. Do you think they could have had a clue typed on their labels?"

"Great idea. I wouldn't have thought about that. Let's add the bottled water to our mental list. What else?"

"Aren't there fountains on the garden paths?"

"That's right. There were a few fountains on the side. I think we have a plan. Let's check out the pool deck this morning. Then we can walk through the paths on our way to the captain's session. If we don't find anything, we can go back to the gym and look at the water bottles."

Bob agreed. "And if everything fails, I am happy to go back on the ice." Morgan swatted his arm and finished her breakfast. Bob went for a second cinnamon roll and claimed that he felt no guilt.

Since *Golden Fortune* was now at sea, the pool deck area was crowded. On port days, most passengers would leave the ship, but sea days meant many more people on the top deck. Morgan spotted little girls splashing in the pool and fathers tossing balls to little boys. She put them out of her mind and made a conscious decision to be thankful for the blessings she did have. Bob gathered towels and found two empty chairs for them to enjoy. They had two hours until they needed to leave for the question-and-answer session with Captain Barone, and they planned to rest for most of that time.

"Let's check out the splash area and the slides," Morgan said. "I'm not sure what we should be looking for."

"Sounds good. But I say we chill after we check everything out. We don't get many Monday mornings to lounge in the sun like this."

"Deal!" Morgan and Bob walked around the pool area and the hot tubs. People were flittering around, so it was difficult to look closely at the surfaces. They then walked toward the children's splash area. Water was spraying everywhere, and children were running around the pirate-themed obstacles. Once again, Morgan noticed the little girls in colorful swimsuits and boys with tiny baseball caps. Despite her efforts, her heart ached while watching the children. The sting of her infertility never left.

The couple did not find anything related to a clue, so they walked back to their chairs. As soon as they sat down, a commotion arose in the shallow end of the large pool. Morgan could hear comments of "It's a clue!" and "Are those numbers?" She looked at Bob, and his eyes widened.

"Let's go look," Bob said. They walked over to the pool as excitement was growing.

Morgan saw a child running to his parents, who were sitting in lounge chairs. He belted out, "It's the clue, Mom! It's numbers!" She nudged Bob to go look. He walked through the crowd to get a closer look.

After a few minutes, Bob walked back to Morgan. "There is something written on the bottom of the pool. This must be the clue. But we don't have any goggles. How can we read it?"

"Wow! I just saw a video of a way to look in water without goggles. You must cup your hands around your eyes and slowly lower your face into the water. If you do it right, you have the effect of goggles."

Bob's jaw dropped. "Are you serious? You saw a video of that? I'm so impressed."

"Go try!" Morgan pushed Bob toward the pool.

"It's a madhouse. There's no way."

"Try."

As Bob walked toward the pool, two lifeguards were placing the passengers into a line at the shallow half of the pool. He got at the end of the line and waited for his turn to peek at the submersed clue. Most of the people ahead of him were children with goggles. Their parents were standing nearby, ready to hear the clue. Bob hoped that Morgan's MacGyver approach would work.

When it was his turn, Bob walked into the water and stood over the wavy characters. He put his hands around his eyes and put his face into the water. Water immediately flooded into his eyes. He tried again and held his hands tighter to his forehead. This time an air pocket formed, and he could see the bottom more clearly. The clue consisted of four sets of characters:

CC

+87

L29

+23

Bob rushed back to Morgan, who was holding her notebook and a pen. "CC plus 87 L29 plus 23." Morgan wrote down the code. Bob then told her that they were written vertically. She rewrote them in a column. "So much for rest."

Morgan giggled. "Sit down. Take a break. I'll work on the code breaking."

"That sounds great. I'll think about the clue. Where is the sunscreen?" Morgan fished the bottle of sunscreen out of her bag and handed it to Bob. "Thanks. And how in the world did you know about the 'air goggle' technique? I can't wait to tell Tony about that. It actually worked."

Morgan enjoyed the sunshine while she thought about the newest clue. She heard Bob softly snoring and was grateful that he was getting a little rest. She deduced that "CC" stood for an action or a location and that the numbers were points or distances. It sounded like a treasure map clue.

Morgan decided to suspend the treasure hunt for a while and enjoy their time on the pool deck. She could see that the continuous search for clues could become obsessive and possibly ruin a vacation. She didn't like to leave things undone, so solving the clues was taking up much of her attention. But it didn't have to. She and Bob were enjoying the sun on a beautiful ship in the Bahamas. That was a treasure of its own.

After letting her mind wander for a few minutes, Morgan found her book and decided to read a little. Christian fiction was her genre; slow and steady was her pace. She was in no hurry to finish the novels and enjoyed the investment into the characters and plot. Her current tale was about a woman left at the alter—literally. Morgan knew that the main character would persevere by the end of the book, but she really didn't see how at this point.

"It's a locker combination." Bob startled Morgan just as the bride in her story was ripping off her wedding gown. "The three numbers are a locker combination. Didn't we see Davy Jones's Locker somewhere?"

"Yes, that was the parking deck. I don't think the clue will be there. Unless the treasure is hidden in the Miami port."

"So where could we find a combination lock?"

"The dressing rooms in the gym have lockers," Morgan answered. "But I really don't think the line would send hundreds of passengers into the dressing area to test dozens of lockers. That doesn't seem practical."

"I agree. That would be too tedious. Anyplace else?"

"We can keep our eyes open for a locker-type combination lock today. And we can try to come up with an alternate idea for the code. I think CC is telling us to do something or go somewhere. Like a starting point."

"Good thinking. I'm starting to realize that an adventure cruise is not the place to rest. Be sure to tell your clients that the clues will take over their week."

"I hope that's not the case. But I do see that it's hard to put them out of your mind. Let's try to chill out for thirty minutes. Then we can make our way to the theater."

"Ahh, air goggles. I still can't believe that worked."

After a little more sunshine, the couple departed for the theater and the 11:30 question-and-answer event. As they crossed the pool deck, Morgan noticed that there was still a line at the pool to see the underwater clue. The hunt for the next directive caused an air of excitement that previous cruises hadn't had. It was just a different atmosphere. The children were clearly enjoying the mysterious clues as much as their parents.

The theater was nearly full when Morgan and Bob arrived. They found two seats near the back and scooted in front of a dozen people to fit into them. On the massive screen was projected a loop of photos from around the ship. Morgan was surprised at how much of the vessel she and Bob had already seen in less than twenty-four hours. They would have to slow their pace down a little. She made a mental note about scheduling intentional down time each day for some rest.

As she was thinking about her schedule, she heard her name called softly. Lucy was in the section to her right and was waving cheerfully. Morgan waved back and motioned for Lucy to meet her when the questions were over. Soon after, spotlights on the stage appeared and five crew members walked forward. They were seated in tall swivel chairs. The audience applauded even as people were still making their way in.

Once the welcome stopped, Captain Barone stood and introduced himself. He encouraged the guests to move forward as the audience was now standing room only. After a minute to let the noise from the crown settle down again, he introduced the remaining crew members as Barry Manning, Hotel Director; Jenny Lu, Staff Captain; Franny Meyers, Cruise Director; and Doc, the ship's head doctor. He announced that the group would be answering some prearranged questions and would then open the questioning to the audience.

The captain stood and held out an index card thoughtfully. "Where is the treasure?" The group laughed. "That is the number-one question I receive. And the answer is that I do not know. The purser's office handles the details of the hunt, and I am only told information as needed and when appropriate. How is the search going so far?" The group clapped, and Captain Barone nodded. He then sat as Franny stood with a question card.

"Where is the treasure?" More laughter as the same question was asked again. "That is also the number one question I receive. And I do not know either."

Public speaking never got easier. The theater stage was vast, and the lighting made it difficult for Luca to see the audience. But the weekly question and answer sessions were part of his job. The team around him was top-notch, so a few questions from paying passengers was not too demanding. The questions were usually the same each week, but occasionally someone would ask about the ship's design or Luca's sailing history. Questions like those were more interesting.

Franny read her next card. "'What is the best part of being a cruise director? And the worst part?' Well, the people are clearly the best part. Each week I get to meet a new group of passengers. And for the most part, they are on their best behavior." The audience laughed. "We do have those who misbehave or complain, but ninety-nine percent of my past guests were gems. Pun intended. You make this job the best in the world. Now, for the worst part. I can honestly say that this is a dream job and I love it. But the pace is a bit quick. We have fun activities planned for you twenty-four seven, and my team does an amazing job organizing the activity schedules for the ship and the incredible island ports. Wait till you see the fun we have planned at our new islands. But whew! A girl stays busy." The crowd applauded after Franny's comments. Her honesty was noted and appreciated.

The next card question was for the hotel director. "'What is your favorite towel animal?' Ha! Clearly the monkeys. Our room stewards are trained to create art out of cotton towels. I love them all. But the monkeys hanging from the ceiling are the best."

"Aww, the monkeys are cute. But I like the swans. Classic and elegant." The crowd snickered. "Hi, I'm Doc. Captain Stubing here is letting me answer one question, so let's see what it is. 'Have you ever performed surgery on a ship?'" Doc turned serious. "In the Navy, I handled many serious events and conducted a few surgeries. But cruise ships are a little different. We only see you for a short time, so we don't usually have serious encounters. But I have seen a few heart attacks and broken bones. We are equipped to handle minor surgeries, but for the most part we stabilize patients to be flown to land-based facilities. Trust me. You are in good hands on *Golden Fortune*. Jenny, I think you are next."

"Thank you, Doc." The staff captain stood. "I'm Jenny, and I'm thrilled to meet all of you. My question is, 'How did you become second in command of a modern cruise ship?' Well, that's a long story. I started working on a cruise ship directly out of college. And I never left. We get to travel around the world and meet new people. It's an amazing job for an extrovert. And for introverts too."

Jenny pointed at Luca, and he responded. "That's true. I don't consider myself terribly outgoing, but one can't help to become sociable in such a remarkable environment. As you can tell, we love our jobs."

Franny took the microphone and invited questions from the audience. The first question was for everyone on stage. "What is your favorite dish from the dining room.?" Franny responded that the grilled salmon was always done well, while the rest agreed that the lasagna was the best dish.

Next, a question was asked about the difficulty in maneuvering a ship in and out of ports. Jenny answered that question with details about the modern technology onboard *Golden Fortune* as well as the highly trained crew members and harbor pilots. She shared that much of the sailing was done with automation, but dockings were done manually.

Questions were asked about the TorpedoX lifeboats, the foster families sailing, and the worst weather the captain had experienced.

The stage party answered with enthusiasm. Finally, each were asked their favorite port. Franny couldn't choose her favorite "child," and the audience chuckled. Barry shared that Treasure Island was mind-blowing and that the audience was in for a treat. Finally, Luca shared that Naples was his favorite port. It was his home and where he had met his wife. Jenny shared that she had been to Antarctica and would never forget it.

Doc stood. "There are over one thousand cruise ports in the world. I want to see them all. My favorite port is always the last port I have visited. I love them all. Well, maybe not Southampton. That was the port *Titanic* embarked from. I'm trying to skip that one." The audience laughed.

Doc clearly had the approval of the audience. He walked toward the center of the stage. "Life is meant to be lived. I encourage you to 'lift anchor' and see the world. Wait! You already did. We are in the middle of the ocean right now. Then let me congratulate you for undertaking this adventure with us. We promise to take good care of you this week. And if you need any help, please call." At that assurance, the audience clapped and began to exit. The stage party stood at the edge of the platform and waved to the passengers. Luca smiled the entire time.

The informative session ended promptly after one hour. Morgan and Bob waited for the bulk of the crowd to exit before they stood. Morgan leaned over to her husband and whispered, "Did you notice the big CC on the screen when Franny was talking about Cutter Cay? That must be what the clue is about. It will be on the island tomorrow. What do you think?"

"I didn't catch that, but that does sound right. We should keep our eyes out for some sort of combination lock today, but expect to find something tomorrow. Are there lockers at Cutter Cay?"

Morgan thought a second. "I think there are lockers at the entrance of the island, but I really can't see the line sending hundreds of people to try every locker. Maybe one of them will have a special notation on it."

"That would make sense. What else could it be?" Just as Bob asked the question, Lucy and Earl called from the end of their row.

Lucy waved again. "Wanna catch lunch with us?"

"Sure," Morgan added. "Buffet or pizza?"

Earl smiled. "Can we do both?"

Bob liked Earl's idea. "I don't see why not."

"Now, gentlemen," Lucy added, "pace yourselves. We have plenty of time to overeat. How about the buffet? I want to try that seafood bisque if they have it again."

"Perfect," Morgan said. "Lead the way."

The group took an elevator to Deck 12. Once again, Blackbeard's Fortress was crowded. And once again, Morgan found a table near the back. She and Bob grabbed some napkins and utensils for everyone while Lucy and Earl gathered their food. They also found the Caribbean punch drinks. Finally, they made their way to the numerous food stations.

Food buffets were a danger to any diet. With unlimited fare that included too much fat and even more sugar, Blackbeard's Fortress was a culinary treasure hunt in its own way. Morgan filled half of her plate with salad items and added a cheesy pasta dish and some grilled fish. That should be enough healthy food to "earn" a gooey dessert, she rationalized.

Once the four were seated, talk immediately turned to the treasure hunt.

"Have you figured out the two *H*s and one *O*, yet?" Lucy asked.

"Yes, we got that one this morning. Do you want a hint?"

"Yes!" Lucy and Earl spoke at once. "We'd like to take a break from the hunt for a little while," Lucy shared. "We talked with the kids this morning, and they were so excited to help us. Kara said that it must mean water. We weren't even thinking that. But we are in the middle of an ocean. There is water everywhere. I don't even know where to start."

Bob looked at his drink. "Hmm, if I were you, I would check out the pool deck after lunch."

"Oh, you would, would you?" Lucy snickered. "We were going to hang out by the pool this afternoon. I'm thinking that may be a good idea."

"Great idea," Morgan added. "We were there earlier. I think we may go back for a little while after lunch. I wouldn't mind getting a little sun and then taking a nap before supper. What time do you eat dinner?"

"We have reservations for 7:00," Lucy said. "I'm not sure if that will be early enough for us to make the 8:00 ice skating show."

"We eat at 6:30," Morgan said. "It will be close, but we are planning to rush to the show. Don't want to miss a bunch of clowns on ice. I'm excited about this one."

"Maybe we can show up a little early. Earl won't mind that." Earl nodded and continued eating his roasted turkey as Lucy updated the Stevenses on their children. The grandparents had been watching them for two nights, and already one child had gotten a knot on her head from running too quickly into the kitchen, and another had refused to pack his backpack for school. Lucy joked that the grandparents may be tied up today as they were outnumbered.

Morgan shared that some of her best memories from childhood were camping with her grandparents. She didn't like the primitive environment, but loved the attention her grandmother gave her and the stories her grandfather would tell by the campfire. "This time with your parents is priceless to your children. And I know your parents are loving every minute of it. Sunday will be here before we know it, and we will be back to our routines. I can't even imagine how much email I will have when I get back to the office. And we will only have a little over two weeks until Christmas. Whew! I'm getting stressed thinking about it. Let's get dessert."

Lucy stood with Morgan as they walked to the vast dessert section. Morgan chose chocolate ice cream with caramel sauce, while Lucy went with red velvet cake. The men didn't get desserts and decided on coffee instead.

After eating, the couples said goodbye and went separate ways. Lucy and Earl went to their cabin to check on the kids and change into swimwear. Morgan and Bob went straight to the pool and found two lounge chairs on the starboard side of the ship. They decided they would spend the afternoon in the fresh air, forgoing a nap in their cabin.

From her chair, Morgan had a nice view of the Walk the Plank feature. Adults and children were walking out on the clear platform over the sea. The littlest children were universally concerned about the see-through bottom, but the teenagers couldn't get enough of it.

Morgan grabbed Bob's wrist. "Let's walk the plank. We haven't seen the view yet."

"We just sat down." He sighed. "Okay. Let's check it out. And maybe grab an ice cream cone while we are up."

"Deal!" The couple walked to the plank and waited for an opening. Morgan stepped out first and immediately grabbed Bob's arm. The translucent floor made her feel like she would fall, but of course she wouldn't. Bob walked her to the rail, and the two looked out over the endless water.

"This is an amazing view! I feel like a bird," Morgan remarked. "It feels like the ship is speeding much faster than it really is."

"It's incredible. We haven't done anything like this on a ship before. The little ones don't know what to think. It feels like we are floating above the water."

"Let's go before we see a shark. I trust the engineers, but I still have a weird feeling."

"Sure. On to the ice cream machines." After serving themselves chocolate-vanilla swirl ice cream cones, the two returned to their chairs. Both agreed that they weren't moving from their seats for at least an hour.

Morgan dozed into a partially asleep state. She could hear some of the sounds around her but was effectively asleep. Bob was quietly reading the ship's information brochure that he found in Morgan's bag. Children were squealing in delight while swimming in the pool as well as when buckets of water were periodically dumping on them in the "fun zone." The air smelled of salt water and sunscreen. And the sun was perfectly warm. Finally, rest was happening.

Suddenly, a loud whistle sounded near Morgan. She popped her head up and saw a lifeguard rushing toward the plank. The crowd around her became silent. Two teenagers were standing on the second rung of the railing, attempting to look farther over the edge of the plank. The lifeguard whisked them down and walked them away from the plank. Morgan's stomach turned because she saw how easily the boys could have fallen overboard. The line would have to raise the railing somehow if children were going to be so careless. For the remainder of the afternoon, a pool attendant stood near the opening of Walk the Plank to prevent anyone else from climbing on the railing.

After the excitement, Morgan and Bob decided to return to their cabin and get ready for dinner. They still had three hours until their 6:30 reservation, so a cat nap was likely. Morgan spotted Earl standing in line by the pool as they walked by. She spotted Lucy nearby and walked over. "I see you found the next clue."

"We did. And the little boy in front of Earl offered to share his goggles."

Morgan smiled. "Bob had to figure it out without goggles. It was hilarious."

"I bet. Enjoy your dinner. We're going to eat at the buffet tonight so we can catch the ice show. I'll look for you when we get there."

"Sounds good." Morgan walked a few steps to Bob and the couple headed toward the elevators. As the car was closing, they agreed that a real nap would be nice. It was a shame to sleep through the fun, but they would have more energy to enjoy the evening if they got a little rest. They were now officially at the "nap stage" of their lives.

Once off the elevator, Morgan and Bob walked completely down the hallway, or passageway, before they realized they were heading in the wrong direction. They turned around and retraced their steps back to the elevators and crossed over to the other side of the ship.

"I am always turned around," Morgan said. "But the extra steps mean extra dessert." Bob laughed and couldn't argue with her reasoning.

After the stage questions, Luca ate lunch in his cabin. He checked for email messages on his desk computer and wrote his sons with an update on the first night of sailing. Luca didn't mind being alone. No one could replace his precious wife, and the quiet times were when he could remember her the best. Sailing the ocean was an exciting adventure that surprisingly provided plenty of peaceful moments. After resting on his couch for thirty minutes, Luca headed back to the bridge.

The bridge team was handling their duties expertly. Luca replaced the second officer at the helm and listened to a detailed update. The weather was expected to remain calm, and the new engines were performing as anticipated. New ships did not have issues with marine growth on the hull, such as algae and barnacles. So far, so good.

Luca stood to make a cup of coffee when he saw a member of the safety team enter. "Captain, may I have a word with you?"

"Of course. Let's step over here." The official explained that two boys had climbed on the railing of the see-through plank on the pool deck and were dangerously close to falling overboard. Luca ordered a lifeguard be placed at the plank during the day and asked for the engineers to inspect the area immediately. "Please report back to me when the engineers have completed their review."

"Yes, sir." Luca watched the young man leave and said a silent prayer for the safety of the passengers. Over the years, he had seen too many teenagers take dangerous risks. He knew that was part of their development to begin leaving the nest, but he was responsible for the safety of every person on board. He recalled the plank and remembered the railing being regulation height. Perhaps additional measures should be taken at this novel spot. He would wait to hear from the engineers before deciding on a plan of action.

The afternoon continued to be routine, which was always good for the bridge crew. Luca handed over the reins at 6:30 so he could get dressed for dinner. He would be eating with Franny Meyers and leaders from the entertainment team in the galley dining room. They had work to do, but also wanted to provide a presence among the diners.

Daily entertainment was one of the efforts that passengers saw up close. And they were quick to criticize when things went wrong. Luca liked to stay on top of the issues and offer help where he could. He knew that scheduling dancers, skaters, comedians, clowns, and musicians with extreme precision was not easy. Fortunately, Franny and Steve Marino did their jobs well.

When Luca opened his cabin door, he was greeted with a huge flower arrangement. It was a mixture of yellow and white daisies. He couldn't remember ever receiving flowers on a sea day. He assumed they were from Jewel Cruise Line's corporate headquarters and was surprised when he read the attached note: *Don't get any ideas, Luci. I just wanted to thank you for carrying us minnows around in the big fishing pond. See you around, Daisy.*

Luca didn't know if he should laugh or cry. Daisy was beginning to become a pest. But was that really a problem? She was just a friendly person and must be lonely. He imagined that she'd decided she would get out and see the world while she still could. Luca was proud that he could get the thousands of minnows on his ship safely around the fishing pond. Or something like that.

Night two of the cruise was formal night. Adults and children would dress their best for dinner. Morgan and Bob did not go "all out" with a formal gown and tuxedo but did try to dress a little nicer. Morgan even brought new clear block heels for the night. They reminded her of the clear floor on the plank. They went with anything, but looked perfect with her pale-blue satin dress with spaghetti straps. She fixed her hair in a loose twist and even added extra mascara.

"Va-va-voom! You look amazing, Mrs. Stevens."

"Why thank you, Mr. Stevens. You look pretty dashing in your gray suit. I forgot how blue it makes your eyes look."

"Of course, my love, that was my goal. Radiant eyes." Morgan giggled and swatted his arm.

"Let's go, Mr. Comedian." The couple made their way to the galley dining room. Tonight, they would be eating alone. Morgan noticed that the bus boys were wearing eye patches. It was a great touch, but she wondered how well they could see with them on.

Once seated, Morgan reviewed the menu. She and Bob usually got the lobster dinner on formal nights. Tonight was no different.

"I think I'll try the Caesar salad as my appetizer. What about you? French onion soup?

"Yep, the soup caught my eye as soon as I looked at the menu."

After ordering, Morgan brought up the risky teenagers on the plank. "Why would someone put himself at a risk like that. Isn't it natural to try to preserve ourselves? They could have fallen into the ocean so easily."

"I don't think teenage boys see the risk. They feel invincible. I still remember Doug and I jumping our bikes over ditches. We built ramps out of scrap wood and treated them like stable launch pads. Even after Doug broke his collar bone, we still jumped the ditch in our backyard. I read about a study in mice where the male mice consistently took more risks than the female mice. And even more when they were around other males."

"Yikes!"

"We just aren't as developed as you ladies when we are teenagers. And we really want to impress our friends."

"I'm sure God made you that way to protect your families. But I'm still amazed. Parenting teenagers must be so challenging."

"Oh yeah. I can't even imagine."

The food arrived, and Morgan chuckled at the huge disk of cheese on top of Bob's French onion soup. "You need a knife for that."

"Don't worry about me. I've got this covered." Bob bowed his head to offer thanks for their food. As Morgan closed her eyes, she put her hand on the saltshaker. Helen had inspired her to remember that she should do her part to bring hope to the world.

The remainder of the dinner was perfect. The couple talked nonstop about their day and the excitement of the treasure hunt. Morgan grinned at each little girl who walked by in a frilly dress. Several had oversize hairbows, and a few had glittery shoes. The familiar ache appeared, but she pushed it away and thanked God for a magical day. She was content with the amazing life that she had and shouldn't wish for something more.

Bob helped Morgan with her lobster tail. She usually had trouble removing the shell without getting lobster juice all over her dress. One time, she sent a piece of the shell flying to a table behind her.

When their server brought their dessert, he was leaning to his left. Morgan wasn't sure if he was having a serious problem. "Are you okay, Minshu?"

"Yes, missus. I am fine. I have to tilt, since I can only see with one eye. The patch is blocking the other." Minshu discreetly moved his patch from his left eye to his right eye. "No problem. I just move the patch. It is many funs."

Morgan smiled. "Please be careful. We don't want you to get hurt."

After dessert, Morgan and Bob made their way to Deck 8 and the ice-skating rink. They looked for Lucy and Earl but couldn't find them. Finally, they found seats in a middle row on the left side of the rink.

As guests were entering the area, festive circus-type music was playing. The logo for the *Bumbling Treasure Hunters* show was projected onto the ice. Characters on the projected logo were periodically falling in silly ways, causing children in the audience to laugh. Morgan noticed a man looking on the ice. He must be trying to find the H_2O clue.

Promptly at 8:00, the lights dimmed, and trumpet music blared. The audience gasped, and skating clowns filled the ice. The one-hour show was energetic and entertaining. Morgan found herself laughing throughout the entire performance, especially when the clowns knocked each other over trying to carry the treasure chest. Talented performers conducting timed acrobatics on ice skates amazed everyone. The onlookers gave a standing ovation at the end.

As Morgan and Bob were exiting the facility, they ran into Lucy and Earl. Lucy spoke first. "Great show! The kids were having a blast. We're heading down to Shipwreck Boulevard. Wanna join us?"

"Sounds great!" Morgan said. "I'd like to try another Cutlass drink." The group went down one flight of stairs and walked into a hub of excitement. A live band was playing a popular line dance tune near the dance floor. At least sixty people were dancing in unison. The smell of fresh popcorn and hot wings filled the air. Fun was being had by multiple generations.

Bob spotted a table for four on the right and led the group to it. "Who wants a Cutlass? Tonight seems like a good night for another cherry lime slushie."

Lucy raised her hand. "Order four . . . on us! Here's my room bracelet. We're having too much fun with you guys. I'll get us some popcorn."

The group enjoyed talking and people-watching for over an hour. Twice, the ladies joined in the dancing. Despite the clear heels, Morgan moved all over the dance floor without falling. At one point, she twirled along with a young girl in a frilly dress. She commented to

Lucy that the late nap was the secret to her having any energy that night. In their younger days, Morgan and Bob could go full speed from breakfast till late-night pizza. These days, they had to build in breaks.

Just as the group was about to break up, several officers from the ship's crew joined the dance floor. They were wearing eye patches and white dress uniforms. Franny, the cruise director, was wearing a colorful dress and led the group. Morgan knew they must be tired, but all were good sports and danced along with the passengers. When the second song started, Captain Barone and Doc appeared in complete pirate costumes. The crowd cheered and formed a circle around them. Doc did a weak attempt at break dancing and then pointed to the captain. It was clear that Captain Barone was not comfortable in the center of a dance mob, but he was a good sport and did a little shimmy.

When the crew members left the dance floor, most of the passengers did too. Several children continued twirling in the middle of the floor. The couples finally called it a night. Morgan gathered two more empty Cutlass glasses and said goodbye to her friends. "Cutter Cay tomorrow. It will be nice to walk on land again."

Earl agreed. "I'm looking forward to a peaceful day on the beach. Do you guys think that the CC in the clues is for Cutter Cay?"

"We do," Bob answered. "We think we have an idea but aren't entirely sure. I hope we can find the next clue quickly so we can enjoy the rest of the day in peace."

"Yep," Earl agreed. "I won't be running around the island if we can't find it quickly."

"We'll see about that," Lucy added. "We can't quit on day three. Tonight was a lot of fun. We will probably see you tomorrow. If not on a beach, probably at the lunch grill."

"Sounds good," Morgan said. "Which beach do you think will be best?"

"Emerald Beach and Jade Beach are the closest, so they will probably have the most people. Earl and I are planning to walk to Pearl Beach. I read that they each have identical activities and food stations, so it probably doesn't matter."

"We were thinking the same thing," Morgan added. "Have you checked the weather?"

"I checked this morning. Looks like temps in the seventies and lots of sun. Not bad for early December."

"I totally agree. Let's take the stairs, Bob. The elevators look busy."

"Sure," Bob agreed. "Let's go."

Luca had not planned to dance at Shipwreck Boulevard, but Franny talked him into it during dinner. He had to admit that it was fun. Doc was a much better dancer, but dancing was all about having fun. Or at least that was Luca's belief. He noticed lots of smiles tonight, especially from the children. The cruise line must be happy with the approval ratings so far. Luca hadn't received any major complaints from guest services yet.

Before retiring to his cabin for the evening, Luca visited the bridge. He checked the most recent reports and was delighted that the ship was running smoothly. He wished everyone a good evening and promised to return soon. They would arrive at Cutter Cay at 7:00 a.m., so Luca needed to be at the helm by 5:00.

That night, Luca dreamt of Dahna. It was a short dream but very vivid. He saw her dancing in the living room of their small apartment. Before children, the couple would sit on their balcony and listen to radio music. They would talk and occasionally dance. Luca looked forward to the days he would have in heaven to dance and talk with his Dahna again.

The alarm sounded at 4:00 a.m. Luca did sit ups and pushups for twenty minutes before showering and dressing. He would eat on the bridge, so he walked directly from his cabin to the command center.

The corridors on the ship were quiet. Passengers were getting much-needed rest before another day of adventure. The skies were especially dark with a new moon. Luca could see a few lights from Cutter Cay in the distance as he entered the bridge area. The control panels provided a greenish glow to the room, and Luca could smell coffee and cinnamon rolls.

Tito would be boarding the ship at 5:30 a.m. Luca knew that the process was dangerous and said a prayer for his friend's safety. He gathered the navigation team and discussed the two sand bars they must avoid. "The port pilot is very knowledgeable, so we will let him guide us here and here. We shouldn't have any traffic, but please check the sensors as usual." Further preparations were made as the group awaited the pilot.

"My jack. There he be!" Tito's voice rang through the bridge.

"Good morning! It's great to see you, my friend. How is Myrna?" Tito shared that his wife and nephew were doing well and decided to eat one of the cinnamon rolls before assisting the crew. Luca sat with him and slowly finished another cup of coffee.

Golden Fortune docked at 6:48 a.m. with no trouble. Tito praised the team and asked for a quick tour of the authentic pirate ship before he left. Luca could not leave the area and asked an officer to show his friend the highlights.

Tito and the officer walked around the pool deck by Walk the Plank and back to the movie area. Then they toured the soda shop area complete with the working juke box. Finally, they visited Shipwreck Boulevard and strolled down the middle garden path.

Tito was impressed and returned to the bridge to tell his friend. "This is quite a ship, my jack. I am worried that real pirates will jump out at us."

"Yes, the decorations are very nice. I am enjoying this assignment more than I expected."

"I'm so happy to hear that. Enjoy your day, and I will return for your departure."

"See you this afternoon, Tito."

"Blessings!" Tito left the area for the small craft awaiting his return, while Luca reviewed weather reports. Today promised to be sunny and calm. Perfect for a day on a tropical island.

CHAPTER SEVENTEEN

December 3, Day Three: Cutter Cay

Once again, Morgan woke first. She and Bob had decided the night before that they would skip their exercise this morning. Instead, they would enjoy a leisurely breakfast and disembark early. Morgan could see from the balcony that the ship was already docked at Cutter Cay. Passengers would be allowed to leave the ship at 8:00 a.m. She dressed in a peach-colored swimsuit and added a blue-and-white-striped cover-up.

While she was waiting, Morgan started up her laptop. But the computer never came to life. Ugh! She needed Mikey. But he was six days away. She shut it closed and plugged it into the charger. Sometimes a little charging would do the trick. Bob awoke fifteen minutes later and was dressed and ready in less than ten minutes. The two went straight to Blackbeard's Fortress for breakfast.

Bob found a table near a window on the starboard side. He and Morgan would be able to watch people strolling onto the island while they ate. The turquoise-blue water was breathtaking. The two took a full minute before they gathered their food to take in the stunning color. Morgan looked at Bob. "How does He do it all?"

"I know. Only God could create such a beautiful color."

Morgan gathered her food quickly. Bob took longer, and Morgan finally realized that he was getting a made-to-order omelet. As she was waiting for him, she noticed several young people driving jet skis back and forth across the closest beach. They didn't seem to be part of a tour group. When Bob arrived, she asked him about the parade of jet skis.

"I don't know. Looks like they are meant to be there. Maybe they are extra lifeguards? Or they might be warming up the motors for upcoming passengers. Interesting. We'll ask someone if they are still out there when we settle down."

"So, do we have a plan for the clue? I say we find a spot to leave our things and then go search."

Bob wasn't so sure. "If we are discounting a locker combination, the numbers would have to be steps. I think they would have to be from the entrance. Otherwise, the starting point could be anywhere. What were the numbers again?"

Morgan knew the clue by heart. "Plus eighty-seven, *L* twenty-nine, plus twenty-three."

"That must mean eighty-seven steps forward, twenty-nine steps to the left, and twenty-three steps forward again. I say we try that from the entrance to the island. If that doesn't work. We'll find some chairs on Pearl Beach and look for some sort of sign marking the start. We should try to beat the heat."

"I like your plan. Let's be sort of subtle about counting our steps. We may be the only ones with this idea."

Bob smirked. "If we are the only ones, we are probably wrong. But I agree, we can walk the steps without being obvious. If you see the next clue, take a picture of it quickly. We don't want to bring too much attention to it."

"Deal!"

After breakfast, the couple gathered supplies into Morgan's beach bag. They had plenty of sunscreen, plus two books, hats, sunglasses, and water bottles. Towels were provided at each beach, so they didn't need to add that bulk. Bob threw in the folding shovel and gloves, just in case. They left their room and took an elevator down to the gangway.

When they exited the elevator, Morgan and Bob were swallowed by a mass of people in tropical attire. The after-breakfast crowd was eager and ready to be one of the first to check out Cutter Cay. Fortunately, the line moved quickly, and the beachgoers were soon walking on the large pier toward the island.

Morgan was quiet as she approached Cutter Cay. She was carefully scanning the entrance for any sort of marking indicating a start. She was about to give up when she heard a child squeal. "Look Dad, X marks the spot." Everyone in the area looked at the large yellow X painted at the end of the pier. To Morgan's surprise, every person in the area continued to walk past the marking. She quickly realized that getting their children settled at the beach was more important to them than hunting for elusive treasure.

Bob whispered to Morgan, "Keep walking. I'll count. And when I get to eighty-seven, I'll squeeze your hand." Morgan said nothing and walked along with Bob. This was happening too quickly. But they couldn't stop and discuss it. They would just go with their plan for now.

After the appropriate number of steps, Bob squeezed Morgan's hand, and the couple turned to the left. She kept the count in her head this time and turned to the right in sync with Bob. The final leg required twenty-three steps, but an oleander bush was solidly planted at step number twenty. Morgan looked behind the bush and was surprised to see a small sign with even smaller words printed on it. She pretended to be taking a picture of flowers on the bush and snapped a quick photo with her phone.

Bob then led her quickly to one of the brightly painted pathways. "Did you get it?"

"Yes, but I didn't read it. Let's get to our chairs." The two walked casually down the path past Emerald Beach. About a third of the beach chairs were taken. Children were playing on a sandy playground, and a game of beach volleyball was underway.

Morgan and Bob continued to Pearl Beach. More chairs were available there, and no children were playing on that playground yet. Bob walked to a towel hut and picked up two towels while Morgan found two chairs in the front row. She scanned the area for Lucy and Earl but did not see them.

"Hurry! What does it say?"

Morgan found the photo on her phone and quietly read the clue, which was written in a very small font.

Congratulations! Your steps in the sand were right. Now you must find a parrot perched late Wednesday night.

"Well, that one is obvious. We'll be on the ship Wednesday night. That must be the large movie area at the front of the pool deck. I can't think of any other perches."

Morgan nodded. "That must be right. And do you know what the best part is?"

"We have a huge break from clue hunting."

"Exactly, we can stop and rest our minds for the remainder of the day and most of tomorrow. Perfect!" Morgan stretched out their towels and reclined on her chair. They were covered by a colorful umbrella and surrounded by the most amazing blue water. It was almost the color of Bob's eyes.

"I'm not moving the rest of the day," Bob joked. "This is perfect."

"Me neither. Let's forget about getting back on the boat. I could live here forever."

"Your mom would never forgive me if I don't get you back to Florida on Sunday. But we can enjoy every minute of today."

Morgan and Bob were silent for twenty minutes before they heard Lucy softly calling. "I thought that was you. We won't bother you. Just wanted to say hi. Our chairs and in the next row over there."

"Great," Morgan said. "We will be here all day doing a lot of nothing. It is so peaceful here."

"It is," Lucy agreed. "Not at the lockers though. Did you see all the people trying the locker combinations on Emerald Beach? We watched for a little while but never saw anyone open one. There must be more to the clue."

Morgan felt guilty about keeping the clue from Lucy and Earl. She would ask Bob about it as soon as they left. "No. We came in a different way."

"I think people were going down the line trying each locker. Did you notice the boys on the jet skis?"

"We did. What is that about?"

"Earl asked that lifeguard over there. He said they are 'shark scrubbers.' They run at the beginning the day to keep sharks away from the shore. Apparently, reef sharks like to get too close in the mornings."

"And they aren't the only types of sharks out there," Earl added.

"Oh, my word!" Morgan declared. "I would never have thought that. Should we tell our clients? Or would that information scare them away from a Bahamas vacation?"

"Good question," Lucy said. "I may leave that on a need-to-know basis. We must admit that Jewel Cruise Line has thought of everything. That may be why they developed those torpedo lifeboats. Too many sharks in the area to waste time."

"Good point," Morgan said. "We're going to stay on land this morning. Come get us when you go for lunch. I'm already thinking about it. There is just something about a hamburger on the beach."

"Will do. Have fun doing nothing."

"On it!" Bob declared.

At 10:00 a.m., Luca was free to leave the bridge. He informed his officers that he would be taking a break and walked to the top deck. From the starboard side, he could see the passengers spilling onto Cutter Cay. He watched couples walking together hand in hand and families moving toward the nearest beach. He noticed several individuals traveling with the help of scooters. They reminded him of Daisy and her Southern charm. God made us as different as snowflakes, which was an unusual thing to think about on such a sunny day.

After watching hundreds of treasure hunters disembark, Luca treated himself to an ice cream cone. The free food was a hazardous perk of living on a cruise ship. Luca bargained with himself that he must exercise as much as he indulged in sweets.

As he turned to leave, Luca noticed Walk the Plank nearby. A young lifeguard was standing guard, although no one was in the area. Luca greeted her and asked if she had seen the teenagers the day before.

"Yes, sir. I saw them. They were just being teenagers. I don't think they were going to jump."

"Good to hear," Luca said. "But they could have easily lost a grip and fallen overboard. Thank you for keeping a watch. I haven't received a report from the engineers yet but expect they will plan to improve this railing when we return to Miami."

"That sounds like a great idea, Captain."

Luca made his way to the garden paths on Deck 7. It was one of his favorite places to think. Today, he chose the far-left path and walked halfway before taking a seat at a bench. A couple walked by and waved before the captain was alone. He took out his phone and checked for any email messages. Sonja had written about the boys and asked for pictures of the hidden treasure dessert. She had read about it on a social media site and couldn't wait to try it in April. Luca made a mental note to order the special dessert the next time it was offered.

Before returning to the bridge, Luca ate an early lunch at Blackbeard's Fortress buffet. He was invited to join a family with two small children and agreed. He made a simple sandwich and added some fruit to it before sitting beside the youngest child.

"Annie, this is the captain of the whole ship. It is an honor for him to eat with us," her dad said. Annie looked up briefly and returned to her French fries. The dad continued sharing with the kids the important roles of a ship's captain. Annie's older brother asked who was driving the ship while the captain ate, and Annie replied quickly that the ship was "parked." The adults laughed before Luca explained the jobs of junior and senior officers, as well as the rest of the bridge team.

"So, what do you like best about *Golden Fortune*?" Luca asked.

"Ice cream!" the children cried out in unison. Their mom explained that they had eaten ice cream at all lunches and dinners and still couldn't get enough of it. Luca joked that the best part of the one-billion-dollar ship was a bowl of ice cream.

"Don't forget the cones," the dad added. "Those are great too."

Luca learned that the family was from Texas and had given up on the treasure hunt. The ship had plenty to offer without the hunt for clues. The family shared that they visited Cutter Cay early and left after two hours to return to the ship and enjoy the pool deck while it was less busy.

As Luca left, he commended the children on their manners and wished them a fun week.

"Don't forget to wear your seatbelt," Annie warned. Luca smile and promised that he would drive safely.

Around noon, Bob declared that it was time for lunch. The smell of grilled hamburgers and hot dogs had reached the beach. Morgan found her cover-up and shoes and waited for Bob to put on his T-shirt. As they turned toward the nearest food station, they noticed Lucy and Earl walking toward them.

"Smell getting to you too?" Earl asked.

"Yep. I'm ready," Bob said. The foursome walked through the sand to the beach grill. The area was set up as a buffet with lines starting on either side. Morgan followed Bob through a line. She opted for a cheeseburger off the grill and fresh fruit. Bob went with a cheeseburger and a hot dog, plus French Fries. They found an empty picnic table and waited for Lucy and Earl to join them. Three drink stations were near the tables, and Bob got glasses of Caribbean punch for everyone.

"This is so nice," Lucy commented. She offered thanks to God for the food and realized that she had missed the condiments for her hamburger.

"I missed them too," Bob said. He and Lucy took their burgers back to the food station to find some toppings. Morgan ate a few bites of watermelon as she waited for the two to return. Her back was to the food, so she was surprised to see Earl gasp. Morgan turned around to see Bob covered in what appeared to be blood. She jumped up and ran toward him.

"What happened? Are you okay?"

Bob rolled his eyes. "Yes. I'm fine. The ketchup pump must have built up pressure because it exploded when I pressed the lever. It even got in my eyes."

"It got on me too," Lucy laughed. "But you look like a murder victim, Bob. We must get you cleaned up." An older couple sitting nearby rushed over to the group.

"My husband is a retired EMT. Please lie down." The woman was more assertive than Morgan expected.

"Thank you, but this is ketchup. I'm fine. Just didn't know my own strength." The couple didn't appreciate the humor and returned to their table. Bob sat his ketchup-soaked plate down and walked toward a bathroom. "I'll try to rinse this off. But my shirt will be soaked."

Morgan stood. "I'll get a towel." As Bob was walking toward the restroom, two employees ran up to him. Morgan could tell by their body language that they thought Bob was bleeding profusely. He must have reassured them because they walked away slowly. One spoke into a walkie-talkie, apparently calling off the reported emergency.

Morgan found a towel hut and grabbed a beach towel for Bob. She figured that his shirt would be soaking wet, as well as stained red. A towel was the only thing she could think of to use as a covering. When she returned to the table, she discovered that Earl had made a fresh plate of food for Bob and that Lucy had cleaned up his mess. Morgan appreciated her friends more than they realized.

When Bob returned, he was holding his dripping shirt. "I think this shirt is toast. Don't tell your mom, Morgan. She gave it to me for my birthday." Morgan handed him the towel, and he wrapped it around his shoulders.

"We made you another plate. And I let Lucy add the ketchup. She seems to have the touch." Earl waited for Bob to sit before he did.

"Thanks, man. I'm scared to eat."

Earl patted Bob on the back. "Watch the punch. It's tricky too."

The four enjoyed the rest of lunch, and Morgan retrieved snow cones for everyone for dessert. They all agreed that lunch in the Bahamas was a pretty good way to spend a Tuesday. Lucy commented about the clue. "Should we split up the lockers and try the combination? Earl and I could take the ones at Emerald Beach, and you two can check the ones at Jade Beach. We would be happy to share with you whatever we find."

Morgan glanced at Bob. They had to tell their friends what they found. It was only right.

"It isn't a locker combination," Morgan said.

Lucy seemed surprised. "It isn't? How do you know?"

"We figured that it would be too disruptive for hundreds of people to be checking every lock, so we went with another angle. And it worked. We found the next clue this morning."

"Oh my!" Lucy looked at Earl. "We never even considered another angle."

Earl sat his snow cone down. "Is it steps? Like on a treasure map?"

Bob tried not to smile. "Very well could be."

"But where would we start?"

"At the beginning," Bob said.

Earl's faced showed that he knew exactly how to find the next clue. He and Lucy decided that they would enjoy another hour lounging on the beach before searching for clue number four. Morgan and Bob helped them clean up the table and walked with their friends toward the beach.

"We'll probably spend another hour or two at the beach before we get back on the ship," Morgan shared. "I wouldn't mind spending a few minutes in a hot tub before we make our way back to our cabin. Let us know if you have trouble with the clue. We tried our best to be stealthy. Not sure if we were."

"Thanks a lot. We can't leave this island without our next directive, so we will come to you for a hint if we need it. Happy resting." The couples separated to their chairs. Bob hung his massacred shirt over the back of his chair.

Morgan took her book out of her bag and settled back under the umbrella. Bob was clearly on the verge of a relaxing beach nap. Before he fell asleep, he looked over at Morgan. "Lucy and Bob are great friends. We have a lot of friends, but not many 'great' friends.

You should have seen Lucy when I emptied the ketchup container on myself. She just shifted into 'mom mode' and got me out of there. Let's make a point to plan something with them when we get back home. I don't want to take blessings like them for granted."

"That sounds like a great idea. Maybe we can invite them to a game night when my mom and Aunt Margaret are visiting. We could even get a bunch of pizzas and include the kids."

"Sounds like a plan. Did you see the lightbulb go off for Earl when we said that the clue wasn't a combination? He knew instantly what the numbers meant. They won't have any trouble finding the hidden note. Now we just wait until Wednesday night. I hope 'late' isn't late-late."

Morgan and Bob ended up spending three more hours on the beach. Bob took a solid nap, and Morgan finished her book. (The jilted bride ended up marrying the groom's brother two hours after the original ceremony was to take place.) As they were leaving the island, they saw a family of four secretly counting out steps from the entrance. It hit Morgan at that moment that the adventure was strengthening families. Moody teenagers were brainstorming with their parents. Toddlers were following older siblings in the search. Grandparents were helping their grandchildren figure out hidden meanings. Couples without children were working together as a team. And cell phones and tablets weren't needed to find the treasure. She would add her thoughts to the FAQ she was building for the cruise. So many benefits came from the added team-building exercise on *Golden Fortune*.

After lunch, Luca rested in his cabin for two hours. He was able to catch up on emails from his family and Jewel Cruise Line. The boys and their families were doing well. Everyone was getting excited about the upcoming Christmas holidays. Luca would spend this Christmas on a ship, as he had done many times. Celebrating with thousands of guests was better than celebrating alone, without Dahna. He didn't mind manning *Golden Fortune* for the holidays. He changed into his evening uniform and returned to the bridge. But not before stopping at Oro for a quick slice of pizza.

Tito was already at the bridge speaking with the second officer. He smiled when he saw Luca. "You're good to go, jack. We had two party boats anchored in our path, but the authorities have moved them. I don't see any trouble but would like to guide you through the sand bars."

"Thank you, Tito. We appreciate your help."

"I have something from Myrna." Tito reached into his backpack and pulled out a small package wrapped in red tissue paper. "She made this for your last week."

Luca unwrapped the paper and found a wallet made from sisal straw. It was very nice. Luca could tell that Myrna has spent some time braiding it. Inside the wallet, he found a card with a note written in a beautiful script: *I have come into the world as a light. John 12:46.* In the lower left corner of the note was a sketched image of a lighthouse.

Luca was touched. "This is very nice. Please, thank Myrna for me."

"Of course." Tito shook Luca's hand. "You are our famous lighthouse on the sea. Don't forget to point others to Him." Luca marveled at Tito's commitment. He and his wife lived their faith without shame. Luca felt inspired to try to be more like his harbor pilot friend.

The ship sailed away from Cutter Cay with no issues. The party boats had moved out of their way, and the sand bars were easily cleared. After saying goodbye to the pilot, the crew next set sail for Mermaid Cove. They could reach it in under two hours but took a longer route so the ship would arrive in the early morning as planned.

At 6:00 p.m., Luca left the bridge for Blackbeard's Fortress buffet. He was scheduled to meet with the foster children on board and their families. Franny had planned a pizza and ice cream party at 5:30. She designed it to be a low-key affair with families eating in one section of the buffet restaurant. Luca would try to meet as many people in person as possible. Photos slowed things down, but he hoped to accommodate all of the children.

The captain of a ship played an important role in navigating the vessel and managing all aspects of the cruises, but he or she also served as an important link to the passengers. Luca knew that he was one of the "faces" of the cruise line, and he took that role seriously. He informed the second officer that he was taking his dinner break and walked to the busy restaurant.

At the buffet, Luca found dozens of families eating pizza and ice cream. When he arrived, all eyes lifted in his direction. "*Buonesara*! It is good to see you all. I am Captain Barone, and I welcome you to *Golden Fortune*. I was going to tell you a joke about pizza, but it's a little cheesy." The group shared a collective laugh and continued eating. Luca tried to sit at each table and have an authentic conversation with those seated while Franny also met with different groups. He heard stories of excitement and unease. Whenever a parent shared that a child was concerned about the ship sinking, he reassured those around him with information on the safety of such a modern vessel. The children listened intently.

Before the cruise, Luca had heard anonymously the backgrounds of some of the foster children. One girl had been born to a drug-addicted mother and had never even met her birth parents. Two girls were in care because their mother was serving ninety days in a Dade County jail for writing bad checks. Four siblings had been in the system for over four years and had given up hope on being adopted. The stories were heartbreaking, but the children were fighters. They had been dealt a bad hand in life but developed skills to survive. Luca was proud of the line for generously offering a week of adventure to these children and their substitute families.

"Where's your ice cream?" A pre-teen boy noticed that Luca wasn't eating.

"I don't have one. Will you show me where to go?"

"Sure, Cappy. Come with me." The boy stood and his guardian mom nodded her permission for him to take Luca to the ice cream station.

"Wow!" Luca was surprised to see the display. Franny had arranged for a larger than usual choice of flavors and toppings. His grandchildren would love this.

"Pick your flavor." The boy was clearly excited to help the captain with his dessert.

"Okay! I choose vanilla."

"That's what I got."

"And what is your name, young man?"

"I'm Ja'Michael, but my mama calls me Jelly 'cause my name starts with Jam. She's in jail. They said she stole money from her job, but I know she didn't do it. The Cooks are watching me till she get out. They have a dog named Snickers, and I have my own room. Maybe you can come to my real house when my mama get out. She makes good hot chicken."

"Thank you, Ja'Michael. I love hot chicken. Will you help me with my toppings?"

"Yes, sir. I get the chocolate syrup first so everything else sticks. They let you get extra jimmies. I like the rainbow ones, but you pick what you like, Captain."

Luca smiled. He knew that ice cream toppings were very important to children.

After selecting rainbow sprinkles, gummy bears, chocolate chips, and a chocolate pirate coin, Luca found a seat at Ja'Michael's table. He learned that Jelly, as he preferred to be called, was in the fifth grade, and his sister, Ta'Maya was in the seventh grade. They had been in foster care for nine months. Their foster parents had a biological son also in the seventh grade. Luca enjoyed hearing the children share their excitement about the cruise. And he answered many questions about pirates and sinking ships.

When he finished his ice cream, he excused himself to meet with other families. The hour went by quickly as he answered more questions about pirates and the potential of the huge ship sinking. Several asked who was steering the boat while he ate ice cream. A teenage girl asked about the training required to become a ship's captain. Luca enjoyed the encounters but had to return to the bridge at 7:30. He would have to thank Gayle Parker for inviting the families to sail with them.

"So, what is on the schedule for tonight? I haven't been thinking about anything but the beach today?" Bob held the door for Morgan to enter their cabin. He was still wearing a beach towel as a shirt.

"We have the mermaid show at 8:00, and there is a "Gold" dance party at the Oro at 10:30. I'm thinking buffet tonight. What about you?"

"That sounds great. Do I have time to crash for a few minutes? I need a small nap after my big nap."

"Ha!" Morgan laughed. "Sure. We've got an hour before we need to get ready. I need to check my laptop." Morgan unplugged her laptop and opened it. Nothing happened. She tried the power button, but it stayed black. Not sure what to do, she put it back on the desk and went to take a shower. She had no way to contact Mikey, who would be able to revive the machine in minutes. *What does he usually do?* she thought. Morgan never really paid attention. She decided to deal with the laptop later. Maybe more time was all it needed. She showered and dressed in a shimmery top and white capri pants. The Gold party was advertised as a time to wear "treasures and jewels." Bob agreed to wearing a solid black shirt. That was as far as his theme-wear would go.

An hour later, Morgan and Bob left their cabin to go to Blackbeard's Fortress. They were early enough to beat any sort of crowd. Morgan immediately noticed a group of children in the back of the room. Captain Barone was standing in the very back talking with the children. Morgan gathered her food and asked a passing server what was happening at the back. Her nametag showed that her name was Abigay, and she was from Jamaica.

"Oh, Captain is hosting an ice cream party for special guests. They can have all the ice cream they want, plus lots of pizza."

"How fun!" Morgan knew something special was going on but didn't ask further questions. She sat at a nearby table and waited for Bob to arrive with his plate. Instead of Caribbean punch, they opted for ice water to drink.

Bob thanked Jesus for the food and started on a bowl of vegetable soup. "Did you find anything about the gathering over there?"

"I asked a server, and she said it was an ice cream and pizza party for special guests." As soon as Morgan finished her sentence, the group of children burst into laughter. "Captain Barone is clearly working the room well." She watched the captain move from family to family before he was escorted by a young man to the ice cream station. The boy was talking nonstop, and the captain was engaged with what he was saying.

After eating her dinner, Morgan decided on chocolate ice cream for her dessert. She walked by the crowd and waited as a crew member scooped out her choice. The ice cream station was expanded tonight, with at least twenty topping choices. A woman from the group stood behind her in line for more ice cream. Morgan asked her if the group was celebrating a birthday.

"Oh no," the woman answered. "Those are foster children from Miami. The cruise line reserved one hundred cabins for local children and their families. My husband and I are here with two fosters and our biological daughter. We are having the best time."

Morgan was surprised. "I had no idea. What a wonderful thing to do."

"It is. Our three children are quite into the treasure hunt. Holidays are hard, so this diversion has come at a perfect time."

Morgan received her bowl and wished the woman safe travels. She rushed back to Bob to share the new information. "They are foster children from Miami. Jewel gave away one hundred cabins on this cruise for local foster families. Isn't that wonderful?"

"That is great. The captain seems to have them fully entertained." Bob decided on ice cream as well and left to get his go-to vanilla. As he was gone, Morgan watched the children. They seemed so cheerful, but Morgan knew that their personal lives were probably anything but happy.

When Bob returned with his vanilla ice cream, he declared that he chose the best flavor. "Most of the children were choosing vanilla also. Of course, they all covered their ice cream with gobs of toppings. But I think you are the outsider today with chocolate." Morgan laughed and finished her treat.

After dessert, Morgan and Bob walked on the pool deck for a few minutes before making their way to the theater on Deck 6. The moon was a tiny sliver, so the stars shone extra brightly. Morgan didn't remember seeing stars this clearly since her days of camping with her grandparents. The sound of the ocean waves gently crashing on the ship completed the peaceful atmosphere. The ocean was both dangerous and peaceful at the same time. She could understand why it was sometimes called a mystery.

The theater hosting *Mermaids Ahoy* was nearly filled when Morgan and Bob arrived. Once again, they found two seats near the back. After being seated, Morgan couldn't help but stare at the large screen behind the stage. An image of the ocean was being shown, and it was so realistic that it looked like a window looking out of the ship. Passengers all around were mesmerized by the scenes. Occasionally, a silly crab would "high step" across the screen, and the children in the audience would laugh. Morgan looked for any of the foster children she had seen earlier but didn't recognize any in the dark theater.

Lively music began from an orchestra hidden from sight. After a short introduction, two mermaids—actually one mermaid and one merman—floated in air, giving the illusion that they were swimming in the ocean around them. The audience gasped in unison. Morgan was amazed at the technology used to simulate swimming. There must be wires somewhere, but they were nearly invisible.

The show included a sweet story about a mermaid who couldn't sing like her friends. The plot was simple, but the special effects were extraordinary. And the music was buoyant. At one point, bubbles were released from machines onto the audience. Morgan loved the one-hour show and left the theater smiling when it was over.

"That was fun," Morgan said as she led Bob toward the dance hall.

"I couldn't see the wires. They looked like they were really swimming. Can you imagine the core muscles it would take to keep from spinning around?"

"It was amazing!"

"Wanna sit in the dance hall for a little bit?"

"Sure. Sounds good. Then we can check out the Gold party."

Morgan and Bob found seats near the right of the stage in the dance hall. The band was playing fifties music at a deafening volume. Morgan had to yell to say anything to Bob. She finally gave up and watched young and old passengers dancing to the Twist. After the band rocked around the clock and tutti-fruttied, they started "Earth Angel." Bob took Morgan's hand and walked her to the dance floor. This wasn't like him, so Morgan knew he must be enjoying the evening. After the dance, they tried to hand jive but decided they would leave that fun to the younger crowd. Morgan suggested that they move to Oro on Deck 8. The Gold party had just started, and she wanted to see the fun.

The festivities at Oro involved more high-energy dancing. This time, current pop music was playing from the jukebox. Tables were moved to the side, and disco balls hung from the ceiling. Morgan spotted Franny Meyers in the crowd sporting a gold sequined dress and delicate golden wings. Crew members were handing out large necklaces and rings with plastic jewels on them. One man was dancing in a gold star costume.

The scene was fun but had little seating. Morgan and Bob stayed for a few minutes and decided to go down one deck to the garden paths. She wore her shiny top with plans to enjoy the Gold party a while, but the day in the sun had drained her energy. On the center garden path, they found an empty bench and sat down. In the distance, a musician was playing a harp. The atmosphere was peaceful and romantic. A perfect way to end the relaxing day.

"It's nice to take a break from the hunt," Bob said. "We couldn't keep up that pace."

"Yep. The trip wouldn't be much fun if it kept that intensity. I can't wait to share these details with my clients back home."

"And your mom. I think she would love this garden area. We need to find a pickleball game tomorrow and get some pictures. The sisters will be asking about it."

Morgan nodded. "Good idea. Please help me remember."

After nearly an hour on the bench, Morgan and Bob called it a day. They returned to their cabin and declared the day a "terrific Tuesday." If all went as planned, Wednesday would be wonderful.

When Luca returned to the bridge, the food and beverage manager was waiting. The captain first checked with the navigation officers and, when convinced that everything was under control, met with the manager.

"How's it going, Ivan?" Luca asked.

"Very well, sir. The menus are still popular. We've had no issues plating the meals, and the Cutlass is selling better than expected."

"What about the eyepatches on the servers?"

"They didn't like them at first, but quickly adapted. I think we are okay for now . . . if they only wear them once per week. We received several comments that the passengers enjoyed the authenticity of their appearance."

"*Bueno.* Let's keep the patches for now. Anything else?"

"Two things, sir. And they are minor for now. First, we misordered on ice cream at Blackbeard's. The figures show that eighty percent of the guests are ordering vanilla. The standard has been closer to forty percent. We're not sure if this is a trend or, as you say, a cough."

"I think you mean a 'hiccup.'"

"Yes, hiccup, sir. We doubled our order of vanilla for next week. But I need your approval for the large increase. Would you please approve the spreadsheet tonight?"

"Yes, of course. I'm curious to see if that trend continues. I usually prefer chocolate, but just ate vanilla myself tonight. Maybe the vanilla fits with the pirate theme more. And what is your second issue?"

"Some of the ketchup dispensers on Cutter Cay sprayed ketchup on passengers. We were able to address it quickly, and there have been no formal complaints, but we aren't sure what happened. They worked for a while, then built up pressure or something. The grill crew has been alerted, and I will keep you updated. We don't want pictures of passengers covered in ketchup to be paraded on social media."

"I agree. Contact the supplier and update me tomorrow. There is probably a simple fix, but pictures of children with ketchup sprayed in their faces would be problematic." Luca had seen plenty of condiment failures over the years, but the prolific use of camera phones made them too visible to the public. This was a fire he couldn't leave burning.

"Right away, sir. Good night."

"*Buona notte.* And thank you for your good work." Thinking back on the numbers, Luca wondered why vanilla ice cream was so popular this week. Could it really be related to the pirate theme? Or did it have something to do with the holiday season? He would have to check around the internet about this when he returned to his cabin. And he would say a prayer for Jelly and his sister. They clearly loved their biological mom, and rainbow sprinkles.

CHAPTER EIGHTEEN

December 4, Day Four: Mermaid Cove

Day four started early. Bob woke first, and Morgan was up immediately after him. They decided that an early walk on the ship's exercise track would start the day off well. As Morgan was tying her shoes, she told Bob about a dream she'd just had. In it, she and Bob lived underwater. They could swim and talk like mermaids. But they were wearing shiny gold shirts and played harps all day. "I would miss our family and friends, but playing music under the sea might be nice."

Bob laughed. "You might be on to something. There wouldn't be any yardwork for me to do, and you could plan cool trips for the other sea creatures."

"This might be a solid plan." Morgan giggled as she walked out of their cabin. She almost forgot about her fast-paced job and responsibilities at home. Almost. "I really need to check my email. Will you help me get my laptop working when we get back."

"Sure. I don't think I'll be much help, but maybe we can will it to work if we stare at it together." The two made their way up two flights of stairs to Heave Ho Gym on Deck 11. On the perimeter of the right side of the gym was a walkway that led to sliding doors. Outside of the doors was a marked track that circled half of the ship. It was open to the air on all sides but one, which was an indoor tunnel crossing from one side of the ship to another. The sky was still dark as Morgan and Bob began walking. They were passed by a man jogging and a couple walking at a faster pace.

After a minute walking in silence, Bob said, "What do we have in store today, Mrs. Cruise Director?"

"Well, I will answer you, but only because you are my favorite passenger, Mr. Stevens. We should arrive at Mermaid Cove in less than an hour. I'm surprised we don't see any lights from the island yet. This island was built for children, so we may not stay that long. But who knows? You've been known to be a kid at heart before."

"That's true. But I run out of steam quickly."

"Yep. We don't have the energy of children anymore. This island has a big beach and a bunch of kiddie splash areas and slides. It has one grill area serving child-friendly food. I'm sure we can get 'beach burgers' and ice cream cones, so we should be fine."

"I'm looking forward to seeing everything and watching the kids romp around. And you know I can't resist a beach burger. The best part is that we don't have to search for a clue until tonight. So we can enjoy the island and come back after lunch. Maybe we can find some chairs close to the pool to relax until dinner."

Morgan was about to respond when they turned a corner and stopped. She and Bob gasped at the sight of the sun rising over the water. As they moved from the track and out of the way of joggers, they watched the pink color quickly turning to red and orange. As more of the sun appeared, rays of gold appeared. Morgan wondered to herself how God could orchestrate such a masterpiece day after day. He truly was the Master Artist.

When the sun had fully risen, Morgan and Bob continued walking. There weren't any words necessary to describe the beautiful sunrise. They walked in silence. Finally, Bob remarked that it was a shame that the sun comes up every day, but they rarely see it. Morgan agreed and suggested that they try to catch a few sunrises at the beach when they returned home.

They decided to take two more laps around the track and picked up their pace. Mermaid Cove was now in sight and getting nearer. Bob noticed a small boat rushing toward the ship and pointed it out to Morgan. Once again, the couple stopped. They watched the boat approach and were intrigued to see a man climbing out of the boat and onto a platform extending out of the ship. The exchange looked precarious, but the man executed it with ease.

"That must be the local pilot," Morgan said. "He will advise the captain on the local conditions. I can't believe we got to see him. There is so much we miss while we are sleeping."

"It does seem that way. I'm hungry. Wanna get some breakfast now?"

Morgan nodded. "Definitely. The little teashop beside the spa looked nice. Should we try it? I saw bacon."

"If it has bacon, I'm in," Bob added. He and Morgan found the teashop and ordered their breakfast by pushing trays along a food station cafeteria-style. The food was tasty, and Bob went back for extra dollar pancakes and bacon.

The two leisurely sipped coffee when Bob asked about the laptop. "Do you think we can get it running?"

"No, I can never get it to work. Mikey is the only one who can make it run."

"Does the ship have a computer center? It must have something like that."

Morgan took out her phone. "I'll check the app." She quickly found that the internet café was found on Deck 5 near the medical center. "Let's go there now." Bob finished his coffee and followed Morgan to the elevators.

At Deck 5, the elevator door opened near the medical examining rooms. Morgan spotted Doc reading a file or chart of some sort. She waved, and he saluted back to her. Bob found the computer facility and helped Morgan find an available terminal. She sat down and read the instructions. The first ten minutes of usage were free for every passenger. The cost was fifty cents per minute after that.

"Read fast," Bob added.

"I will. I just need to make sure there aren't any emergencies. Mikey should have everything under control." Morgan logged into her email account and was surprised to see that she had thirty-seven unread messages. "What in the world?"

Morgan quickly scanned the messages and noticed that half of them were from the Andersons, the couple spending their honeymoon in Paris. Morgan found the first one and opened it. "Help! It's James. Our room is full of poinsettia plants. They are everywhere."

The next message. "At first, we were okay with the poinsettias, but now we want them out of the room. They are on the bed and in the tub. Kathy called the front desk. They haven't answered."

Morgan continued reading. "The man at the front desk didn't understand what we were saying, so we went down and asked him to come see our room."

Message four. "The manager said that they cannot remove the poinsettias. We must keep them. But there is nowhere for us to sleep."

Morgan looked up at Bob. "It's bad. I think the hotel filled a honeymoon suite with poinsettias instead of rose petals. I need to read the rest of the messages." Morgan didn't want to read further, but she had to . . . even at fifty cents per minute.

Bob patted her shoulder. "I'll find some coffee. You keep reading."

In the next message, James said that Kathy was breaking out in hives. They weren't sure why. Next, she was itching and wheezing. They were going to find help. Morgan said a silent prayer for the couple, even though she knew the reaction happened two days earlier.

Morgan continued through the email messages from James Anderson. The hotel concierge had called a local doctor and helped them get a taxi to go to the closest hospital, Institute Hospitilier Franco-Britannique. Morgan was relieved knowing that she added travel insurance to all overseas trips. Health care in France is generally affordable, but a serious emergency could be expensive.

The next message explained that Kathy was allergic to poinsettias. It's a rare condition and is related to her latex allergy. Kathy's breathing was becoming severely restricted, but the professionals helped her immediately. Morgan's heart rate increased. This was serious. Bob returned with two paper cups of coffee. "Thank you, but my nerves can't handle coffee right now. The bride had to go to a hospital." Bob sat in the chair next to her and urged Morgan to read the rest of the messages.

The next four messages were sent within five minutes. "The doctor wants Kathy to stay overnight. She's breathing okay, but her oxygen level is a little low. Did you order all those plants? The concierge said you requested them."

And "Kathy's parents want to fly over tomorrow? Can you make their arrangements?"

Next, "The hotel just called. You requested 'rose petals.' The head housemaid translated that to 'poinsettias.' Ha! Isn't that funny?"

And finally, "Great news! The hotel is moving us to the Presidential Suite. We'll have a kitchen and two bathrooms! The in-laws aren't coming, so don't plan anything. And they gave all those flowers to a nursing home. I took some pictures. You won't believe it."

Morgan didn't know what to think. She had never had anything like this happen to one of her clients. Most travel problems involved stomach issues from either ultra-rich or undercooked food. A few people had fallen and broken bones, but none had been admitted to a hospital overnight. She felt guilty for not answering any of James's messages, but also relieved that Kathy would be okay.

James sent two messages yesterday. First, he thanked Morgan for the "awesome" suite they would enjoy for the week. And then he was excited to add that their story was picked up by a local television reporter. The couple was given a special dinner at the base of the Eiffel Tower for sharing the details. Morgan smiled and read the last notes out loud to Bob. She typed a lengthy response, apologizing for the mix-up and wishing Kathy well. She then accepted the coffee Bob had offered earlier and logged out of her account.

"God worked it out, Morg," Bob said. "He always does."

"Yes, that was totally God. I didn't even know all of that was happening. Let's go check on my laptop. If it doesn't start, I'll have to come back here this afternoon."

"Lead the way, Mrs. Stevens." Morgan and Bob went back to their room and changed for the beach. They planned to spend a few hours at Mermaid Cove and to return to the ship after lunch. As expected, the laptop didn't start.

Luca marveled at the beautiful sunrise from the small window in his cabin. He had seen literally thousands of sunrises over the ocean but was still amazed that God could create such stunning colors. They were especially breathtaking over the turquoise blues of the Bahamian waters.

After showering and dressing for the day, Luca ate a room service breakfast at his desk. He answered email messages and approved invoices and schedules. The work was routine, and he began to appreciate the opportunity to work again. If Jewel Cruise Line hadn't called, he would probably be sitting alone somewhere. Commanding a new ship gave him something to live for and the mental energy he needed to spend quality with his family. Dahna would be happy that he was sailing again.

When finished with the virtual paperwork, Luca readied to go to the bridge. The second officer oversaw navigating Mermaid Cove, and Luca chose to let him handle today without his assistance. From the view out his window, the docking was perfect. Luca saw the shark scrubbers out on jet skis, but they kept a safe distance from the large ship.

Luca made a cup of coffee before walking into the bridge. The second and third officers were talking with the local harbor pilot, and Luca carried his coffee toward them. They reported that the ship handled beautifully, and the docking was uneventful. Guests would begin disembarking soon, and the pilot left. He would return at 3:00 to guide the ship away from the island.

At 10:00, the captain and senior officers would explore Mermaid Cove. Luca had seen it last week, but without passengers. Today would provide their first glimpse of the much-anticipated fun found on the island. They especially wanted to see the mermaids swimming near the beach.

Luca planned to walk the colorful pathway and eat lunch at Landlubber Café. The purser had shared that the first treasure would be hidden on Treasure Island as most expected. Plans were underway for extra photographers to be in the area to capture the moment. *Golden Fortune* would arrive at Treasure Island in two days, or on day six of the cruise. With the fortune found, families could enjoy the last day of the cruise without the concerns of clues and hidden treasure. They could lounge by the pool or splash in the kiddie area while at sea all day.

Luca reviewed the weather alerts and communication reports. All was well. He pulled out of his pocket the wallet that Myrna had made. He didn't need another wallet, especially on the ship. But the handiwork was so nice. And Tito and Myrna were great friends. Not good friends, great friends. The wallet was a reminder to Luca that God saw him and that he should point others to Him.

Mermaid Cove was a child's vacation paradise. Morgan was fascinated with the pastel colors and cheerful music. As she and Bob walked the main pathway around the island, they saw endless splash areas and slides with children happily playing. The beach area had plenty of lounge chairs and storage boxes with lots of sand toys. The entire area was one huge water park. And passengers were loving it.

Morgan secured two chairs near the farthest part of the beach while Bob searched for two Cutlass drinks. She couldn't help but watch the parents enjoying a beautiful day with their children. For some reason, she didn't have the usual ache to have children of her own. The reason was obviously God. He had been working on her heart, showing her that He hadn't forgotten about her. He still had a perfect plan for her life. She just had to let go of her plans and accept His. Letting go wasn't easy, but growth rarely ever was.

Bob returned with the drinks and declared the next hour to be "do-nothing time." Morgan agreed and decided to start by reading a chapter in a book. Since she had finished her jilted-bride book, she decided to peruse Bob's book. He was currently reading a firsthand account of the Battle of Iwo Jima. This was not Morgan's typical literary choice, and it was surprisingly interesting.

After a few pages, Morgan started dozing along with Bob. She could hear giggles from children mixed in with ocean waves and palm leaves rustling. How does God do it all? After what seemed like a few minutes, she and Bob both woke to squealing youngsters. They saw a commotion near the shoreline and sat up to see what was causing the excitement. They finally stood and walked near the gathering crowd. Something was in the water.

The cheers were for life-like mermaids swimming past the beach. It wasn't clear to Morgan how the women were able to swim so effortlessly with artificial tails, but the effect was quite realistic. And the children were loving it. The mermaids didn't stop to greet the children but continued out of sight to leave the impression that they truly lived in the ocean. What an amazing effect for the cruise line to add. Morgan figured that the flock or pod or school of mermaids would make passes throughout the day. She also assumed that the "shark scrubbers" would be working along with the mermaids. The site was almost unbelievable.

After the excitement, Bob suggested that they take an early lunch. The smell from Landlubbers was enticing. Morgan agreed and found her mint-green-striped cover-up in her bag. She could hear children talking about the "real" mermaids as they were walking toward the picnic tables in the area. Each table was painted in a different pastel color and covered with a matching umbrella.

After gathering cheeseburgers and French fries, Morgan and Bob sat at a yellow table. Bob joked that he did not take any chances with the ketchup dispenser. Morgan offered to get some on a plate for him, but he declined. He would avoid beach ketchup for a while.

"Didn't those mermaids look real?" Morgan asked. "I wish I had gotten some pictures. It didn't even occur to me to take any. I would love to share them with my clients."

"Very real. And I imagine plenty of people will get pictures of them before the day is over. I can see them used in marketing going forward."

"Maybe. But the surprise of them added to the authenticity. This is a fun island." Bob agreed and suggested more resting after lunch. Morgan added that soft-serve ice cream cones should come before a nap.

Back at their chairs, Morgan resumed the book while Bob closed his eyes. The sun was directly overhead, and the chatter from energetic children had diminished. It was a perfect beach day for an adult couple on a kid-centric beach. Morgan spent so much time planning vacations. She thought out every detail. But sometimes, a peaceful afternoon happened spontaneously. Once again, she thanked God for His blessings.

An hour later, the couple declared that they were adequately rested. Morgan gathered their things and looked at Bob. "I'd like to check my email before we go back to our cabin. I'm praying there are no more mishaps with the Andersons. And I promised to send some pictures to my mom. She must be getting a little worried since I haven't written."

"Definitely. Let's go." They walked back to the ship slowly. Morgan took pictures of the beach area and the picnic tables. She also made a note of the menu items at Landlubbers. It offered more kid-friendly options than Cutter Cay. And she noticed large wagons that families were using to transport beach supplies as well as weary children back to *Golden Fortune*.

Thankfully, there was only one message from James Anderson. He attached a picture of the presidential suite. Morgan could see the faint outline of the Eifel Tower in one window. The couple was enjoying their honeymoon, and there were no poinsettias to be found.

After sending three pictures to her mom, Morgan logged out of the shared computer. She suggested to Bob that they take a long way back to their cabin to get some blood flowing. Bob agreed and followed Morgan. They made their way to the top deck to check out the Parrot Perch area. There weren't any obvious clues. Of course, it was early, but it didn't hurt to check.

Back in their cabin, the couple cleaned up and changed into comfortable clothes. They sat on the couch as Morgan made more notes about Cutter Cay. To Morgan, the mermaids were the best part. To Bob, the low-key atmosphere was the best. Both agreed that today was turning into a "wonderful" Wednesday.

Luca ate lunch on the island with the other officers. They chose a yellow picnic table near the edge of the dining area and gathered their food. The group was commenting on the realistic mermaids when someone shouted, "Captain!" Luca turned to see Jelly running toward him. He was wearing a lime-green bathing suit with blue whales on it. Jelly's foster mom was running behind him. Before she could suggest that he let the captain eat his lunch in peace, Jelly started speaking.

"I've got a joke for you, Captain Barone."

"Oh, you do? Let's hear it." The officers stopped eating and listened to Jelly's joke.

"What is the only vegetable not allowed on cruise ships?"

Luca thought for a few seconds and said, "I do not know."

"Leeks!" At that, the entire group laughed. The second officer commented that it was true, and Jelly laughed some more.

His guardian finally spoke. "Okay, Jelly. Let's let them eat their lunch. And thank you again, Captain Barone, for sitting with us last night. Ja'Michael and Ta'Maya talked about you all night. They both declared at breakfast that they will be ship captains when they are grown. They would never have seen the ocean like this without Jewel Cruise Line making such a generous offer. Our son, Davey, is even asking questions about becoming a ship's captain."

"How wonderful! I will ask Franny about arranging a tour of the bridge for your family. We could show the three children how we navigate and how we communicate. It would be our pleasure."

"Oh, that would be wonderful. Thank you for thinking of us." The mom put her arm around Jelly's shoulders and guided him back toward the beach. Luca thought about the thousands of children on this week's cruise. Would any of them become sailors? How many would work in the cruise industry? The love of the sea is a condition only cured my more sea.

After lunch, the crew walked back to the ship. As they walked the long pier, the group heard a motorized scooter approaching. "Loo-chie! Loo-chie!" They turned around and spotted a woman in a bright yellow jumper and yellow water shoes racing her motorized scooter directly at them. Luca knew immediately it was Daisy. He shooed the others back to the ship and told them he would be at the bridge soon.

Luca turned to the yellow flash on the scooter. "Daisy. It's great to see you. Did you enjoy Mermaid Cove?"

"I sure did, Loo-chie. You don't mind me calling you that, do you? Luciano is so starchy."

"That is fine, but I am usually called Luca."

"Okay. Thanks, Loo-chie. You're harder to find that an empty spot in the back row of my church."

"Ha!" Luca didn't know how to respond.

"Gracious. If you keep being this hard to find, we gonna have to put a 'Hot Now' sign on you like they do at the Krispie Kreme. I'll spot you for sure then."

"It's nice to see you, Daisy. May I help you?" Luca often dealt with overbearing passengers. But, like Daisy, they were usually harmless. Many saved for years to take a once-in-a-lifetime trip and were over-impressed with the captain and the cruise director. Daisy had a simple charm to her, and Luca didn't mind giving her a few minutes of his time.

"Yes, sir. I saw the real mermaids twice today. Do you think you could get me an autograph from the yellow one? She is the best one." Daisy made her request with a straight face, so Luca could only assume that she was serious.

"An autograph? I'm n-not sure a-about that," Luca stammered. "I think they stay in the water all day. And we sail away in a few hours."

"Please, please. Pretty please. I'm in a tizzy. I just have to get her autograph for my collection."

Luca knew that he wouldn't be able to reach the Cove talent before they sailed. "I don't know, Daisy. But I will contact Franny Meyers. She will know who the yellow mermaid is. If anyone can contact her, she can. I'll do my best."

"Thanks, Loo-chie. Let me let you go. I'm gonna head over yonder to that big lunch buffet." Daisy steered her scooter around Luca and drove full speed toward the ship. He continued walking down the pier. He would stop at his cabin to change into his evening uniform and return to the bridge to observe the sail-away. And along the way, he would find Franny and ask about the popular yellow mermaid.

PART THREE

Stormy Seas

243

" When you pass through the waters, I will be with you;
and when you pass through the rivers, they will not sweep over you.
When you walk through the fire, you will not be burned;
the flames will not set you ablaze."

Isaiah 43:2

CHAPTER NINETEEN

December 4, Continued

Night four was the seventies theme night. Morgan dressed in an old tie-dye shirt with a peace sign design and some blue eye shadow. She also wore tall wedges and white pants. Bob once again opted out of the themed attire and went with a light-blue polo shirt. They didn't have a show scheduled for tonight, so they planned to find a comfortable spot to "people watch." Late night pizza was also a possibility.

Morgan and Bob made their way to the galley dining room on Deck 5. Tonight was American night, and Morgan was looking forward to fried chicken. The ship's chicken would be smaller than the chicken back home, but delicious nonetheless. She was also hoping for some creamy macaroni and cheese or tangy potato salad.

As the couple was seated, Morgan spotted Lucy and Earl sitting at a table near the window. The two women waved at each other, and Morgan followed Bob to their table. Bob looked around and commented about the crowd. "The dining room seems quite lively tonight. I guess the kids are still excited about seeing 'real' mermaids."

"It was a special day. I'm sure families will be talking about Mermaid Cove for years. I hope my pictures will look nice on the web page. Mikey may have to help me brighten them a little."

"I hope you got some good shots of those mermaids."

"I did! And the yellow one really glowed."

The waiter took their orders. Morgan selected a cheese plate, fried chicken, and chocolate treasure cake. Bob went with a crab cake, barbecued brisket, and warm apple cobbler. The servers were wearing tie-dye, button-up shirts with black pants. The women had colorful headbands. A maître di was walking around the dining room in a white suit complete with a black shirt and black platform shoes. The crew were participating in the seventies theme as much as the guests.

"The seventies party isn't until 10:00 tonight. What do you want to do after we eat?" Morgan looked at Bob.

"It's a little windy out there. I think we are passing through a storm. Maybe we should stay inside. Perhaps rest on one of those garden paths?"

Morgan thought for a few seconds. "You're probably right, but I would like to check out the pool deck tonight. We haven't spent any time up there at night. Will it be too windy?"

Bob smiled. "I guess there's one way to find out. The moon is just coming back, so it should be dark enough to see some stars. We can find a quiet place to chill out before the groovy party. Since the clue said, 'late on Wednesday night,' I think we won't be able to find it until after the party. Do you think 'late' would be before 10:00?"

"No, I think 'late' will be midnight. But that will be difficult for families with children. Maybe something will appear during the party."

"We can catch up with Lucy and Earl if we get a chance to see them before we leave the dining room." The appetizers arrived, and Bob marveled about the crab cakes as always. Tonight marked the middle night of the cruise, so the cruise was nearly half over. Morgan was enjoying this time with Bob. She couldn't wait to get back and prepare the information on *Golden Fortune* for her clients. She would be busy with Christmas and looked forward to the visit with her mom and Aunt Margaret. Holidays with children must be extra special, but the life God has gifted Morgan was more than she deserved.

The entrees and desserts were done very well. Morgan's fried chicken was much better than she expected. And the chocolate cake lifted the day to officially "wonderful."

"Bob, why do you think people are so fascinated by the sea? It seems that most people like to be around an ocean or a lake."

Bob thought for a minute. "That's a good question. I'm not sure. Maybe God built that into us to prepare us for heaven."

"The water is so calming yet can be dangerous at the same time." Morgan remembered a time when the water became perilous. She was camping with her grandparents and was swimming with two boys from a nearby campsite. They dared her to swim to the floating dock and back without stopping. She knew that she had never swam that far before. But she wanted to show them that she was as strong as any boy. Unfortunately, she wasn't and had to be rescued by two college students who were fishing and heard her yelling for help. After that, the lake never felt as comforting as it used to. But Morgan still loved being near it with her grandparents. And she enjoyed the ocean even more.

Bob ordered coffee to finish his meal, and Morgan marveled at the realistic mermaids they had seen earlier. "They were so authentic." When they finally exited the dining room, they noticed that Lucy and Earl were no longer at their table. The two decided that they would let them enjoy their evening alone but would invite them to rest on the pool deck if they found them. Morgan hoped it wouldn't be too windy. Evenings under the stars were so romantic. Strong winds would change that.

On their way toward the elevators, Morgan and Bob spotted a woman dressed in a yellow top with orange leggings and white go-go boots. She was leading a crowd of people in dancing the Hustle while they waited to be seated for dinner. Apparently, she had a portable speaker in the basket of her scooter. The scooter was decorated with battery-operated fairy lights and a miniature disco ball.

"C'mon! Join the fun!" The woman waved Morgan and Bob over toward the group. Morgan ran to join them, but Bob moved toward a wall. He took out his phone to capture a few photos of Morgan spontaneously dancing in the dining room lobby.

The woman was clearly having the time of her life. "All right, everyone. Let's start a "Daisy chain" and cha-cha through the dining room!" A line started forming behind the woman, who must be named Daisy. Quickly, the hostess steered the group toward the elevator banks to avoid chaos among the diners.

Morgan peeled away from the cha-cha line when she got near Bob. "I don't spontaneously cha cha every day. That was fun."

"You were great! I took a few pictures. Those must go on your website. The whole group was smiling and laughing, especially Daisy the leader."

Bob and Morgan found an elevator going up and waltzed in. Three others joined them and were laughing about the "Daisy chain." When they stepped out on Deck 14, Morgan immediately noticed the wind had increased from earlier. But the breeze wasn't enough to cause her to leave. "Let's find some chairs in the corner. They won't have as much wind. This is nice though."

Bob agreed. "Good idea. Are you warm enough?"

"Actually, I'm a little chilly. But I'll be okay."

"Why don't I run and get you a sweater? Is that white one okay? I want to change into my other dress shoes. You find two chairs. I'll be quick."

"That would be lovely. Thank you, kind sir." Morgan gave Bob a side hug and looked toward the chairs on the starboard side of the ship. "Don't take too long. If you can't find my sweater, anything warm will do. And please bring some sort of clip for my hair. I can't see anything with it whipping in my face."

Morgan found two chairs near a wall. Just like last night, the moon was a tiny sliver, and Morgan could see the stars clearly. "Thank You, God. Just thank You. I have so much, and I know it is from You. You made those stars out of nothing. And You created the seas. I don't know why You care about every detail of my life, but I know that You do. So, thank You."

Morgan closed her eyes and was listening to the ocean breeze. The air temperature was warm enough that the wind was welcomed. There was just something special about a warm ocean breeze. The deck was quiet. Apparently, the treasure hunters onboard were waiting for much "later" to check out the Parrot Perch. Suddenly, Morgan heard a girl's voice. "Stop!"

Luca had another Captain's Table event tonight. He sat at a large table with three families. Each had one person who was a member of a large, nationwide travel agency. The children were well-behaved and interested in ship's life. One asked where the fresh water on the ship came from, and one asked if Luca could drive a car on land. He, in turn, asked them about their studies and their favorite hobbies. The meal was one of the highlights of the trip so far. And that crabcake— *delicioso!*

While eating, Luca heard a commotion in the dining room lobby. At one point, everyone at his table turned to see what was happening. They could see a group of people dancing, and Luca assumed it was a large family celebrating a birthday or some other special event. Perhaps Franny planned something special for the group.

After dinner, Luca returned to the bridge. He stopped for a cup of coffee on the way. The night would be a long one. He was scheduled to make an appearance at the seventies party on Shipwreck Boulevard around 10:30. Franny had a large wig for him to wear with bell-bottom pants. Luce cringed at these types of costumes but knew that the passengers loved them. He could hear Dahna telling him to "lighten up and be a good sport." Walking around the area and greeting passengers wasn't exactly a terrible way to spend an evening.

On the way to the bridge, Luca stopped by Franny's office. He could hear her voice while still in the hallway. Franny was wearing an orange and yellow dress with white flowers in the design. She had on a long wig that made her look a little like Cher. She was speaking with two members of the entertainment team when Luca walked in.

"Captain, good evening. May I help you?" The others walked toward a nearby table and began looking at some sort of spreadsheet on a computer.

"Yes. If you have a minute."

"Of course. What do you need?"

"There is a special passenger on board who is asking for an autograph."

"Oh my. I have a folder of signed photographs. Let me get one for you."

"No. I apologize. The autograph is not yours. She would like an autograph of the yellow mermaid who was swimming around the Cove today. I know the request is a little outrageous, but I was wondering if you had any sort of swag related to the mermaids. They were a big hit, by the way."

"Yes, I have heard that the mermaids made quite a splash." Franny laughed at her own joke and swung her hair just as Cher would have.

"We won't see the girls again until next week. But I do have their email addresses. I can find out who the yellow one was and ask her to send me a personalized message."

"That would be great. The guest's name is Daisy . . . Abilene something. If you could get me a copy of the message, I will get it to her."

"Sure thing, Captain. I'll see you in a little bit at the party. It's gonna be groovy."

Luca rolled his eyes. "Can't wait."

Back on the bridge, Luca discovered that the ship would be heading near a pop-up shower. The storm shouldn't affect the ship's course but could cause a little chaos on the pool deck. He would order a few crew members to patrol the area at the peak of the rain in an hour. He would also warn hospitality to set out umbrellas near the Parrot Perch movie screen.

Tonight's clue would be projected on the screen during the scheduled movie. Rain could cause a problem with the movie, so Luca called the purser's office. Luca was relieved to hear that the team had a back-up plan. They would play the movie as scheduled and project the clue on an interior wall if rain started. Apparently, tonight's clue would lead the guests to a bench on one of the garden paths near

Shipwreck Boulevard. The paths would be full of excitement late tonight. Oro Pizza was prepared for a larger-than-normal crowd.

All was calm at the command center despite a headwind of thirty knots. Passengers usually find the swirling winds bothersome, so they would most likely find an interior activity tonight. The seventies party would be well-attended. Of course, half of the ship would be making their way to the Parrot Perch later to find the latest clue. This would be the penultimate clue. It would lead a passenger or passengers to the last clue before the treasure.

Luca was staring at the choppy seas, deep in thought, when the purser called to him. "We've got a small problem, Cap'n."

"What is it, son?" Luca knew that the evening was going too smoothly. An issue was bound to come up.

"This is awkward. The line sent us a secure box with gold coins, but they did not send a chest. The coins came with a certificate, so I assume they are valued at $50,000. Franny found us several chests that will work, but they aren't entirely waterproof. Our plan was to send the 'hide party' out tonight, but the weather is declining. We also have seen some jet skis circling near the island. I don't think they are looking for the treasure to be hidden, but I do think they may see something."

"Do you have a suggestion?" Luca had learned over time that those closest to the situation often had the best answers.

"Yes, sir. I think we can wait till tomorrow for the rain to pass. Then we can send out the party. Two of the crew members will work on setting up the bonfire while two will hide the treasure box. Those people will remain on the island to guard the gold and ensure that the treasure box does not become wet tomorrow night. The original plan was to let the permanent security team in on the location. Should we keep that plan?"

Luca thought for nearly a minute. The permanent team was comprised of locals. They could inform friends or family members of the location and affect the integrity of the search. "Let's stick with the original plan. Let the hide party know your concerns and we will revisit this issue at the executive committee meeting on Sunday. Thank you for your hard work. Your efforts will be critical to the success of the entire cruise line."

The purser left, and Luca checked the weather reports. Winds were increasing slowly. But the ship should be able to avoid any heavy rain. He discussed the reports with the navigation team and sat down to observe tonight's activities before the party.

"Stop!"

Morgan heard a girl pleading again. She got up and casually walked toward the voice. Despite her hair blowing in her face, she could tell that three teenagers were on the Walk the Plank platform. No one else was nearby, although an increasing number of people were hanging out at the Parrot Perch movie screen at the front of the ship.

As Morgan got closer, she saw that a boy was standing on the railing, simulating a scene from *Titanic*. He was facing the wind with his arms stretched out. The other boy was trying to get a girl to stand on the rails beside him. She was wisely refusing. But the boys continued to insist that she play the part. One boy lifted her up and sat her on the rail. The girl screamed and fell backward. She hung by her knees toward the water with one hand on the railing. Without thinking, Morgan ran to the girl at the same time one of the boys tried to pull her in. Each grabbed a hand, and the girl started kicking.

The girl was panicking as she was dangling over the water. Morgan tried to calm her. "You're okay. Stop kicking. We'll pull you in." The girl continued to jerk as she attempted to get back into the boat. Suddenly, lightning struck close to the boat, and the girl straightened her legs in an involuntary response. Her weight pulled Morgan and the boy over the edge with her. All three fell into the water.

It felt like three or four seconds before Morgan hit the water. She was plunged into darkness and thought she would never stop descending. Immediately, she began kicking to the surface. Strangely, her wedges were glued to her feet and didn't come off. Morgan's lungs were screaming for air. She had no idea where the surface was, so she continued to kick.

Finally, she emerged from the water and gasped for air. She coughed a few times and was surprised that she was floating easily. The water was very cold, and Morgan could hear rain nearby. But for now, she was floating in utter darkness. The wind seemed to be calmer at the surface.

Morgan turned to her right to see the massive ship sailing away at a rapid pace. "Wait! Wait for us! Please stop! Help! Help!" *Us? The teens. Did they survive the fall?*

Morgan called out and was relieved to hear the girl cry out for help. "I'm over here. Help! It's so dark. Help!"

"We'll be okay. They have cameras. They know we fell over. Are you hurt?" Waves were crashing over Morgan's head, and she was struggling to keep from swallowing the sea water.

"My shoulder. It hurts. But I am still floating." Morgan could not see the girl and wasn't certain of the direction of her voice. The ship was becoming smaller and smaller as it sailed away. And the waves were the same color as the sky. Morgan was completely enveloped in darkness.

"Okay. Keep fighting. Your friend is getting help right now. They will come after us any minute now. Just keep floating." Morgan realized they hadn't heard from the boy who fell in. *Please, God. Please!*

"Oscar! Oscar! Oscar!"

Bob was opening the cabin door to leave when he heard the distress call. He knew that the Oscar message meant that someone had gone overboard. He walked into the cabin and sat on the couch. His stomach instantly knotted. "Lord, please guide the crew to find that person. Protect that person this very minute." As soon as he finished, a chill went down his spine. Morgan! She was on the top deck. She might have seen what happened. Bob left the sweater and ran out the door. He took the steps two at a time to get to the top deck.

"Oscar! Oscar! Oscar!"

Luca heard the call and took immediate action. "Which sector?"

The third officer responded. "Starboard Aft, sir."

"Release the boat. Number four. Now! Release it! Jonathan, mark the coordinates and send them to the Coast Guard immediately. Engines full astern! It will take us thirty minutes to stop and turn around. You can do it. Take the helm. I am going up deck."

Luca took a service elevator to Deck 14. He prayed while he waited for the car to reach the top of the ship. Once outside, he saw a crowd gathering around Walk the Plank. The wind was blowing, so it was difficult to tell what was being said. Luca heard three names being called: "Lizzy. Morgan. Will." Why so much confusion? Who fell overboard? Did anyone see him or her? Did the person jump? Or was there a criminal on board?

"It's not my fault. The lightning scared her. I didn't do it." A teenager was sitting on a chair, trying to convince the crowd that it wasn't his fault. Luca saw a nearby crew member and asked for an update. He also told the man to record the teenager's name.

"Yes, sir. We believe that three people have fallen. Passengers threw all the rings overboard. It is too dark to see if any survived the fall."

"Okay. Monitor the—" *Whoosh!*

The TorpedoX lifeboat was released, and the sound was nearly deafening. An eerie quiet fell over the deck. Luca could hear the boat but could not see it. The cries from passengers then continued.

"Morgan! Morgan! My wife. Is she here?"

"Lizzy! Lizzy! She was with you and Will. Where are they?"

A team of security officers arrived, and Luca sent them to address distraught family members. "It appears that we have three overboard. Move their families away from the crowd and get as much information as possible."

Luca looked at the water and saw nothing but darkness. Clouds covered any stars in the sky. This was the blackest of nights. And the wind took away any sound. He asked God to help the passengers in the water. *Please let them still be alive. Please let our rescue be successful.*

In the last Oscar distress call Luca directed, a teenager tried to jump from a balcony onto a lifeboat attached to the side of the ship. He slid off the small boat and into the water. Surveillance cameras saw everything, and the boy's body was never found.

Luca had overseen success stories also. A schoolteacher from New Jersey was found twenty hours after she fell from her balcony. She was sitting on the railing while capturing a picture of the sunset and lost her balance. An immediate rescue was initiated, and she was found floating in the water the next day. Only God dispensed miracles. Luca prayed for three of them tonight.

The crowd on the deck was growing. Onlookers made their way to the top deck as soon as the Oscar message was announced. Most wanted to offer help and prayer, but some just wanted to snap photos of the crisis. One passenger organized a prayer circle near the kiddie splash area.

Luca asked the security team to send onlookers downstairs, if possible. He then walked toward the two large smokestacks near the mid-aft of the ship. The funnels on *Golden Fortune* were disguised with flags and a makeshift crow's nest but were substantial in size. Luca opened a locked gate with his master key and began climbing the narrow ladder on the side of the starboard stack. A member of the security team followed him.

At the top of the stack, Luca stepped precariously onto a small ledge. The man following him did not fit and had to remain on the ladder. "What are you doing, sir? This is not safe. I must ask you to come back down."

"We must be the light. We must be the light," Luca mumbled.

"Sir, please get down. The winds are too dangerous for this."

Luca ignored the security officer and leaned over the narrow railing. He knew every inch of this vessel, and he knew that there was a high-beam spotlight on the sides of each stack. They were used during the building of the ship and should still work.

The noise from the stack combined with the wind from the storm prevented Luca from hearing anyone on the deck. The exhaust from the funnels was hot and acidic, but the high winds were working in Luca's favor in this area. He didn't have to breathe the acrid fumes. He leaned farther and found the spotlight attached to the funnel. It was mounted on a swivel and could be aimed in nearly any direction.

Luca searched for the power switch but couldn't find it in the dark. *Please, Father. Grant me this miracle. Please let me find the switch.* He continued fumbling with the spotlight as the wind threatened to send him flying from the railing.

"I must insist. Please come down, Captain." Luca ignored the officer. His single goal was to illuminate the spotlight. The officer tried to force Luca down, but was unable to reach the railing.

Luca finally discovered that the light did not have a switch. It had an indented groove in which a socket or wrench was placed and turned to provide power. Of course, Luca didn't have any tools with him. *How, Lord? How?*

The only thing Luca had in his pockets were his cell phone and a jump drive with information on shipping channels of the Bahamas. He took out his phone and quickly discovered that it was too large to fit into the groove. The jump drive was his only hope. Luca inserted the drive into the indentation and turned. The drive turned easily and did not grip the interior groove. With one last prayer, Luca removed the cap from the drive and inserted it into the groove sideways. The cap snapped into place, and Luca began to turn. After a few seconds of maneuvering, the spotlight shone brightly.

Thank you, Jesus. Thank you!

Bob scrambled around the deck and quickly discovered that Morgan was not there. He ran to the boy, who was claiming that it wasn't his fault. "Who went overboard?"

"It wasn't my fault." The boy was trembling and not providing much information. A security member asked Bob if he were missing anyone.

"Yes, my wife. She was waiting on me to bring her sweater. She's wearing a seventies-style shirt." Bob could hardly speak over the howling winds.

"The boy said that a woman in a tie-dye shirt went over with the children. Could that be your wife?"

"Oh, no! That could be her. I can't find her." The man led Bob to some chairs near the pool. He spoke a few sentences into his walkie-talkie, but Bob couldn't understand what he said. His mind was whirling. Maybe Morgan went back to their cabin. No, he would have passed her on the way. Maybe she took the elevator when the Oscar alert was sounded. But she was wearing a tie-dye shirt. Oh, no! How could she have possibly fallen into the water? She was just sitting on a pool chair.

"Stay here. We want to get information from you. Don't worry. We have deployed a lifeboat and informed the Coast Guard. We have the best technology available to retrieve your wife."

Retrieve? That sounded ominous. Bob kept thinking about the word *retrieve*. What did that mean? He couldn't possibly sit here while Morgan was fighting for her life, or worse. But what could he do? The ship was well past where she fell, so he couldn't jump in and try to reach her. He was helpless. There was absolutely nothing he could do. Retrieve? What did that mean?

As Bob sat on the pool chair, he told himself to focus. He knew how to put out fires at work. He could put out this storm. He just had to think. Storm? Of course, he was in a terrible storm. And the only way out was through the One who calms the storms. Bob knew that the only battle plan he had was prayer. But he also knew that was the only battle plan he needed.

"Help, Jesus. Help! She's out there, and You know exactly where she is. Please, let the Coast Guard find her and bring her back onto the ship safely. Please!" Bob got on his knees and decided to pray until Morgan was returned. He didn't like giving up control but knew that he was powerless. His all-powerful God knew exactly where Morgan was. And the two other people. Bob prayed for God's to save all three of them. Three women who were nearby kneeled by him and prayed with him. Only God could calm this storm.

Luca knew what to do. He knew exactly what to do. He turned the spotlight toward the water and searched for the TorpedoX lifeboat. When this day was over, he would speak with the designers about adding an automatic light to the boats. For now, he would provide the light. After a few seconds, he saw the craft bobbing in the water and aimed the large spotlight at it. The ship was slowly moving away from the it, but the spotlight could still reach the drifting boat. Luca could clearly see it silhouetted in the dark. His singular focus now was to keep the light on the boat.

"What is he doing?" someone in the crowd shouted. "What about the people in the water? We can't see them." A crowd of people was gathering around the back of the ship. Each person was looking for any glimpse of life in the dark water.

"The captain is a fool! We don't need to see the boat. We need to find the people. Aim the light at the water."

"I can't see anyone. There isn't anyone in the water."

Luca didn't listen to the crowd. He knew that the light should be aimed at the boat, not the passengers, so he kept the spotlight aimed directly at the lifeboat. *Please, God. Let them find the boat. Let them be saved.*

Morgan could see the ship getting farther and farther away. And her shoes were still on her feet. How strange.

"Are you still there?" the girl called out.

"Yes, sweetie. I'm here. I'll try to find you. It's just so dark."

"I'm scared. I can't do this. And I hear that boy who fell. He's in the water somewhere. But I can't see him. I can't see you. Help!"

"He may be swimming toward the ship. We wouldn't hear him well with the wind and the waves. I'm coming." Morgan tried to swim toward the girl, but the current kept pulling her away. A bolt of lightning went across the sky, and Morgan got a glimpse of the girl's head. "I see you! I'm coming."

Slowly, Morgan made her way closer to the girl. Staying afloat was not difficult, but moving in a forward direction was. As they got close enough to talk, Morgan asked the girl her name.

"Elizabeth Grace Fleming. I'm fourteen. And I'm cold."

"Hello, Elizabeth. It's nice to meet you. I'm Morgan. Let's not think about being cold. How is your shoulder?"

"It's moving forward. But I don't think I can lift it up." The two were bobbing in the water and slowly drifting closer to each other.

Morgan kicked toward the girl. "Okay. I'm here. Do you know the boy's name. I haven't heard him."

"I think it's Will. He and Bobby dared me to stand on the rail. I knew it was dangerous." Just then a huge wave went over Morgan and Elizabeth's heads. They were completely submerged and popped up, coughing. Morgan knew that they had to get out of the water soon. The waves were getting higher.

"We're gonna die. I'll never see Fifi again." The girl's voice was getting weaker.

"No. We aren't. Did you hear that loud noise earlier? I think that was a lifeboat torpedo." Morgan was yelling now. The wind was whipping up the waves higher and higher. She knew that the lifeboat was somewhere in the water, but she didn't want to tell Elizabeth that chances were very slim that they would find the boat.

Morgan tried to keep Elizabeth focused on survival. "They will come find us. The ship is slowing down. It will take a while to turn around, but it will come back. We need to lookout for—"

Flash!

A bright light shone from the ship to the left of Morgan. "We need to go where the light is, Elizabeth."

"I'm too scared. I can't move. And people call me Lizzy."

Morgan couldn't help but smile to herself. "Okay, Lizzy. You must move. We have to go to the light. Do you see it?"

"But I'm okay here."

"No, sweetie, we must move. It's the lifeboat. We must get to the lifeboat."

"I'm scared!" Lizzy started crying, and sinking.

"No. Lizzy, I am begging you to come with me. I can't make you. But you must trust me. Kick your legs and move to the light. Now!" Lizzy didn't respond, but Morgan could tell that she was kicking toward the end of the light.

Morgan hadn't heard from the boy and feared that he didn't survive the fall. "Will! Will! If you are out there, swim toward the light. Swim now!" No response.

Back on the bridge, officers were in touch with the Coast Guard. A rescue helicopter was eighteen minutes away. The third officer was maneuvering the ship in an arc to return to the "overboard point." He made regular announcements to passengers on the status of the Oscar alert.

Franny made the decision to continue with the seventies party. Families were arriving with and without costumes. Keeping them entertained would prevent them from gathering on the pool deck. She informed other venues to continue with their scheduled programs and activities and was grateful that the officers were making ship-wide announcements. It kept the passengers from asking her for updates.

Doc and his team made their way to the top deck. They brought warm blankets and electrolyte drinks in the hope that the overboard passengers were returned to the ship. He also watched family members for their reactions to the stressful situation. When he arrived, he saw two groups of people kneeling and praying. He found the families and walked over to provide any comfort he could.

Luca did not leave the railing by the smokestack. He aimed the spotlight at the bobbing lifeboat and prayed that the three passengers were still alive. Once the Coast Guard arrived, they would take over and provide better lighting. But for now, he would shine the light on the only hope in the sea: the TorpedoX lifeboat.

In the water, Morgan and Lizzy continued to move toward the inflatable boat. Morgan didn't know how the light was aiming at it, but she was grateful. Without the light, she and Lizzy would not know where to go. She kicked her feet until her legs began to burn. She had to make it to the boat. She had to make it to the light.

"We're almost there, Lizzy. You're doing great."

"I think I saw a shark! It's going to eat us. Help!" Morgan hadn't thought about sharks and started to panic herself. Lizzy began splashing around. Was the light attracting sharks? Should they swim away from the boat? Their efforts seemed pointless. No. The boat was the only way. They had to focus on the lifeboat. It was their only hope.

"Lizzy, sharks aren't going to get us. But we must get into the boat. I promise we will be safe when—"

Another wave overtook them. Morgan feared that they wouldn't have the strength to make it to the boat. *Please, God. Help us get into the boat.*

Lizzy surfaced coughing and crying. "I can't. Go on without me."

"No! We're going together. Kick. That's all. Just kick." Amazingly, the boat moved closer to Morgan and Lizzy as they made a strenuous effort to kick. "We did it! The boat is right here." Suddenly, a large wave lifted the boat and it crashed onto their heads. Morgan felt stunned as her neck bent in an awkward angle. But she was still floating. She turned around and found Lizzy holding onto a rope attached to the lifeboat.

Lizzy looked exhausted. "What do we do now? This thing is crashing into us. I'm so tired."

"There must be a ladder. That spotlight is so bright that I can't see. But we found the boat. We found it." Morgan made her way around the boat, which stood above the waves several feet. "Over here! Over here! There are steps over here. Come to my voice, Lizzy."

Morgan waited at the steps and was overjoyed when she saw Lizzy swimming toward her. The girl's blonde hair was covering her face, and she was swimming with pure grit. Morgan helped her step up the side steps and pushed her into the boat. She then climbed up the steps and fell beside Lizzy.

Thank You, God. You saved us.

Lizzy began crying, and Morgan could feel her shaking. Was the girl going into shock? Or was that just something that just happened in movies? Thankfully, the light continued to shine on the lifeboat. Morgan crawled around and found several large sacks. She opened one and found what looked like emergency flares. They probably didn't need to use those. The next bag held blankets and possibly clothing. Morgan pulled out four blankets and scooted over to Lizzy. She wrapped three of the blankets around the girl and one around herself. Now, they would just wait for someone official to find them.

After a few minutes, Lizzy stopped crying. But her shaking continued. Morgan could tell that she didn't want to talk. And Morgan didn't feel like talking. What was taking so long? Shouldn't someone be coming for them. Then she remembered the boy who fell in. Will. Was he still out there?

Morgan knew that she was safe in the lifeboat. But Will was still in the water. How could she rest knowing that he could be clinging to life. The waves were calming a little, but the boy was not safe. He was probably dazed and confused. He may not survive much longer.

Morgan made the decision to get out of the lifeboat and search for Will. She told Lizzy that she would be right back. The girl made a small whimper and curled under the blankets. Morgan searched the other bags for life jackets. She didn't find any but did find plastic tubes that looked like they would float. She put two tubes across her chest and under her arms and headed for the side of the boat near the steps.

As she stepped out of the boat, Morgan prayed to find Will. *Please let him be alive. Please let me find him.* She lowered into the water and was surprised at how cold it was. Was it this cold earlier? Morgan decided that she wouldn't be able to stay in the water for long. The light was still aimed at the lifeboat, so she pushed into the darkness in the direction of the massive ship.

"Will! Will! Are you out there? Follow the light. Don't go to the ship. Find the end of the light. Are you there?" Nothing but the sound of the wind. The boy probably didn't survive the fall. Or a shark got him. *Shark! Oh my!* Morgan had forgotten about the sharks. She had jumped back into the water without thinking of the sharks. She felt totally helpless, but also totally safe. If God could keep lions away from Daniel, he could keep sharks away from her. She just hoped that safety from sharks was God's will.

Morgan wasn't sure what to do. Her mind suddenly pictured Bob. He must be frantic. Surely, he knows by now that she had fallen overboard. Everyone on the ship must know. Morgan's mind was racing through scenes from her life like a movie reel. She should get back into the lifeboat. There was no sign of Will, and the cold water was affecting her thinking.

As Morgan began to kick toward the lifeboat, she heard a voice. "Bobby? Bobby?"

"Will! Is that you? Where are you?"

"I don't know. I'm so tired." The boy was clearly running out of time. Morgan kicked toward his voice and found him clinging with one arm to a red life ring. *Thank You, God! Once again, thank You!* Morgan wrapped one of her arms into the ring and began kicking. She had a strange image of herself ballroom dancing and began to laugh. Was she going into shock also? She really wasn't sure, but she knew to aim for the end of the bright light. Always aim for the light.

At the lifeboat, she calmly ordered Will-Whatever-His-Name to climb up the steps. But he refused. "I'm fine. I'm fine in the water."

"No, you aren't fine. You need to get into the boat." But the boy just hugged the ring and refused to climb. Knowing that she wasn't strong enough to lift him, she asked one more time. "This is the only way. You must get into the boat. There is no other way."

The boy didn't budge, so Morgan climbed up the steps and tried to pull him in. Lizzy poked her head up and saw that Morgan was struggling with someone. "Is that Will? Did you find him?"

"I did. Can you help?"

Lizzy crawled toward Morgan and looked down at Will. "There are sharks in that water." Will's eyes widened, and he reached for Morgan's hand. He managed to climb the steps while still hugging the life ring. Once the three were on board the lifeboat, Morgan wrapped everyone in a blanket and sat down. She began crying. The danger was over. They were all saved. God rescued them. He provided a Light.

After what seemed like hours, the group heard a helicopter. Morgan sat up on her knees and saw the lights of the helicopter getting closer. Just then, the bright light from the ship stopped. For a moment, the lifeboat was completely dark. Nobody moved. Morgan would never forget the feeling of safety amidst the dark and stormy sea.

When the helicopter was nearly overhead, it shone a light onto the lifeboat. This light was directed into the boat, and for the first time Morgan could see the faces of the teens. They looked so young . . . and relieved. They had survived.

A voice over a loudspeaker announced that a rescue swimmer from the Coast Guard would descend into the boat to help each person into a harness. The ladder would pull them into the chopper one by one. As soon as the message finished, a woman dropped down on a ladder.

"Hi! I'm Sabrina. Is anyone hurt?" The three just stared at her. No one could speak. "It's okay. We are going to safely lift you onto the helicopter and then return you to the ship. We are good at this. You will be just fine."

Still, no one spoke, and Sabrina conducted her mission flawlessly. Morgan pointed to Lizzy. Sabrina put a harness on Lizzy and attached it to the rope ladder. Slowly, the girl was raised into the air. Morgan became overwhelmed at the graveness of the situation and strangely missed Lizzy as she entered the helicopter.

The ladder returned, and Sabrina brought the harness toward Morgan. "No, please take the boy next. He is struggling." Sabrina nodded and carefully assisted Will into the hovering helicopter. Finally, Morgan was lifted to safety. As she took a mental picture of the ship and the lifeboat in her mind, she wondered how life could change course so quickly—and how her shoes were still on her feet.

"You did it, Captain. All the passengers are on the chopper. They will be brought to the helipad within minutes. Doc has three gurneys ready to take them to the medical facility." Luca heard the report but wasn't sure who was speaking. His eyes hadn't adjusted to the dark yet. He carefully crawled down the metallic ladder with shaky legs. The night could have ended in a tragedy, or three. But God spared their lives. Only God.

"The families are eager to see their loved ones. We have told them that immediate family should report to Deck 5."

"Thank you. I will go to the bridge to file a preliminary report and make my way to the medical area afterward. Please thank everyone you see for their competent actions."

"Will do, sir."

On the deck, Luca walked toward Walk the Plank. He looked into the water. It was so dark and furious. Three of his passengers had been in that water and he could not see them. But God did. God was with them in the storm.

Morgan awoke in one of the examining rooms on the ship. Bob was holding her hand. Her fall into the ocean wasn't a dream. She was covered with several blankets, but still shaking.

"Mrs. Stevens, we are so glad to have you back on board. I'm Doc, and I'd like to check your vitals." Morgan nodded as Doc listened to her pulse. She couldn't look at Bob because she knew she would start crying. They had been so close to losing their future together. "Sounds good. I would like for you to sip on this broth. It will raise your body temperature slowly and give you some energy. I'll be right back."

"Doc? How are the children?" Morgan was afraid to ask but had to know. They were younger and smaller.

"They are fine. And will have an amazing story to share when the return to school."

After about thirty minutes, a nurse helped Morgan into some dry clothes and walked her into the main waiting area. Bob never let go of her hand. Morgan saw Lizzy with wet hair sitting beside her parents and a boy who must be Bobby, her brother. Will was sitting with his father. Morgan and Bob sat in chairs near the closest examining room. As soon as they sat, Captain Barone entered the room.

"Greetings, all of you. On behalf of Jewel Cruise Line, I would like to express my sincere thanks to God that you are all okay. We have begun an intense investigation into the cause of this misfortune and will be reviewing video footage from the pool deck."

Will looked up. "It's my fault. I was daring Lizzy."

"I was teasing her too," Bobby chimed in. "We never thought she would fall in. The lady was trying to stop us."

"Thank you for your honesty, men," Luca added. "We will have more questions for you soon. For now, you each have the option of staying on the ship for the remainder of the cruise or returning to Miami tonight with the Coast Guard. We will make you as comfortable as possible either way."

Morgan finally looked at Bob. "I think I would like to go home." He nodded and was about to put his arm around her when Lizzy ran over to Morgan and hugged her tightly.

"Don't go. I just met you." Lizzy was wiping tears as she continued to hug Morgan.

"Lizzy! Mrs. Stevens wants to go home. And I think we should too." Lizzy's mom did not approve of the spontaneous hug.

"You should listen to your mom," Morgan said.

"She's not my mom. She's my foster mom. My mom died from drugs." Lizzy broke down crying, and the whole room grew silent.

"Oh my. How sad. I think it might be best if we all went home." Morgan hugged Lizzy and patted her wet hair.

"Please stay. Please." Lizzy's plea was heartfelt now.

The foster mom spoke up. "I'm fine with staying. Paul and I have the week off from work, so we have nothing better to do. And Bobby can wash dishes or something to pay for that huge Coast Guard rescue." Bobby's stunned face drew a laugh from the crowd.

Morgan's heart calmed. "I would be happy to stay if you want me to. We could meet for breakfast tomorrow. I would love to get to know you. And you, Will. We will share this crazy bond for life." The families decided to get some sleep and meet for breakfast at 9:00 at the buffet restaurant.

Back in their cabin, Bob hugged Morgan and swore that he would never let her go. "I felt so helpless. There is no way I will sleep tonight. I just want to sit here and hold your hand." He helped her sit on the couch and took off her shoes. "I'm really going to stare at you all night."

"I will take you up on that. I won't even notice because I feel like I could sleep for days." Morgan took a hot shower and went straight to bed. As promised, Bob sat beside her and held her hand until he fell asleep hours later.

When Morgan woke, she felt energized. Bob was sitting on the balcony. Morgan quickly dressed and went outside to join him. "God gave us another day together!"

Bob stood and gave Morgan a bear hug. "Yes, He did. I don't think I'll ever be able to thank Him enough for last night's miracle. And please don't stand so close to the edge."

"You know, I'm not the least bit afraid of falling over. Last night's experience was scary, but I never felt alone. I knew that God was back in 'headquarters,' arranging my rescue. Plus, my mind was occupied with Will and Lizzy. I still can't believe that happened. Did you see Lucy last night?"

"No, I don't remember seeing anyone. The officers were making announcements, so she knew what was happening. I'm not sure if she knew it was you." Bob hugged Morgan once again. "I think we should tell them in person."

"I imagine that I will receive a ton of messages once my name gets out there. I can't think about that right now. And I hope this doesn't affect Jewel. The line did everything they could to solve a problem they didn't create. I will do my best to let the world know about Captain Barone and his crew."

"Are you hungry?" Bob asked.

"Yes, starved! And I can't wait to talk with Will and Lizzy. Let's go now. Maybe they will be there early." Morgan walked back into the cabin and found her white sweater. She still had a slight chill.

"Sounds good. Doc wants you to come by the medical facility after you eat." Morgan led Bob all the way to Blackbeard's Fortress. She walked on her tiptoes most of the way. When they exited the elevator, they saw Lizzy standing alone at the entrance to the buffet. She was wearing pink shorts and a navy hoodie.

"Where is your family, sweetie?" Morgan asked.

"They didn't want to come. They are eating at the soda shop. Will's family went with them. Here, I made you this." Lizzy handed Morgan a handmade card. Her name and a message were written in a beautiful script.

"Thank you. This is beautiful. Where did you get the stickers?"

"I do a lot of journaling. My kit comes with stickers." Lizzy looked down at her feet.

"Well, I will keep this forever. Let's eat!" The trio found a table near a window and gathered their food. Morgan was concerned that Lizzy didn't eat much. She was also concerned about her shoulder. And why didn't her family come with her?

"I don't usually eat breakfast," Lizzy added.

"Oh, we never skip breakfast," Bob joked. "I would eat two breakfasts if I could." Lizzy laughed awkwardly, and Morgan changed the subject by asking about the girl's interests.

It turned out that Lizzy loved writing and wanted to start a blog when she turned eighteen. She was in the eighth grade at a large school near Little Havana. She had been in three foster homes during the last two years. She cooks a lot for the family and is in the junior photography club at school. Morgan could have listened to her talk all day but had to stop the conversation when they finished eating.

"Are you going to see Doc this morning?" Bob was still concerned about the health of both.

"Yes. Mrs. Bryant is taking me. She told me to meet her in our cabin at 10:00."

"Okay. You better get going. Maybe we can hang out tonight. We'll be near the pizza place." Morgan didn't want to say goodbye.

"I'll look for you. Thank you, Mrs. Stevens. Thank you for everything." As Lizzy walked away, Morgan thought of a million things she should have said. *Lord, please give me another chance to talk with Lizzy. Really talk with her.*

Bob led Morgan to the elevator on their way to the medical center. Their trip had taken such a sudden turn. Families were scurrying about on their way to swim or play. Someone would find the treasure, probably tomorrow. Life carried on. But he would never be the same. Not after feeling so helpless. Not being able to see Morgan or contact her. That left a lasting impression. He had to fully trust God, probably for the first time in his life. Bob felt a comfort knowing that God saw him. And cared for him.

As they entered the elevator, Morgan blurted out, "I want her!"

"What?"

"I want Lizzy. She's been in foster care for two years. She doesn't have parents. I want her. She needs us. She needs us, Bob." Tears began to fall down Morgan's face.

"You can't just have her, Morg. There are rules."

"I want her. Let's find out about the rules. God set this up. Don't you see?" Bob was concerned for Morgan but had to admit that the whole situation did seem like something only God could have orchestrated.

"We can ask, but please don't get your hopes up. This must be very complicated."

At the medical facility, Morgan met with Doc one final time. He was pleased that she seemed to have no adverse effects from the fall nor the exposure to the cold ocean water. He asked the couple to wait a few minutes. The captain wanted to speak with them privately. As the couple waited, the Bryant family arrived. Morgan smiled at Lizzy who stared at her shoes.

Lizzy and Mrs. Bryant went into one of the examining rooms along with Doc and a cheerful nurse. Bob started a conversation with Mr. Bryant. "How is she doing?"

"She's fine. Slept like a rock. These kids are resilient. They've been through so much in their lives and seem to bounce back every time."

"How's Bobby?" Bob asked.

"We have a meeting with security after lunch. They have videos of him taunting Lizzy. I'm not sure what will happen since he's a minor. I guess we'll see."

Morgan leaned forward. "Is Lizzy up for adoption?"

The man's eyes widened, and he sat up straighter. "Yes, she is. But she is too old to get adopted. Most couples want babies. She is on the lists for two different girls' homes in Dade County. We have fostered several girls who have moved on to the group homes. There they learn how to support themselves. You know, they no longer have care when they age out at eighteen?"

Morgan's heart dropped. She couldn't let Lizzy "age out" and fend for herself. "We want to adopt her. How do we go about that?"

"Wow! You just met her. She's kind of moody in the morning. And she writes in notebooks all the time."

"I want to do this. Bob, are you okay with this?" Morgan held Bob's hands and looked him straight in the eyes.

Bob answered softly. "I am okay with pursuing this, but you can't get your hopes up. You bonded during a traumatic event. That doesn't mean the relationship should be permanent."

Mr. Bryant was nodding his head. He took out his phone and searched for a contact. "Here is the name and number of Lizzy's case worker. You should call her and get details. In the meantime, we would be happy for you to join us for dinner tonight. You might get a glimpse of that moodiness I warned you about." Morgan cheered inside. This was meant to be. Lizzy needed a family, and the Stevens had room in their home and in their hearts for a child.

Morgan stared at the number. The case worked could change their lives. This person—Felicia Underwood—would hold their future in her hands. Morgan couldn't wait to get back to shore to make the phone call. In her mind, Lizzy was meant to be in their family. It had to be God's plan. She right away began thinking about the classes she and Bob would have to take to become legal guardians and the furniture they would have to buy to turn the spare bedroom into Lizzy's room. Her mind sped to Christmas mornings and youth group trips and braces. Don't all children need braces? Her thoughts were overwhelming, and Morgan knew that she should slow them down. But she couldn't. Her heart was already invested.

When Lizzy and Mrs. Bryant exited the examining room, the others stood. Doc declared that everyone was fine and could continue their fun for the remainder of the cruise. The Walk the Plank feature was barricaded and not currently available.

Morgan smiled at Lizzy and told the girl that she would see her at dinner. She and Bob would join the Bryant's in the main dining room at 7:00. "And Lizzy, you mentioned Fifi when you were in the water. Is she a cat or a dog?" Bob was highly allergic to cats, so a cat would be out of the question. Perhaps Bob could take allergy shots?

Lizzy laughed. "Neither. Fifi is my sister Sofia. She's eight, so she isn't old enough to go on this cruise."

The meeting with Captain Barone was a blur. He was going over details, but Morgan missed all of them. She couldn't stop thinking about Lizzy and her sister. Two girls. At once. Did God plan this all along? The captain mentioned something about a press conference at disembarkation. Morgan agreed. She was eager to share her story with the media. She and Bob thanked Captain Barone once again for risking his safety to shine the light on the lifeboat. As soon as they left the facility, Morgan looked at Bob and said one word. "Two!"

CHAPTER TWENTY

December 8, Disembarkation

Morgan and Bob were escorted off the ship separately from the other passengers. They were taken directly to a briefing room in the Jewel Cruise Line terminal. Dozens of reporters sat in chairs and snapped photos of each group arriving. Captain Barone stood at the podium. Bob and Morgan were on his right, and a family from Louisville,

Kentucky, were on his left. Morgan quickly learned that the family found the first treasure on aptly named Treasure Island.

Hands were in the air, but the captain ignored them. He began with a prepared speech. "Ladies and Gentlemen, I am pleased to share with you two exciting stories from the inaugural sailing of *Golden Fortune*. God's blessings were with us the entire week. First, please meet the Franklin family from the United States. They found the hidden treasure early Friday morning. It was hidden behind a towel hut on Treasure Island. The Franklins have agreed to answer a few questions before they take a chartered ride to the airport.

Morgan heard a flurry of questions and responses about cash and taxes and college funds. The mother of the family was a travel reporter for a local television station, and the father was a chemistry professor. He couldn't wait to tell his students about the "two *H*s and one *O*" clue. Morgan did not focus on them. Her mind was distracted. God had orchestrated this entire week. The entire journey. And Morgan had one chance to share that with the world.

Please give me the words.

Captain Barone then took a more somber tone. "As you have probably heard, we had an Oscar situation on this cruise. Two minors were daring another minor to do something dangerous. Mrs. Stevens here took it upon herself to protect the girl. In the process, she and two of the teens fell overboard. Through heroic action, Mrs. Stevens was able to aid both children into a lifeboat. Our new TorpedoX lifeboat performed perfectly, and the three passengers were safely rescued by the U.S. Coast Guard. A full investigation is still underway, and a detailed press release will be issued soon. We will also be awarding Mrs. Stevens with a Silver Seas Award of Valor. At this time, Mrs. Stevens would like to say a few words."

Morgan stepped to the podium. All she could see was a bank of smartphones aimed at her. But she knew that there were reporters behind the phones. And she knew that whatever she was about to say would be relayed around the world.

"Thank you, Captain Barone. And thank you to the amazing crew of *Golden Fortune*. We had a wonderful week and will continue to sail with Jewel Cruise Line.

"In the Gospel of Matthew, Jesus tells His disciples that they are to be the 'light of the world.' I have had issues with that concept because constantly directing a light at Jesus seemed arrogant to me. I now see it as the most merciful thing we can do on God's Earth.

"When I was lost at sea, I was in utter darkness. I knew there were sharks in the water and two teenagers. But I couldn't see them, and I couldn't see a way out. Captain Barone heroically climbed a smokestack and found a spotlight. He risked his safety to turn on the light. And he didn't aim the light at us as bystanders were yelling for him to do. Instead, he aimed the light at the lifeboat and continued until we were safe. To survive the dangerous seas, I needed to see the boat. I needed to see the rescuer. We all need to see the Rescuer. And we need to shine our lights on Him. Daily. I see that now.

"Sometimes we need to get out of the boat to save others. I wouldn't have found the young man if I had gotten comfortable in the boat. You may have to leave your comfort zone by talking to a new neighbor or traveling to a foreign country on a mission trip. The lost are worth it. I encourage you to jump out of your lifeboat and find the lost souls near you.

"And to those of you without a relationship with Jesus, I urge you to get out of the water and into the Lifeboat. The sharks are seeking to 'steal, kill, and destroy.' Find a Bible-believing friend or church. Don't ignore the Savior. He is the most important element of your life. He is your Deliverer. Don't get too comfortable in this world. It will deceive you into thinking that this world is your home. But it isn't.

"Our goal is to be rescued from Earth and brought into heaven. God takes us according to His will and His timing, just as the brave Coast Guard members brought us one by one into the rescue helicopter. As I was waiting for my turn, I reflected that all believers will be rescued. We are waiting for our turns. We will miss those who get rescued before us, but we will rejoice with them when it is our turn.

"In this world we are surrounded by sharks, but we have a Lifeboat in our Savior. His name is Jesus. We must get into the boat to be safe. And I challenge all believers to aim our lights at Jesus. The world needs to see Him. Don't let your light dim.

"Captain Barone's first name is Luciano, which means 'light' in Italian. He provided the light for us to be rescued. Please use his strength and courage to motivate you to shine your light every day. His last name happens to mean 'brave.' What a fitting name for a hero on Earth.

"Thank you, Luciano, my heroic light-giver. You saved my life."

Luca thought of his precious Dahna being rescued before him. The Coast Guard analogy eased his pain a little. He would do the work he was called to do until his heavenly Father lifted him off the Earth at his appointed time. He would remain in the lifeboat until God directed him otherwise. And he would gather as many others into the Lifeboat as he possibly could.

CHAPTER TWENTY-ONE

September 8, Adoption Day

"Mom, you're not wearing clear shoes, are you? They won't look right. And we need to hurry. It's after 9:00."

"For the courthouse? My shoes won't look right?" Morgan was still amazed that Lizzy cared about her fashion choices. "Grammy and Aunt Margaret are almost here. As soon as they get here, we will load up the van. Don't worry. The judge can't start without us. If Fifi ready?"

Bob walked behind Morgan and gave her a hug. "This is really happening. Can you believe it? The case worker said that the process could be sped up some, but I had no idea we could become parents in nine months. Well, I guess that is how it normally works. But you know what I mean."

"We are witnessing firsthand that all things are possible with God. I hope that Luca can join the hearing virtually. He said that he should be able to since today is a sea day." Morgan squeezed Bob's hand.

"Earl texted that he and Lucy are on their way. They decided to bring all the kids. And Greg and Marsha will be there. We will take over Pizza-Rama."

Morgan laughed. "I love it! And our girls will be getting pineapple on their pizza. I knew you were the weird one."

As Morgan went to her room to change into "Lizzy-approved" shoes, she thanked God for the millionth time. It was true that His timing was perfect. He planned for the four of them to be a forever family, but in an unconventional way. She found Lizzy in the middle of the ocean, just like God found her. They were lost and afraid, but they knew where to go thanks to the light. She was found by the Light.

Today was a sea day, and Luca had no trouble slipping away from the bridge to watch the adoption ceremony. He would stop at Shipwreck Boulevard for a cup of coffee and stroll down one of the garden paths before returning to his cabin to watch four people become one family.

Luca would never forget the fourth of December. God worked in a very mysterious way as He blessed the Stevens family. What could have been a tragedy turned into two welcomed additions to a childless couple. Only God could have orchestrated such a turn of events. And Luca was thankful to play a part in His design.

A new group of passengers boarded yesterday. The first clue had already been solved by many. Nine months after the inaugural sailing of *Golden Fortune,* interest was still high in the treasure hunt at sea. Media reports of families, couples, and individuals finding fortunes in the Bahamas only fueled the attention. Bookings for *Plunder* were higher than those of *Golden Fortune.* The Jewel Cruise Line had created a hit. His grandsons were still talking about the endless pizza and "real mermaids" from their trip in April.

When the elevator doors opened, Luca was nearly knocked down by two flashes of gold on motorized scooters. They zipped past him and spun around in unison.

"Loo-chi! Loo-chi! We've been trying to find you." Luca couldn't believe his eyes. It was Daisy from the inaugural sailing. The other woman on a matching scooter had to be her sister. They were dressed in identical gold tops and were smiling ear to ear.

"Daisy! It's great to see you."

"Hey, Loo-chi! This is my sister Eloise. We call her Aster. We've been saving our nickels to come back on the treasure cruise. Aster was madder than a wet hornet when I didn't take her last time. We're hunting for the treasure this time. We're hunting for real."

"We are happy to have you return." Luca was truly happy to see Daisy. He regularly met with return passengers, but none as colorful as Daisy.

"I was hoping we hadn't buttered our biscuits too late," Aster replied.

Luca had no idea what Aster meant but was genuinely looking forward to the Southern charm of the sisters. "I'm delighted to meet you, Aster. I have a 10:00 appointment to make but would love for you both to join me at dinner tonight. How does 8:00 sound?"

"We'd be happier than tap shoes in canola oil to join you. I told you, Aster, Captain is a doll. Wait till you see him in his seventies costume." Daisy expertly turned her scooter 180 degrees and headed toward an open elevator door. Aster followed swiftly.

Luca said his goodbyes and walked toward his cabin. *Extra lasagna tonight*, he thought. *We're having double the fun.*

About the Author

Christine R. Whitlock is a wife, mother, Sunday school teacher, and chemist. She and her husband Robert have been married for thirty-five years and have one incredible son. They have also cared for twenty-four foster children. They love to travel, especially cruising in the Caribbean. Christine has a bachelor's degree from Huntingdon College and doctoral degree from The University of Alabama. Her entire professional career has been as a chemistry professor at Georgia Southern University. Outside of the lab, she enjoys jogging, pizza, and jigsaw puzzles.

Visit her online at ChristineRWhitlock.com.

Coming July 2024